Beauty Shop for RENT

LAURA BOWERS

Beauty Shop for RENT

...fully equipped, inquire within

Harcourt, Inc.

Orlando ° Austin ° New York ° San Diego ° Toronto ° London

www.HarcourtBooks.com

Library of Congress Cataloging-in-Publication Data
Bowers, Laura, 1969–
Beauty shop for rent: fully equipped, inquire within/Laura Bowers.
p. cm.
Summary: Raised by a great-grandmother and a bunch of beauty shop buddies,
fourteen-year-old Abbey resolves to overcome her unhappy childhood
and disillusionment with the mother who deserted her.
[1. Mothers and daughters—Fiction.   2. Interpersonal relations—Fiction.
3. Determination (Personality trait)—Fiction.]   I. Title.
PZ7.B6766Bea   2007
[Fic]—dc22   2006016761
ISBN 978-0-15-205764-0

Text set in Bodoni Book
Designed by April Ward

First edition
A C E G H F D B

Printed in the United States of America

For Broc, Cooper, and my husband, Bob,
who told me I could do this

In loving memory of
Stacy L. Kjeldgaard
(1969–2000);
You are missed.

Prologue

I'll be a millionaire by the time I turn thirty-five. Successful. Independent. Abbey Garner—self-made financial genius. Then, and only then, will I consider getting married and having kids.

Not like my mom, who traded her pom-poms for diaper duty at the age of sixteen. Only two years older than me and walking around high school with the scarlet letters *D-O-O-M-E-D* etched on her forehead. Not like my grandmother Evelyn Somers, pregnant with my mom at seventeen. Or my great-grandmother Polly Randall, having a daughter at sixteen.

Of course, Granny Po said her generation got married young, had children young, and that's the end of that, but I think there's more to the story.

I think it's a curse. Not only did the women in my family inherit overly fertile eggs, they each married men who were total, complete, and absolute duds.

But it all stops with me.

I'm not going to continue the family tradition. Two simple rules will guarantee I won't. Number one: Be financially successful so I'll *never* have to rely on anybody but myself. Number two: Always remember that fairy-tale endings rarely last after the final page. It's sad but true, and after hearing all my mother's stories, I should know. I've seen what happens when love ends and desperation begins.

So I'm lucky. Most people don't know their future until they're too old to do anything about it. I do. The story of my life will never be written by a curse.

And never by a man.

Chapter One

"**H**ypothetical Question of the Week: If you were forced to have an extra body part implanted on your back, which would you choose? A finger, ear, breast, or nose?"

"Abbey Lynn Garner!" Granny Po exclaimed from the manicure table, pointing at me with her emery board. "Where did that crap come from?"

I smiled and held up a wrinkled tabloid. "From *your* magazine."

Granny Po rolled her eyes and went back to filing Caddie's nails. "Hmph. Well, what are you doing reading that trash, anyway? Not exactly appropriate for a fourteen-year-old."

"Fifteen," I reminded her. "My birthday's in a few weeks."

My great-grandmother shot me a look that said the extra year didn't amount to much. I could be twenty and she'd still think it's not appropriate. The beautician's chair squeaked as I leaned back and propped my feet up. Tabloids really aren't my style, anyway, but there was nothing else to do. I'd already cleaned, folded towels, organized a messy array of curlers, and taken a quick inventory. We hadn't had a single customer all evening except Caddie, but she practically lived at Polly's Parlor and didn't count.

"Come on, Granny Po. Answer the question," I teased. "You know you wanna."

"No, I don't wanna. Sounds like something from all those reality shows on TV. Lord." Granny Po sighed. "Well, if I must . . . then, no breast. Couldn't sleep with a boob on my back."

Caddie, named after her father's Cadillac, turned from the table with a confused gaze, her dangling pearl earrings slapping back and forth against her plump neck. "I don't understand the question. Good heavens, why would someone want a body part on their back?"

"Nobody's *really* going to do that," I explained. "It's a hypothetical question, Miss Caddie. You know, just for the *p*'s and *g*'s of it."

"What, pray tell, are the *p*'s and *g*'s?" Granny Po asked, as the shop door opened and Edith walked in, her cowboy boots thumping on the hardwood floors.

"Poops and giggles," Edith said, pulling off her barn jacket and throwing it on the sofa. "You never heard of that? Abbey, how about a quick trim. No shampoo."

Granny Po picked up the cuticle lotion. "Should have known. Edith Jones, don't you corrupt my Abbey with your talk. Lord knows what else she's picking up from you."

More than that. At her horse farm next door, Edith uses a *different* word for poop. I stood, pulling up on the low-rider jeans that always make me feel like my rear is about to pop out, and reached for a cape from the shelf. Edith sat and raised her chin as I snapped the vinyl cape around her neck and repeated the question.

"A finger, ear, breast, or nose. Interesting," Edith mused. She grimaced, pinching her nose shut with weathered fingers. "No nose. I wouldn't want to walk around with a nose on my back, and I don't think I gotta explain why."

"Why?" Caddie asked, picking up a frosted beige polish. A look of comprehension crossed her face. "Oh, . . . never mind."

Edith grinned. "If you picked a finger, you could scratch your own back!"

"Or stick yourself up," I added, raising her chair by pumping my foot on the lever. The worn hydraulics moaned with each inch.

"Well, I still don't see what's funny about the question," Caddie said, in her soft Southern accent, while taking out the new hearing aids that always made her uncomfortable. "If the good Lord wanted something extra on our back, He'd put it there Himself."

Caddie primly smoothed the floral smock over her rounded hips and accidentally dropped her hearing aids to the floor. The seams of her pants stretched to capacity when she reached down for them.

Granny Po snorted, her eyes taking on a mischievous gleam. She said, "Yeah, and I think the good Lord certainly gave Caddie something extra in the rear-end department."

"Like two giant pumpkins stuffed in polyester," Edith added, while Caddie grabbed the table ledge to keep from falling out of her chair. "Just like her dearly departed husband, Gary, after eating her greasy cooking for thirty-one years, God rest his soul."

"God rest his soul," repeated Granny Po.

I tried to hide my smile but wasn't quick enough.

"What'd you say, Polly? You *know* I can't hear good without my hearing aids." Caddie strained to sit up, then glanced at me. "Abigail, dear, are these nasty women making fun of me?"

I sprayed Edith's gray hair with some water, then picked up my scissors. After living with Granny Po for the past four years, I've learned it's best not to get in the middle. But still, I couldn't help myself. "Miss Caddie, if you chose an ear, you'd hear everything they say behind your back."

Edith laughed and reached back for a high five. Caddie frowned and patted a curl, looking like a kicked puppy. "And here I thought you were on my side, Abbey darling. Well, if y'all keep this up, then I'll just leave."

"Caddie? The beauty queen? Leave before your nails are done?" Granny Po said. "There's a better chance of Edith winning an Oscar than you leaving with tacky fingertips."

Edith clutched a wrinkled hand to her chest. "I'd like to thank the Academy, my agent, my momma, and all the people I had to sleep with or kill to get to the top."

Poor Caddie. Even though they've been friends for years, she always takes their banter seriously. I gave her a sympathetic grin while shaping Edith's hair. "Ignore them, Miss Caddie. You know they're just jealous."

"That's right. Sick, jealous women." Caddie selected a bright pink polish and pointed it at Granny Po. "And don't y'all say a thing about my beauty-queen days."

"Beauty queen my foot," Granny Po said. "You were a *farm* queen, and farm queen is not the same as beauty queen. And the reason you won is because the only other person competing against you was Louise Demmings. She looked too much like the pigs she raised to ever have a crown on her head."

"Why, Polly Randall, that was downright mean! No wonder nobody wants to rent this shop from you, what with all this negative atmosphere!"

Granny Po squinted, putting a fist on her plump hip. "Caddie Daniels, I cannot believe you just said that!"

Hoo-boy. The antique cuckoo clock above the parlor's door, which was always five minutes too fast, chirped while Granny Po stared at Caddie. For two years Granny Po's been trying to rent the shop so she can retire to a life of lingering morning coffee and afternoon soaps. But every potential renter who's visited the parlor has turned it down. Fast. The white sign on the front lawn that reads BEAUTY SHOP FOR RENT . . . FULLY EQUIPPED, INQUIRE WITHIN now has rust spots, so everybody knows it's a touchy subject.

Even Caddie.

Caddie really was the 4-H Farm Queen in 1961. She once showed me the pictures, a shiny tiara perched on her then blond hair and a white sash draped across her then slim body. Granny Po told me she raised only one small hog, just enough to qualify for the contest, and she bribed her older brother to do all the farm work. That pig went straight to the butcher, after it peed on her leg in the show ring, but the crown was hers and don't you forget it.

It was time for me to diffuse the situation. I reached for the remote, buried under newspapers, and turned on the television. "Hey, *Wheel of Fortune* is coming on in five minutes."

Nothing could stop their bickering faster than *Wheel of*

Fortune. Caddie turned her chair to face the TV. Granny Po stopped worrying about her shop and stood. "I'm hitting the ladies' room. Abbey, fetch us some iced tea, will ya?"

"Oh man! I don't want to miss the first puzzle!"

"You best hurry, then! And bring those cheesecake cookies while you're at it." Granny Po ducked into the hallway that led to the bathroom before I could respond. So much for *please.* Edith glanced in the mirror at her hair, then took off her cape, even though I wasn't finished. "Eh, that's good enough. It's not like the horses are going to care."

She reached into her pocket for a folded wad of money and pressed it into my palm. I didn't open my hand until I walked through the door that separated the beauty shop from the other side of the duplex, where Granny Po and I live. Twenty-five dollars. Fifteen for the haircut; ten for me.

Awesome.

Edith is a good tipper, and every good tip gets me closer to my goal of having a million dollars by my thirty-fifth birthday. Which is why I'm glad Granny Po hasn't rented the shop yet. The money's good, you can't beat the commute, and if a new owner came in, there's a big chance I'd have to say, "Good-bye, job."

As I put the money in my pocket, I heard a stereo's pounding *boom, boom, boom* coming in through the open windows. Even the lace curtains seemed to sway to the beat. I didn't need to look to know it was Mitch Anderson, a junior from Winchester High who's mowed Granny Po's lawn twice a week for the past three years.

I crept to the front family room and peeked out the window. Mitch was sitting in his old Chevy with the door wide open, listening until the song ended. But it wasn't rock that blared. Or rap. Or even Top 40; nothing normal. He listens to cowboy music, stuff like Roy Rogers and Gene Autry, singing about tumbling tumbleweeds and get along little dogie—music that could get a guy beaten up. Mitch has an obsession with old black-and-white Westerns. When we were younger, he'd sometimes bring over his favorite John Wayne or Rex Allen movies for us to watch on Sunday afternoons, and I'd annoy him by laughing at the corny plots and typecast characters.

But our Sunday matinees slowly came to an end after Mitch asked me out. On a real date. I told him no, and even though we're still friends, there's no more tumbling tumble-weeds and get along little dogie.

Mitch climbed out of his car, wearing a stained football jersey and sporting some serious helmet hair from practice. He shot a glance in my direction, causing me to drop the lace curtain and press my back against the wall.

Real smooth, Abbey.

In the kitchen, I fished around the leftover chicken casserole for the iced-tea jug buried in the jam-packed refrigerator. A plate of cheesecake cookies sat next to a perfect Jell-O mold with a note—FOR BINGO, TOUCH AND DIE—taped on top, giving me a sudden urge to poke my finger into the jiggling mass.

"Abbey! Stop picking your nose and get back in here! Show's about to start," Edith bellowed from the other side of the duplex. She's a good tipper, yes. Patient, no.

With the glasses teetering dangerously on a wooden tray, I fumbled at the parlor door, trying to hold it open with my foot.

"Need any help?" Granny Po asked, just as I set the tray on the counter.

"Um, not now."

The parlor door opened with a flourish. Crisp October air chilled my ankles as Rosemary Lewis walked in, wearing the lavender raincoat she'd bought in Baltimore, and her hair held down with a chiffon scarf.

"Ladies! Hello! How nice, all the Gray Widows are here." She threw her designer handbag on the sofa, away from Edith's barn coat. "My, what a day it's been. I was stuck in York all afternoon, dealing with those horrid annual inspections for my rental properties. I'm much too old to be running around like that! *Wheel of Fortune?*"

"In a few minutes," I answered, squeezing lemon into my tea. "Why don't you hire a property management company and have them do all that work?"

Rosemary took off her coat. "Because my husband, Thomas, never trusted management companies, and after he died, I guess I felt duty-bound not to as well, God rest his soul."

"God rest his soul," they repeated, shaking their heads.

"Besides, what else am I going to do? Oh, and I brought you a little something, Abbey." Rosemary handed me a book, *The Millionaire Within* by Rob Keith. "Just finished it last night and thought you'd like it. There're several chapters on real estate."

I read the inside cover. "With over thirty-five years of experience, Rob Keith will teach you secrets that separate the leaders from the followers." My heart quickened at the author's photo revealing a perfectly cut designer suit and a sparkling diamond watch.

That's going to be me. Not the suit or diamonds; spending

thousands on clothes or a watch is ridiculous, and no, I don't want to be a man.

It's his success I want. With security, and a guarantee that I'll never live like my mother, hopping from one crappy apartment to another, never owning her own property, and always relying on other people for her happiness. If I have to give a thousand haircuts and sweep a thousand pounds of hair to get there, then I will. Too bad Caddie and Rosemary won't let me cut their hair, but they haven't let anyone but Granny Po touch their curls since the Gray Widows came together.

The Gray Widows. All over sixty—some by miles; some by meters. All with gray hair, though most of them colored it once a month. And all of their husbands dead, like the mates of a female black-widow spider. My great-grandfather died in a car accident when Granny Po was only thirty-four years old. She scraped together enough money to open a beauty shop, and Caddie was her first customer. Caddie's husband, Gary, died after a massive heart attack, and all joking aside, it probably was from her cooking. She's a firm believer a meal isn't a meal without a cup of lard and is always trying to fatten me up.

Rosemary's husband died from an aneurysm. After he passed away, and she was suddenly left with twenty-nine rental units to manage, Rosemary wandered into Polly's Parlor for a manicure and cried the entire time. But when Edith lost her husband to cancer, she cried only once. The first and only time in her adult life.

"No sense in crying over the past, something you can't change," she told me. "You gotta look ahead."

With that, I couldn't agree more.

"Oh, dang." Caddie sighed. "Pat Sajak's not on. I *hate* when they have a replacement host! You know what it reminds me of? Eating a hot dog on white bread because you ran out of hot-dog buns. It's just not the same."

Rosemary nodded. "Mmm, I love hot dogs on potato rolls."

Granny Po brushed polish on Caddie's nails with the precision of a skilled surgeon. "I wouldn't know. Abbey here hasn't let me eat a hot dog in the past four years, since they're so *unhealthy*."

"Please, do you have any idea what's in them? We're talking scraps," I said.

"Scraps, craps," Caddie exclaimed. "Years ago, they said butter would kill ya. Then they said it was healthier than margarine. Just wait—five years from now, hot dogs will be the new diet trend, like all the Atkins and Zone nonsense. Celebrities will swear by it, posing with their hot dog on a stick. They'll call it the Weiner Zone, or something."

I opened my mouth, but Granny Po quickly cut me off. "Girl, whatever you're about to say, I'm not gonna like, so forget it, Abbey."

Darn. It was pretty funny, too; but the first puzzle was starting, anyway. Four words; the clue was "noun." Game on.

Life around here is put on hold when *Wheel of Fortune* is on. It's a sacred ritual, as important as going to church on Sunday or flossing extra good before a dentist appointment. To the other Widows, it's just a fun show; but it means much more to Granny Po, and to me.

Granny Po hardly knew me when my mother left me here four years ago. She had no clue what to do with an eleven-year-old who mostly cried in her bedroom. And I had no clue what to do with her, this stranger, who my mother barely talked about, let alone visited. One week later, I silently joined her on the sofa, exhausted and my face tearstained as I curled into a ball on the opposite end. Granny Po didn't say a thing. She just turned on the television as the game show began. I stayed quiet during the first puzzle. Tried not to act interested in the second. By the third, I blurted out the answer, a second before Granny Po.

She accused me of cheating. I called her a sore loser. We tuned in same time next night. And the next night. And every night since that we possibly could.

After all these years, she's still a sore loser and hates when I solve the puzzle before her. Which is pretty much all the time, like now, even before Vanna White turned the sixth letter. "Mocha latte with foam!"

Granny Po groaned. "Big deal. I don't know all those dang coffees, anyway."

The second contestant did; I could tell by the confident swagger in his stance. But instead of solving the puzzle, he reached forward to spin the wheel, trying to get more money even though he already had $4,250.

"Oh my gosh, don't spin! Solve the puzzle, you moron!" It would be totally stupid to spin now, since there was a good chance he'd hit bankrupt or lose-a-turn. If it was my hard-earned money on the line, I'd solve the puzzle quicker than Granny Po could wax off a mustache.

"Bet a dollar he hits bankruptcy," Edith said.

"You're on," Rosemary countered, always willing to make a bet.

Edith won. The next contestant pounced, solving the

puzzle with only five hundred dollars in the bank. But at least *nobody* could take that five hundred away.

"Idiots. Always greedy for more," Granny Po said, shaking her head. "Just like my late husband, who'd spend our last dollar on some junk car, saying he'd make thousands once he fixed it up. And he never did, God rest his soul."

"God rest his soul," the ladies repeated.

I sat down at the manicure table while Rosemary handed Edith a dollar. I've never met my great-grandfather, but in a way, my mother sounded so much like him. She would use the last of the rent money on clothes or that silver jewelry she loved so much, just to ease her depression. And it never did.

"You okay, honey?" Caddie asked me.

"Sure. Fine," I said, picking up a glittery blue polish and opening the bottle. I pretended to concentrate on my nails, but my mind flashed back to that rainy August night. How Mom drove nonstop from upper Pennsylvania to Maryland until she reached Granny Po's front porch. I remember clinging to Mom, careful not to bump the white bandages on her wrists that protected the fresh wounds from her suicide attempt. The oversized men's sweatshirt I wore hung past my knees, heavy with dampness, like the cold, empty feeling in my heart when I realized she was leaving me.

"It's not forever, sweetheart," she promised. "Just until I find a new place and a job. I swear, by winter, we'll be together."

And then she was gone. Leaving me with a puzzle I've never been able to solve.

Why?

Chapter Two

Back then, I believed her.

There had been no doubt in my mind that by winter, Mom would return. Her depression would be gone, the wounds on her wrists would be healed, and we'd be together again. She just needed time, even though I didn't understand why . . . or why she couldn't have me around.

Granny Po had enrolled me in sixth grade, and waved as the bus drove away, taking me to a middle school that seemed ten times larger than my old school in Pennsylvania. None of the other girls spoke to me—not on the bus, not at lunch—but it didn't matter. It was senseless to make friends, anyway, because in a few short months, my mom would return for me. Every day after school, I checked the mailbox for her letters, and jumped for the phone if it rang. I ran to the door whenever someone knocked, thinking it might be her on the other side wearing a big smile and saying, "Pack your bags. I found a great apartment, and we're going home!"

But winter came and passed. Snow melted and the grass

turned green. Mom did call a few times. There were a few letters, and she briefly visited that Easter. But it wasn't until the hot July sun scorched the grass to a dull brown, nearly one year after arriving at Granny Po's doorstep, that I began to realize: She's not coming back. She'll never tell me we're going home.

And most times, I'm glad.

Because this is my home now. At the beauty shop for rent.

"Abbey, you didn't call me last night!" Kym Hughes was walking down the hallway toward me with her backpack slung over one shoulder and her blond hair in a high ponytail. Sarah Diehl followed a few paces behind, frowning at her cell phone and almost hitting Kym in the rear with her violin case.

Shoot. I forgot to call Kym, and she always thinks something's wrong if you don't call or instant-message her at least once a night. "Sorry, I worked at the shop and then had a ton of homework."

"Bummer." Kym dropped her backpack to the floor and pulled out a sheet of paper. She held it up with a devious smile. "You could have been the first lucky soul to hear my brand-new list! Who wants to see it?"

"Another list? You just did one yesterday," Sarah said, grimacing as a gang of basketball players crowded by, pressing her against the lockers.

Kym watched them pass with a hopeful gaze, but none of them noticed her. She reached into her sweater to adjust a wayward bra strap, then passed her list to Sarah. "Well, that was before Tony Clark got his new haircut. He looks totally hot now!"

"Tony Clark is a moron. He had to repeat algebra, twice," I said, trying to force open my locker, which gets stuck every single day. The handle snapped shut, pinching the tip of my thumb. "Crap! I hate this locker!"

"Yes, but he's a hot moron," Kym said. "I'd be willing to overlook his lack of brain cells."

Kym is one of the smartest girls in our sophomore class, but nobody knows it. Not our classmates, not the teachers, and maybe not even Kym. After she made the winter JV cheerleading squad, Kym became obsessed with raising her semipopular, "B" status to the elite "A" level, and she would overlook more than brain cells if it meant getting the right boyfriend.

I moved closer to Sarah so we could both read Kym's infamous list of the ten guys she's in love with. At least for today. "Hey, what happened to Kenny Smith? Is he no longer in your harem?"

Kym sighed and cocked her head to the side. "Sadly, no. And the poor guy doesn't know what he's missing."

I met Sarah and Kym at the beginning of eighth grade, after a major school district rezoning forced me to go to a different middle school. Most students protested the change, but for me, it was a total blessing. I could start over, in a new environment, where no one remembered me as the sullen girl who sometimes cried in sixth grade. Kym and Sarah were rezoned as well, and the three of us merged together the first week.

Sarah and Kym have the most in common. They both love shopping at the mall, or discussing at night what they're going to wear to school the next day, while I'm the one who would rather read *Forbes* than *Cosmopolitan* magazine. But our biggest difference is that, while Kym thinks her greatest high school accomplishment could be securing a hot boyfriend and Sarah's biggest worry is losing her own boyfriend, John Hall, I think dating is a total waste of time.

I jammed my hip against the metal locker in a useless attempt to open it. It was hopelessly stuck this time. Sarah held up her phone again, checking for new messages.

"No calls," she moaned. "John refused to talk about it last night. Okay, yeah, so his parents are moving after the second semester. But there's no reason why he needs to go to another school! His mom said she would drive him here to Winchester High, but *no*, he wants to go ahead and transfer to Layton Park. I don't get it! You would think he'd want to stay with me!"

I leaned against my rebellious locker and looked at Sarah's crestfallen face. Of course Sarah didn't get it. John wants to leave because there's a good chance he could make the Layton Park varsity baseball team, even though he's only a sophomore. The guy lives and breathes baseball. Sarah should know that he'd pick baseball over her, after all the pitching lessons, and batting lessons, and games she watched from the sidelines.

Sarah believes him when he says he still wants to stay together, even though they'll be in different schools. But really, does she think high school romance lasts forever? I mean, seriously, it doesn't.

Just ask my mother.

I've heard the story so many times. How she, Grace Somers, was the popular sixteen-year-old junior dating Dale Garner, the senior quarterback hero. They were the golden couple, everyone's all-American, until the pregnancy test turned pink. When she told him, Dad ran a hand through his hair, paced the school hallway with a stupid football in his hand, then said, "Holy shit, how could this happen? Weren't you careful?"

Hardly the Hallmark moment.

Of course, there were a few fairy-tale moments. Dad said everything would be okay. Mom would give birth, and after she graduated, they'd get married and go to the same college. They could take turns babysitting while the other went to class, and be a happy little family forever.

Instead, Mom's parents, Elton and Evelyn Somers, kicked her out of their house, leaving her no choice but to move into my father's basement. They were married in a courthouse five months later, and Mom quit school. After my first birthday, Dad dropped out of college and lost his football scholarship, thoroughly pissing off his parents, Joseph and Arlene Garner. So, Mom and Dad moved into a rented town house . . . and hated each other ever since.

Which proves how fairy tales are complete and total bull-crap.

"Sarah," I said, thinking of my words carefully, "don't you think . . ."

I stopped. *Don't you think you'd be better off?* Sarah should concentrate on her goal of becoming a concert violinist, not a devoted girlfriend. But instead of saying what she clearly didn't want to hear, I turned back to my possessed locker and the one corner that refused to budge. Mitch Anderson walked up and leaned against the locker beside me. Sunglasses casually hung from the front of his T-shirt and his hair was windblown and messy from the way he likes to drive with the windows down.

He grinned as I knicked my pea green, pain-in-my-butt locker. "Hey, need any help?"

"Oh, hey," I said. "Um, no thanks, I almost have it."

"No, you don't." Mitch edged me aside, shaking his head. Kym and Sarah stood behind him with these awful knowing looks as Mitch pulled my locker handle back, then pushed down so the corner popped open. "There you go. Piece of cake."

"Thanks," I said, trying to ignore Kym, who was sneaking closer to smell his cologne. *Stop it*, I mouthed to her.

"No problem." Mitch shrugged. "I wanted to talk to you, anyway. Any chance you can help out at Edith's tomorrow afternoon? She still hasn't found a new manager yet, and we're short on help."

Edith started Jones Horse Rescue on her fifty-acre farm after her husband died and takes in abused or neglected horses. After seeing how capable Mitch was working for Granny Po, Edith hired him a year ago. During the summer, I help out, because all Maryland students are required to do volunteer work before graduating.

The last manager Edith hired was a disaster who showed up drunk on more than one occasion. Edith gave him the boot when he fed alfalfa hay to a group of horses who were used to timothy hay. The poor geldings had diarrhea for days, and trust me, cleaning those stalls should have earned me *double* community hours.

"Yeah, sure," I said. "I can be there by noon."

"Great. See you then, Abbey." Mitch saluted me and

turned around, heading toward his homeroom. Two freshmen girls watched him pass, with lovesick eyes.

"Could you possibly drool any more?" Kym teased, nudging my shoulder.

I nudged her back and grabbed a handful of books from my locker. "Please, don't even start. Mitch and I are just friends."

Sarah chuckled and linked arms with me as we walked down the hall. "Uh-huh. So explain why you work at Edith's farm for free."

"Community hours, duh! And I like the horses." We rounded a corner and dodged a crowd of girls rushing out of the bathroom. "Please, we are *seriously* just friends."

Kym held open the stairwell door for us. It slammed behind her just as the first morning-bell rang. "Only seventy-five hours are required. You have double that, *and* you don't even like to ride horses. Besides, you know men and women can never be only friends. What about the movie *When Harry Met Sally*, hmm? It was impossible for them to be just 'friends.'"

Oh my gosh, Kym and her romance movies. Her favorite birthday present last year was a subscription to Netflix, so she can see all her favorites. Ten times each.

"No, that's not true," I said as we trotted up the steps. "Harry and Sally *were* friends until they had sex, and that screwed everything up. Harry practically *ran* from Sally after that, remember?"

"*But*, they found love in the end, remember? Just like John and I will," Sarah said.

"Sure they did," I countered, opening the second-floor

door and glancing at my watch. "It was a movie, not the real world! There had to be a happy ending!"

Sarah's pace slowed at my comment.

"But not you and John," I blurted, after seeing the hurt expression on her face. "Of course you and John will make it. I wasn't talking about you guys!"

That was a total lie, but she seemed relieved. The second bell was about to ring, so she waved and took off down the hall while Kym and I hurried to our homeroom. I was about to ask Kym if she studied for Spanish, when we rounded a corner and crashed right into a hulking figure wearing a lacrosse jersey.

"Ouch!" I flew back, dropping my armload of books.

"Aw, dude, you okay?" Before I could answer, Camden Mackintosh bent down to pick up my books, and gave me a playful glance. He was a junior who sat a few rows behind me in Advanced Chemistry and goofed off most of the time. Camden stood to what must be a full six feet, with broad, athletic shoulders. My face burned when he handed me my books. "Sorry about that. You all right?"

Kym quickly shook her hair out of its ponytail and beamed at him. "Oh, Abbey's fine, aren't you, Abbey?"

I glanced at her. She poked me in the ribs as if to say *Come on, say something!* "Yeah, I'm fine. No big deal. Whatever."

"Cool. Then I'll check you later . . . Abbey." Camden gave a sly grin and tipped his chin up in a "hey, baby" gesture that guys somehow think girls find appealing. *Please.*

As soon as he was out of sight, Kym let out her breath and gasped. "Oh my gosh, did you see that? He was totally checking you out. Camden Mackintosh! Checking you out!"

"No, he wasn't, and hurry up. We're going to be late." At least *I* didn't think he was. Not that it mattered, anyway.

Kym pulled on my sweater sleeve. "Don't you know who he is? He's the best player on the lacrosse team and has, like, the most fabulous parties ever! And so totally gorgeous."

So totally not.

"Maybe he'll ask you out!" Kym exclaimed.

"And I'd say no."

"Why? Unless, of course . . . you really do have a thing for Mitch."

Right. The look on my face told her exactly what I thought of that theory.

"Okay, then," Kym said, "give me one good reason why you'd say no to Camden."

I thought for a second, knowing it had to be a good one or she'd nag me for days. "He called me 'dude.' A person with breasts is *not* called 'dude.'"

Kym let out a quick laugh. "Not necessarily."

We made it to homeroom with only seconds to spare. A few minutes later, Kym tossed a note on my desk: *Admit it. Camden is gorgeous. And 100 percent A-list.*

I found a pen from my purse. *Yes, 100 percent A, for* ABSOLUTELY NOT. *He's all yours, baby!*

Kym didn't pass the note back, but I could hear her pen moving feverishly behind me. I bet she's writing another list. With Camden Mackintosh somewhere near the top.

Chapter Three

"Granny Po! I'm going to Edith's now."

I poked my head through the shop door. Granny Po had on rubber gloves, a floral smock, and was squirting perm solution onto Adelle Johnson's tightly rolled hair. She set down the bottle and walked toward me, holding her hands up like a doctor scrubbed for surgery.

She took in my worn jeans and old sweatshirt. "You dressed warm enough?"

"Yes, ma'am. It's a beautiful Saturday."

Granny Po nodded. "Fine. Got your cell phone?"

Even though Granny Po used to be severely opposed to any teenager owning a cell phone, she bought me one when I started working at the horse rescue. She was afraid a horse would kick me in the head and I'd be too incapacitated to crawl to the phone.

I pulled the phone from my pocket and wiggled it. "Yep, got it. And I peed and pooed, too, so you don't have to worry about that."

Edith's barn has only a portable bathroom outside, another concern of Granny Po's. She narrowed her eyes and pointed a gloved finger at me. "Don't be fresh, girl. And make sure you're home by four thirty, tonight being bingo and all. *And,* you tell that Mitch he got a little messy with the Weed-wacker by the back fence, you hear?"

"I hear, Granny Po."

Bodie's ears bounced as he ran toward me, his tongue lolling to the side. I climbed over the fence that separates our property from Edith's and clapped my hands. The blue heeler crouched in a submissive crawl a few steps in front of me, looking scared until I knelt and scratched behind his black-tipped ears.

"Hey, Bodie-bear. How's my good boy?" Bodie sat up, hooking a front paw around my arm. He gazed at me with complete adoration, then licked my face, his breath a combo of sour milk and stink bomb.

"Oh my gosh, Bodie, you stink! You are one rotten dog!"

He wagged his tail and got in one more stinky kiss before darting toward Edith's horses resting beneath an oak tree. Her favorite horse, Ragman, ambled over, switching at flies with his short, almost hairless tail. He had a blanket of white spots on his hindquarters and a huge roman-nosed face that was so ugly he was cute. Edith and her husband used to breed registered Appaloosas, but after he passed, she sold all but three horses and built herself a small stable. She uses the large barn for her business.

I patted Ragman and then walked with Bodie to the old barn where JONES HORSE RESCUE was painted on the silo. What sounded like Western music spilled from the barn, and a couple of thin chestnut horses lounged by the water tub, lazily swishing their tails. A rusted horseshoe hung over the doorway. It rattled as the barn door kicked open and Mitch walked out holding a pitchfork with a dead rabbit dangling from the tines.

He stopped when he saw us, then tilted his head to the side. "I hope Bodie didn't lick you."

Bodie gave me a sorrowful glance, ears pinned back with shame.

Mitch laughed at the expression on my face. "*Eeewwww!* I'm not kissing you today. Lord knows what kind of rotten parasites are crawling on your skin right now."

"Please. You're so desperate, you'd kiss anything," I said, reaching down to reassure Bodie and resisting the urge to wipe my face. Mitch opened a trash can with one hand and dumped the rabbit inside.

"God rest his little bunny soul," Mitch said, in pure Gray Widows style.

"God rest his soul," I repeated. From working at Granny Po's for so long, Mitch knew all their quirks. He shut the trash can and brushed sawdust off the front of his stained shirt.

"How long can you stay?" Mitch asked, leaning the pitchfork against the barn.

"Until four thirty, since it's Saturday."

"Granny Po has bingo?"

"Bingo."

"Cool." Mitch motioned me to the barn. "Come to the office, then. Edith hired a new manager yesterday, and you'll want to meet him."

That was fast. Normally it takes a while for her to find someone, since Edith can't offer much of a salary. "What's his name?"

Mitch looked back at me with a grin. "Oh . . . you'll find out."

I followed him into the barn, noticing a few cobwebs gathered in the corners. I'd have to get them later. Mitch knocked lightly on the door to the office, which is really an old feed area with a wooden desk and medicine cabinets hung on the walls for supplies. A portly man with shiny auburn hair and a face full of freckles rose from the chair, extending his hand across the table.

"Ah, you must be Abbey! Darn pleased to meet ya, young lady. I've heard a lot of good things about you," he said.

I shook his hand, feeling thick callus across his palm, and noticed the age spots clustered on his forearm. Mitch stood behind his desk, smiling. "Abbey, this is . . . Harry Penney."

I almost choked. Did he say Harry Penney? "Uh, who?"

"Harry Penney," Mr. Penney repeated. "Darn pleased to meet ya!"

Mitch seemed to be enjoying himself watching me struggle to keep a straight face, which is hard when your mind is racing with images of hairy copper pennies. "Right. Hi, I'm Abbey Garner."

"Well, darn pleased to meet ya," Mr. Penney said again. "You need anything, just holler, okay?"

I nodded, backing out of the office. Once we were out of earshot, I swatted Mitch on the shoulder. "Jerk! You totally set me up."

He laughed and dodged another blow. "Hey, you handled yourself like a trouper. I really thought you'd crack up at least once."

I busted out laughing. "Not that I didn't want to. Oh my

gosh, Harry Penney? Didn't his parents have any clue when they named him?"

"Could be worse," Mitch said. "My dad knew a kid in school named . . . get this . . . Harry Peters."

"No!"

"Yep, no joke. Saw the yearbook picture myself. Can you imagine the therapy it took to get over that?" He gave me a wink and then pointed to a back stall. "Come see the new arrival."

"Is it hairy?" I asked.

"Very."

I followed Mitch, noticing how his own hair had grown long enough to almost touch his collar. It was nice, if you like that curly-head look. Mitch was the only other person in high school that I knew who worked just as hard as me. He was saving for college, since he didn't want to rely on getting a football scholarship.

Long hair I like. Football I hate.

After I turned Mitch down last spring, I was afraid our friendship would be over. But we knew too much about each other to not be friends. I know how spinning carnival rides make him sick, that he loves going to Virtz's Ice Cream in the summer, and eats his mint chocolate chip while sitting on the hood of his car. He knows that the smell of sauerkraut makes me ill, how I want to be the first woman in the Garner family to get a college degree, and how I have always wanted a dog like Bodie.

Mitch stopped at a stall door. A dirty bay mare pinned her ears back and scooted to the far wall. "Edith picked her up yesterday. Her owners had to move to Kentucky and didn't have time to sell her."

"Was she abused?" I asked, softly clucking to her.

"Nah, she's just cranky about being in the stall. But you know the rules, all new horses are quarantined. Their daughter showed her in 4-H, so maybe we could ride her in a week or so. What do you think?"

I think . . . no thanks. Even though I love being around horses, that does not include actually sitting on one. My father once put me on a neighbor's pony, promising me I would be fine. But the pony reared and took off, dumping me on the hard ground. I've since sworn off riding.

Mitch accepted my silence as a no, then reached for a halter hanging on a tuna can nailed to the wall. Thank God he didn't push like Edith, who's determined to get me on Ragman one day. "That's cool. Then hang around while I clean up the chestnut gelding over there, since some people are coming later who might adopt him. I want to talk to you about something."

Uh-oh.

It's never good news when someone says they want to talk. What if he's asking me out again? Homecoming is coming up. That's all everyone at school is talking about, the big football game on Friday night and the dance on Saturday. Lord knows that's important to Mitch, since he's a first-string running back.

I walked down the aisle and sat on a hay bale, tapping the spot beside me so Bodie would jump up. He nestled close, putting his head on my lap. I took a breath, then casually said, "What's up?"

Mitch led the gelding out of the stall, attaching the cross ties. "Oh, nothing. It's just that homecoming, you know, is this weekend and . . ."

Oh man, he *is* asking me out. I tried to figure out the nicest way to say no.

". . . and I was thinking. About the dance."

Mitch, I value our friendship too much to . . .

"What if I asked Amy Perkins to the dance? What do you think of her?"

Huh?

"I, ah, what? Who?" I stammered, my fingers curling around Bodie's collar.

"You know, Amy Perkins? Brown hair, with those blond highlight things? She's on the varsity squad."

Oh, *that* Amy Perkins. Varsity squad, as in varsity cheerleader.

"What?" he asked. "What was that look for?"

Did I make a look? I shrugged, trying to act cool. "I didn't say anything."

"You didn't have to; I can see it all over your face. What's wrong with Amy?"

He rested his arm on the gelding's withers, waiting for an answer. *Okay, think of one!* I shrugged again, focusing my eyes on Bodie. "Nothing's wrong with her. I mean, I guess she's nice. It's just that . . ."

"Just what? That she's a cheerleader?"

"No, it's not that." *Liar.*

"Then, what?"

I crossed my arms, knowing I couldn't tell him the truth. How the whole cheerleader–football-player thing was nothing but a stupid, tired cliché. Mitch and I may be friends, but he doesn't know the story behind my parents, and I'm not about to tell him now.

Mitch continued to stare, waiting for an answer. I had to give him something. "Okay. You want to know? Fine. Yes, it is because she's a cheerleader. I mean, I don't get why anyone would want to stay on the sidelines, cheering on everyone else instead of playing the game themselves, you know? That's what bugs me about cheerleaders."

Mitch turned and started brushing the horse's neck, clouds of dust flying with each stroke. "Oh, come on, Abbey. Haven't you ever seen a cheerleading competition? You don't think they're athletes, too?"

Yes, they are, and I felt bad for talking like this, considering Kym is a cheerleader. But there's no backpedaling out of this one without looking like a jealous cow. Why didn't I keep my mouth shut? "I'm not saying they aren't athletes. It's just that . . . just that . . ."

"You're jealous," Mitch teased, turning around and twirling a finger in my face.

"Are you kidding me?"

"*Jealous!*" He poked his finger closer. "That's why you still come here for free, just to be near your buddy Mitch."

I jumped up, grabbing his finger. Bodie stood and barked, causing the horse to spook. "Oh *please*. Jealous? Of her? Why, because of the short-ass skirts she wears? My legs are a thousand times better. And besides. This place would go to hell in a handbasket if I didn't come here. Just look at those cobwebs. If Granny Po let me work more during the school year, they'd never be there."

Which was true. Mitch couldn't argue with that one. Since I started working at the farm over the summer, the tack rooms have been organized, the hay and feed ordered on time, and I even installed a program on Edith's computer to help with her accounting.

Mitch pulled his hand back, rubbing his finger. "Fine. So your legs aren't bad. Neither is your grip. Now, could you kindly settle down? You're scaring the horse."

"Fine."

"Fine! Hell in a handbasket. You talk like an old lady, from hanging around the shop so much. Why don't you get to work now, since you're so gifted?" He leaned closer, one eyebrow raised. "I told Mr. Penney how great you are at worming the horses, and he said he'd be mighty grateful if you took care of it."

I rolled my eyes at his smirk. He knows full well how much I hate sticking the syringe in the horses' mouths and injecting the sticky paste down their throats. Seems like I always get stuck with that job. Guess it's because I'm capable, unlike some cheerleader I won't mention.

"Yeah, well, Granny Po is seriously peeved at you for overwhacking the weeds by the back fence," I said, crossing my arms over my stomach.

"Oh man! I was hoping she wouldn't catch that," Mitch said. "Guess I'll be hearing about that later."

"Oh yes, you will."

"Abigail Lynn, you're twenty minutes late!"

I climbed the fence and crossed the backyard to the brick patio. The Widows were sitting at the wrought-iron table with a pot of tea, Granny Po's antique teacups, and a box of Triscuits. I kicked off my dirty boots, walked up the brick steps, and flopped down beside Rosemary. "Sorry, Granny Po. Hope you all aren't going to be late."

"Bingo can wait. Besides, it's too pretty out here to rush," Rosemary said, pouring me a cup of mint tea, the steam rising in the evening air. A fire crackled in the outdoor fireplace, called a *chimenea*, that was shaped like a giant gourd. Thick mums in clay pots lined the patio, and the wind chimes I made in the eighth grade sounded when the wind stirred.

Granny Po sniffed the air. "Abbey, you smell like shit!"

"Polly!" Caddie held a hand to her chest. "Using that kind of language around Abbey, Lord! And you can't blurt out stuff like that!"

"Why not?" Granny Po asked. "It's the truth, ain't it? I could smell her even before she reached the fence."

Rosemary passed me the sugar bowl. "Still, Polly, that's not how one should behave in polite society."

I pulled my sweatshirt to my nose and gave it a whiff. There was a combination of manure, horse, worm medicine, and possibly Bodie's parasite germs. "Yeah, but it's true, Miss Rosemary. I do smell."

"See?" Granny Po declared. "*Thank* you, Abbey. People spend too much dang time dancing around the truth. Like this lady who came in for a perm the other day, even though she had beautiful straight hair. She spent the entire time complaining about how tired she was, how she couldn't keep up with her children, blah, blah, blah. Know what I told her?"

Caddie opened her mouth as though she was going to guess, but Granny Po continued.

"I told her she was too overweight and outta shape, that's why she was tired."

"Polly! My Lord, you didn't!"

Granny Po tucked her chin, eyebrows knitted. "Sure I did! It's the truth, ain't it? If she spent her time exercising and eating right instead of just complaining, then she wouldn't be in that pickle. Somebody had to shake her up by telling her the truth. Might as well be me."

I smiled and leaned back in my chair, sipping tea, while Caddie and Rosemary jumped on Granny Po for being too harsh with the poor mother. Maybe she could be a bit more subtle, but that's what I like most about Granny Po. She tells the truth, even if the truth hurts.

You can always count on people who tell the truth.

Clouds passed in the vibrant autumn sky as I tuned out the Widows' voices, leaving room for the one haunting question I try my best to avoid.

Where is she now?

The last time we spoke on the phone, Mom was living in Gettysburg, working at the Jenny Wade Museum, named after the only civilian killed during the battle. Or, as Mom pointed out, another woman victimized by a man. But she never stays long at any one place. Mom moves as often as the seasons change, always running whenever the wintry storms in her mind change direction. Maybe it was her parents' kicking her out when she got pregnant that gave her a restless spirit, always searching for someplace to call home.

But she never seems to find it.

I drained the rest of my tea, trying to forget about my mother and wondering if I should use Granny Po's policy and tell Sarah the truth: that once John went to a different high school, the chances were slim they'd stay together; that she should let him go, and worry about herself . . . and *her* future, not his.

Granny Po stood, telling the other ladies it was time to leave. We walked inside and she looked at me while pulling on her windbreaker by the closet. "Sure you don't want to go with us?"

I held the front door open for her. "No thanks, I'm going to hang here."

"Makes no never mind to me," Granny Po said, picking up her bingo basket and food containers and stepping out onto the porch. "Just don't be watching any crap on television; do your homework; and do not, *do not*, let anyone in this house unless they're the paramedics coming to save your bleeding soul. Do you understand?"

The same old lecture, each and every Saturday before Granny Po leaves for the United Lutheran's weekly bingo night. I did go with them a few times when I was younger. Talk about a vicious scene: women nervously praying for the right number to be called, anxious eyes patrolling as many cards as they can handle. The wave of outrage that spreads through the room when someone crows out an obnoxious *"BINGO!"* And what happens if you call Bingo by mistake? It happened to me, and from their reaction you would have thought I spat on the holy cross and burned an American flag.

"Yes, Granny Po, I understand. But you didn't say anything about parties in the backyard," I teased, even though the chance of me having a party was slim to none. I've never even gone to a high school party, except for Kym's last birthday sleepover. I'm just not the kind of person who would have a party, and that suits me just fine.

Caddie gave me a wink before swallowing me in a big hug. "Good one, baby girl."

"No, not good, Miss Abbey," snapped Granny Po. "How about: No one allowed on the premises, inside or out! And that includes Mitch, if he comes by for his pay."

"Yes, ma'am, I'll go to *his* place, then."

Granny Po wiggled a finger in my face. "Don't think you're old enough to sass me, little Miss Smart Butt. I can still take you down."

"Oh, lighten up, Polly," Edith said, following us off the porch, wearing her best cowboy boots. "It wouldn't hurt the girl to have some fun instead of doing nothing but work. Maybe act like a teenager for a change instead of a dang grown-up. Quit lecturing and let's go! Time to kick some bingo butt!"

"*Yee-haw,* Gray Widows attack," Caddie said, shaking her keys before opening her car door.

"I don't *make* the girl work! She's the one who bugs me for more hours," Granny Po exclaimed while lowering herself onto the front passenger seat of Caddie's spotless Cadillac. She balanced the sacred Jell-O mold on her lap and gave me a lighthearted snarl. "Oh, go deep condition your hair; it's all frizzy. And your week's pay is by the register . . . and I made an egg-custard pie, just in case you like that sort of thing."

She knows it's my favorite.

Chapter Four

The vacant beauty shop felt strange, with its empty chairs and silence. Hair dryers stood like statues, and the magazines, spewed haphazardly earlier today, were now neatly stacked on a washed-pine table.

In the early seventies, Granny Po's brother-in-law, Sherman, lived in this half of the duplex. But when my greatgrandfather died, his brother moved out and Polly's Parlor moved in. The kitchen cabinets now hold shampoos and beauty supplies instead of dishes, and canisters of cotton balls, curlers, and combs litter the dated countertop. In one drawer is a pile of romance novels available for trade.

My salary was next to the ancient register, an annoying piece of equipment Granny Po really should replace. I counted the money twice, making a mental note to ask Rosemary to deposit it for me at the bank, since Granny Po doesn't drive much. She hardly ventures out except for her weekly grocery store and Wal-Mart runs. Ever since I came here, she has joked about how she can't wait for me to get my driver's license so

I can chauffeur her around, like in that old movie *Driving Miss Daisy*. Guess in a way, she always knew my mother was never coming back.

Remembering Granny Po's deep-conditioning advice, I decided to take a long bath. But just as the water began sinking deep into my tense shoulder muscles and turning my fingers into a delightful, wrinkled mess, the phone rang.

I forgot to bring in the portable. *It's probably Granny Po, and if I don't answer, she'll think someone's kidnapped me, or something.*

I stepped out of the tub, grabbed a towel, and sloshed to the kitchen with hair conditioner running down my back. The answering machine picked up on the fifth ring.

"Hi, Abbey, it's Dad. Are you there?"

My hand froze, suspended above the phone.

"Well, I, ah, guess since it's Saturday night, you're out having fun, so . . . I'll just talk to you later, okay? Take care. And give me a call, okay?"

His voice sounded tired—sad even—like a child who wasn't invited to a birthday party. Maybe I could have picked up, but tonight . . . tonight I wasn't in the mood for his weekly attempt at playing the role of doting father. Every time I hear his voice, it takes me back to *there,* back to the days when empty beer cans lined the kitchen counter and my parents' fighting rang in my ears long after I'd gone to sleep.

I deleted the message so Granny Po wouldn't hear it, then walked to the bathroom to rinse my hair. Whenever he calls, she pushes me to phone back because he's my father, and I was in no mood to be pushed.

There was a time when Dad could have been a real father.

He could have taken custody of me four years ago, but he was more worried about starting a life with his new wife, Sharon, and her kids. It wasn't until *they* divorced, a year ago, that he started calling and, in his words, "trying to get to know" me.

Only about four years too late.

Thoughts of my dad swarmed like yellow jackets as I walked to my room, so I put on sweats and reached for my notebook with MBTF etched on its spine. "Millionaire by Thirty-Five." My savings plan started when I was twelve, after watching an *Oprah* episode with Rosemary. Oprah's guest was a blond sixteen-year-old girl who'd been investing in the stock market for five years and planned on retiring wealthy at twenty-five. *Twenty-five!* It blew me away, someone her age making money like that. Of course, it helped that her parents knew about the stock market, but it got me to thinking: *Why not me?*

I asked Rosemary if she had any stocks. "No, honey, we never got involved with the stock market. Thomas and I invested in real estate—rental properties mostly."

"Oh. Okay. Just asking."

Rosemary must have seen the disappointment in my face. "Are you interested in finance, Abbey?"

"I don't know. I guess, maybe."

The next day, she sat me down at the table, took a book out of her briefcase, and pulled a bookmark from a chapter on compound interest. "Girl, this is something I wish someone taught *me* when I was your age. Look at this chart, Abbey. If you saved twenty-five dollars a week, at six percent interest for thirty years, you could have more than a hundred thousand dollars! But only thirty-nine thousand was the actual money deposited. The rest was all from compounded interest."

I didn't understand, so Rosemary tried again. "See, that's about seventy thousand dollars earned from interest without lifting a finger, just by tucking away twenty-five dollars a week. But the secret is to start saving money when you're young."

Okay . . . young, like me. And as I grew older and earned more money, I could save even more per week. The knowledge made my heart pound. I wanted to learn more, *had* to learn more. So I came up with my million-dollar plan. I'd never live like my mom. Or be like Granny Po, blindsided at thirty-four with a first and a second mortgage when her husband died. The next morning, I already had the coffee brewing when Granny Po stumbled into the kitchen. She had leaned against the counter, eyes half-mast, trying to comprehend my plea for a job at the beauty shop. Any job.

She reluctantly said yes, and at first thought it was only a phase. Caddie even took my picture, *ooh*ing and *ahh*ing over how cute I looked with a broom, while Edith pointed to the spots I missed. Rosemary beamed with pride while at the bank, helping me open my first savings account and teaching me how to fill out a deposit slip.

Now, after all this time, the Widows know I'm serious, especially when I request a yearly raise. They even pitched in to buy me a computer, and last year Rosemary helped me expand my investment options by opening a mutual-fund account. Mutual funds are an easier way to invest in the stock market, since the investment company's fund managers decide which stocks to purchase, not myself. So now, after working in the beauty shop and saving the money my father feels obligated to send on birthdays and holidays, I have over seven thousand dollars—$7,182.64, to be exact, between my savings account and my mutual funds. And I haven't even turned fifteen yet.

I closed my notebook, running my fingers along the worn binding. The alarm clock on my nightstand showed six thirty.

You're probably out having fun.

He probably thinks I'm like other teenagers, who talk on the phone for hours or hang out at the mall with their friends. Maybe that's what I should be doing and Edith is right . . . I am too much of a grown-up.

I glanced at the framed photograph next to my alarm, the only picture I was able to save of Mom, Dad, and me together. I was maybe seven when it was taken, with a funny grin and with my stomach hanging out of a crop top. I can't remember who took the picture—maybe it was the neighbor who always parked in our driveway—but everything else I can remember with perfect clarity. Like how the second porch step had a nail pop that would poke my bare feet, and how a guy named Vince put that tattoo on my father's left shoulder. I remember the smell of Mom's potted marigolds, and how the keys set beside a Coke can were for the used Toyota Corolla Mom hated, because she always wanted a Ford Mustang. But I mostly remember the feel of Mom's hug, and how they sat quietly on the porch after the picture was taken, watching me chase fireflies. And how I thanked Jesus because Mommy and Daddy weren't fighting.

Quiet moments like those were rare, as rare as the times when Mom was truly happy. But for some reason, no matter how bad it got, I never thought that it would end.

It did, though, when I was nine. While Dad was at work, Mom spent the day packing, then loading boxes into a friend's van. I asked her why she wasn't putting them in the Corolla Dad bought her.

"Because he knew I wanted a Mustang," she said, her words like a knife. "Go pack your things."

I was too scared to pack. Mom barged into my room minutes later, throwing clothes in a trash bag and rolling up my bedspread into a messy ball. She shoved it into a box, along with my shoes and winter coat, yelling at me to stop standing there with a stupid look on my face and to *do* something. There was only enough time for me to grab my pillow and slip a few books into the case before she grabbed me by the elbow, pulling me toward the hallway. My father's sweatshirt was hanging on the rail when I went down the stairs. I don't know what made me tuck it under my arm when Mom wasn't looking, but I do know why I grabbed this photograph off the hall table. Because I knew we were never coming back.

I was about to finish my second slice of pie when the doorbell rang. A small jolt ran through my heart, a bad habit left over from the years when I would run to the door if someone knocked, thinking that *maybe* it was my mother on the other side, even though she's only bothered to visit four times.

I threw open the door, ignoring Granny Po's warning. It was a woman. But not the one I was thinking of.

"Hi! I'm Gena Hopkins. I'm here about the sign."

Chapter Five

My hand gripped the doorknob hard as I stared at the woman.

She pointed over her shoulder with a polished fingernail. "Uh . . . the sign out there? 'Beauty Shop for Rent' . . . Is it still available?"

I paused, as dumbfounded as a five-year-old asked to spell *predicament,* and glanced at her Jeep, which was parked right behind Granny Po's old Pontiac. "Um, no."

"No, it's not available?"

Get over it and say something. "Sorry. No, it's not rented yet."

She tilted her head, as if waiting for me to say more. "Okay . . . then is the owner here? Your mother?"

Your mother. I hate when people ask about my mother. Because then I say, "No, I live with my great-grandmother," and they instantly assume the floodgate is open to questions like Why? What happened to your parents? Or your grand-parents, why don't you live with them?

God only knows where my mother is, and Dad is otherwise occupied. My grandparents, Joseph and Arlene Garner, moved to Florida ten years ago, and I wouldn't be able to pick them out of a lineup. Evelyn Somers, my other grandmother . . . Granny Po's daughter . . . killed herself when I was only three. Her husband, my grandfather, moved back to Washington soon after, thus completing the weak sapling I call my family tree.

"No, my great-grandmother owns the shop, and she isn't home."

She nodded. "Okay, then I should come back another time."

Yes, you should, since there were no ambulance lights flashing, no blood; and letting a stranger in the house was against Granny Po's rules. Severely against the rules. I should get her phone number and tell her to come back later, but the words wouldn't come out of my mouth. Besides, there's a slim chance someone as elegant as her would like the shop, anyway.

"Do you, um, want to see it now? I can show you around."

Her eyes flicked to the shop door, as though she really wanted to see what was behind it. "Well, yes, that would be lovely, but only if you feel comfortable doing so."

Granny Po's going to have a cow.

"Sure. Come on in."

I flipped the shop lights on, waking the sleeping hair dryer statues, and stood with my back to the wall. Her footsteps echoed as she crossed the worn hardwood floors, taking in each detail, from the handmade braided rugs Granny Po got at the Amish market to the 1950s prints on the walls of old beauty products. I searched her face for the disappointment that was in the eyes of every other visitor for the past two years.

But there was none, only interest. And, I think, maybe *appreciation.*

She touched the back of Granny Po's beautician chair, spinning it in a slow circle and watching it twirl. "Nice parlor. Very charming. Larger than I thought. My mom used to take me to her friend's beauty shop like this once a week, every week. I'd sit in the corner, watching all the ladies get pretty and wishing I could, too. If I behaved, the owner would give me a lollipop from this huge basket she kept by the cash register. And, if I was *really* good, I'd get to sit in her chair and spin."

I tried to think of something to say, but my tongue felt tied. She was so casual and cool, talking with me as easily as old friends do. I pointed to the basket full of lollipops beside the cash register. Her eyes lit up. "Cool. May I?"

I nodded, watching her open a cherry lollipop and then throw one to me. She popped hers in her mouth and sighed. "But it's sad. You don't see many home beauty shops nowadays because they are so behind the times. Customers today want more."

She was right. Hardly any of Granny Po's clients are under fifty. Sarah may come in for a manicure every now and then, but Kym only goes to a posh spa on Main Street where haircuts cost double.

There was a time when Polly's Parlor thrived, in the mid-1970s when she first opened the shop. Above the manicurist's table is a collage of all her past customers wearing polyester dresses or pointy-collared shirts, getting their hair permed and teased into giant beehive clouds and plastered into shape with Aqua Net. Business slowed in the late eighties and early nineties when the new mall offered hair salon chains with discounted prices, but many of Granny Po's customers stayed loyal. Then as the century turned and her clientele aged, the day-to-day business slowed. Granny Po is frugal with her money, so we do all right, but I know it hurts her more and more as each potential renter turns her down.

It's just like this woman said, customers today want more.

I expected her to politely make her way to the door, but she walked past the shampoo sink, past the counter where Granny Po set the TV, and ran her finger along the manicure table. She gestured toward the back wall. "What's that door for . . . I'm sorry. What's your name?"

"Oh. It's Abbey. Garner. And the door? Um, it leads to two bedrooms and two bathrooms, but nobody uses them anymore. Well, yeah, I mean we use one bathroom, but Granny Po uses the other rooms to store my late great-grandfather's old stuff. My great-grandfather's brother used to live here, although Granny Po said he never paid any rent. There's also a patio out back. It's real pretty, you know, covered and everything. Tables, too."

Oh my gosh, shut up! First I'm a mute, now I'm a blabbering child.

"Mind if I take a look, Abbey?"

I paused, knowing full well if she walked back there, she'd see Granny Po's junk rooms, too messy for any visitor to see. But I didn't want to say no. "Sure, that'll be all right."

Granny Po's going to have a whole herd *of cows.*

It was a little embarrassing for her to see the clutter of boxes, mounted deer heads, and piles of fishing magazines in the back rooms. But if she disapproved, I couldn't tell.

"Hmm, there's hardwood in all the rooms. Good. May I see the patio?"

Why not. I've come this far.

"This is just beautiful," she said, stepping onto the brick patio and reaching out to touch a chrysanthemum that looked like a bronze daisy. It *was* beautiful on the patio, with vivid yellow, lavender, and maroon mums clustered in terra cotta pots Granny Po had let me paint. A sudden feeling of pride and gratitude came over me that she was noticing all the hard work we've done.

She stepped off the patio, her heels sinking slightly in the grass as she walked along the privacy fence, where ivy crawled up and over it like tendrils of hair. I tried not to stare at her, but it was hard not to. She looked like a model, exotic and cosmopolitan, with her long black hair and olive-toned skin. The kind of woman you both envied and admired. I felt plain, resembling my mother, with her honey-brown hair and wide-set hazel eyes.

"Okay. I think I've seen enough."

Does that mean yes, she wants to rent the shop, or no, she's leaving? My pulse quickened, searching for something to say. Maybe I should call Granny Po and have her come home. Talk to her herself. I cleared my throat, trying to shake it off and think of my job instead. Of keeping my job. "Well, thanks for stopping by."

"Actually, I'd like some more information."

Oh.

She reached into her purse and pulled out a business card. "Can you give this to your great-grandmother, Abbey? I'd love to hear from her." She took one more look around the patio, then walked back through the shop.

I didn't look at the card until after she left in her black Jeep.

Slowly shutting the door, I held the card tightly in both hands. Gena Hopkins. The first woman to actually be interested in renting Polly's Parlor.

Granny Po will have to see this. Soon. A feeling of dread filled my stomach, but it wasn't because she might punish me for breaking the rules. That, I could handle. But could I handle another change?

Things are actually good now. I have a job, one where all I have to do is walk through a door to get there. I'm in control; I'm saving money every week, so everything is going according to plan. Who's to say Gena would give me a job? Yeah, she's nice, but not a lot of salons hire fourteen-year-olds, even if they'll be fifteen in a few weeks.

Gena could ruin everything, and yet . . . part of me really wanted her to come back.

I went to my room and propped her card beside the photograph of my parents. Gena couldn't be much over thirty. Thirty-one, thirty-two, maybe. I focused on my mother's face, mentally comparing the two women and resenting myself for it.

After Mom and I left my father, we were happy at first. Mom rented an apartment in Pennsylvania, miles from the constant fighting with Dale Garner. She bought a used sports car and found a job bartending at a place called Alfred E's. Mom said she loved bartending—how the patrons would sit on their bar stools, talking to her, watching her, needing her, if only for a drink. She took me one Saturday afternoon, while covering another woman's shift. I watched as she lined the drinks up on the bar, occasionally spinning a liquor bottle in her hand, like a pro. She flitted from one customer to the next—in control, smiling, in the spotlight. And when Mom smiled like that, she was the prettiest woman there.

Soon, she started dating a customer named Brad and would sometimes invite Brad and her coworkers to the apartment, splurging on beer, crabs, and steamed shrimp. Before they arrived, Mom would primp in the mirror, with rollers in her hair, leaning forward to layer on mascara, her mouth drawn down in a long O. Later in the evening, I'd crack open my bedroom door to watch her dance, her hair swinging long and free, to a favorite Lynyrd Skynyrd song.

But after about a year, the parties dwindled. Then the music faded to a distant memory. Mom and Brad broke up, the rollers went unused, and Mom spent long, empty hours in her rocking chair, a cigarette dangling from nail-bitten fingers. Bills piled up on the coffee table, since Dad never sent child support, and a storm slowly brewed in her eyes. I spent each day walking on eggshells, avoiding anything that might set her off.

When divorce papers from my father's lawyer arrived, whatever thread that had held her together finally broke. She locked herself in the bathroom, sliced both wrists with a razor blade, and sat there bleeding until I unlocked the door. Mom survived her suicide attempt, but our life together died. She snuck out of the hospital the next night, wrists covered with bandages, telling me once again to pack and get in the car. I remember the windshield wipers slapping back and forth, her knuckles as white as her bandages. "Where are we going now, Mom?"

Her voice was weak, like a rope swing after many years of hanging. "You are going to stay at your great-grandmother's."

Not we.

Headlights flooded the front window as Caddie's huge boat of a car pulled into the driveway. Granny Po and the Widows, home from bingo. I could hear Granny Po's voice before she opened the front door.

"The nerve of that old bat Loretta Scott, calling my Jell-O mold lopsided and saying that Rosemary's angel food cake was too sticky." Granny Po walked in, throwing her purse and empty plate onto the kitchen counter. "And what did she say about the chocolate frosting, huh?"

Edith followed, greeting me by lightly punching my shoulder—her sign of affection. "Something about it being too runny and tasting like—"

"Tasting like generic Halloween candy! Can you believe that, Abbey?" Granny Po grabbed mugs from the cabinet while Rosemary put water in the coffeemaker. From the look Caddie gave me, I could guess that Granny Po had been complaining the entire way home.

"Nope, can't believe it," I said.

Caddie carefully measured out four scoops of French roast decaf. "But, Polly dear, you did say that her chocolate soufflé looked like a big old cow pie, didn't you?"

Granny Po paused. "Yeah, well it did. Darn thing was creepy, all brown and lumpy; and I swear it had eyes that watched me. Besides, she had it coming. Here I thought I got away from that witch by leaving the church years ago, and now she starts coming to *our* bingo nights, with all her snotty friends, just to stir up trouble. Bingo is *my* turf."

If she didn't look so serious, I would have laughed at the image of Granny Po and Loretta Scott, slugging it out *West Side Story*-style about their "turf." Granny Po's beef with Loretta Scott goes way back. They hated each other in high school and hated each other even more as adults, even though they both belonged to Granite Hill Methodist Church until Granny Po stopped going eleven years ago. Granny Po told me it was because Loretta Scott bossed everyone around, acting like she owned the place because she was the church treasurer *and* a trustee. But Caddie once confided that Loretta had gossiped about my mother getting pregnant at sixteen and, three years later, talked bad about my grandmother Evelyn when she killed herself because of depression. Granny Po has never set foot on Granite Hill's property since, even though my grandmother—her daughter—is buried there.

Granny Po handed me a mug of coffee and then felt the ends of my hair. "Thank God, you deep conditioned. Anything happen while I was gone?"

I looked at her face as she checked my hair for split ends. Her forehead was furrowed and the corners of her mouth turned down, the look she always gets when she's questioning me. I glanced at the answering machine, with no messages blinking, and then thought about the business card on my nightstand. Granny Po would want to see the card—*should* see it—but I just couldn't give it to her.

"No, nothing."

Chapter Six

I carried the card in my pocket all Sunday and into the next week. I looked at it every now and then and by Wednesday morning had it memorized. Her name, her Baltimore address, her cell number.

During first period, it sat on the corner of my desk, its edges now worn and fuzzy. I gazed out the school windows at a few runners circling the track, their faces and legs flushed pink from the sudden drop in temperature. Mrs. Langdon droned on about *The Catcher in the Rye*, but my attention drifted to the stadium clubhouse, where our school mascot, the wildcat, was painted in fighter's stance and ready to attack. Below it were past football championship titles, printed in black, and although I couldn't read them from here, I knew two of them by heart.

AA Maryland State Champions, 1987 and 1988, two years in a row.

My father had loved to talk about his high school glory days and winning those titles. He'd sit at the table, drinking a beer, dressed in his machine-shop uniform, which always smelled like week-old sweat and motor oil no matter how many times Mom washed it. And later, when he took his drink to the sofa to watch whatever sport happened to be in season, I would fill in the blanks with all the stuff he hadn't said. Like how he had to give up his football scholarship because Mom got pregnant, and how he resented me for that, even though he'd never say it out loud. He didn't have to; I could tell, whenever he looked into my face.

To this day, I hate the smell of beer. It reminds me of waking in the morning to a row of empty cans lining the kitchen counter, or of my dad's drinking buddies leering at my mother when no one else was watching. Dad was drunk when he married Sharon, a cocktail waitress, of all things. It wasn't until one year ago, when they divorced, and Dad lost Sharon, that he checked himself into rehab. Guess losing me wasn't enough to make him quit drinking.

My father asked me to go to an Alcoholics Anonymous meeting with him once, but I'd rather drop dead first. Granny Po said she would come with us, but she doesn't realize I know the truth, that two days after Mom left, I *heard* her on the phone talking with him, saying with certain clarity, "Dale, are you sure you don't want custody of Abbey? Have you thought this through?"

Obviously, he has. During the two years Mom and I lived in Pennsylvania, he never once asked for custody, or even weekend visits. And in his divorce papers, there was nothing about me either, so I don't know why Granny Po wants me to give my father a chance. I don't know why she doesn't hate him, since he was the reason Mom tried to kill herself. Especially when Granny Po's own daughter did kill herself.

"Abbey, would you care to answer my question?"

I jerked my head up, to find Mrs. Langdon and the rest of the class staring at me. Mrs. Langdon tapped her foot as my face burned to a deeper pink than the runners' outside.

"I . . . ah." *Crap!*

Mrs. Langdon crossed her arms, black hair frizzing out of a messy ponytail. Granny Po would cringe if she saw her split ends. "I'm waiting, Abbey Garner."

Oh God, just shoot me now. From across the room, a guy named Will Grover tried to mouth the answer, but I couldn't understand him.

"Well then, Abbey, since you don't have a reply, perhaps you should work on one tonight. By doing a typed—two-page, double-spaced—synopsis on our current study book. And then, next time, you'll pay attention, correct?"

Great. I nodded like my lesson was learned. The bell rang, sparing me from any further humiliation, but my face was still burning when I reached my locker. Which, of course, was hopelessly jammed. I slapped it with my palm. "You have *got* to be kidding! Not *now*!"

"Ah, the battle continues. Young Abbey Garner against the villainous school locker."

I wheeled around, clutching my sore hand, to see Sarah, grinning at me. "Yeah, well, I surrender. Maybe the school could assign me a new locker, because this one hates me."

"Step aside, you big quitter." Sarah lifted the locker handle and jammed her hip against the metal. Of course, the stuck corner instantly popped out.

"How come everyone can open this locker but me?" I whined.

"It's all in the hips, baby," Sarah said, spanking her side. "All in the hips."

She waited while I grabbed my jacket, then walked with me to the front lobby, where students crowded in separate groups, drinking sodas from the vending machines and talking so loud there was a low roar. Camden was standing with some other lacrosse players by a bulletin board. He stopped talking when he saw me and tipped his chin up in that "hey baby" gesture I never found oh-so-attractive. *Please.* I gave him a casual wave, anyway, so I didn't look rude. Thank God Kym wasn't around to witness it.

"So, where's John?" I asked Sarah. Normally he's waiting in the lobby so he can kiss her good-bye.

Sarah opened the door. "Oh, his father picked him up. He's taking John to buy another bat. His old one has a dent from hitting a ball so hard—you know, because he's such a great player."

"Yeah, of course he's a great player," I answered, not sure of what else to say.

"So . . . I should be happy for him, you know, that he's probably going to play varsity baseball next spring, right?" Sarah pulled down her sweater sleeves when we stepped outside, covering her hands as though they were freezing.

"Sure," I said. "And he should be proud of you for being selected as a soloist for the band's winter performance. That's so incredible."

Sarah was too focused on John to think of her music. As we reached the buses, she stopped, bringing a covered hand to her chin. "And like Kym said, I'll be able to wear his letterman's jacket next year. That would be pretty cool, huh?"

"Yeah, cool." Leave it to Kym to come up with that little detail. "Look, Sarah. Like you said, John wants to play college baseball. And you want to study music, right? I mean, you guys are going in different directions eventually."

Sarah let go of her sleeves and faced me. "So, what, I shouldn't be sad about him leaving? You've never been in love, Abbey. You don't know how it feels to lose someone you care so deeply about."

Yes, I do.

"Sarah, I'm sorry. Really, I am. You've just been bummed out about this for so long, and he's not even leaving school until the end of second semester. You still have plenty of time to be together."

Sarah stepped in the direction of her bus, looking back over her shoulder. "Two and a half months is not plenty of time, Abbey. Not when you love someone."

She walked away before I could say anything more.

That Friday night, Granny Po stood at the shop door, looking out at the empty driveway. With a deep sigh, she turned the OPEN sign to CLOSED earlier than usual. "What'd we have, only three customers tonight? One manicure, one eyebrow wax, and one haircut, although Jillian Klein should count as half a cut, seeing how the poor woman is half-bald. Lord. I swear, I'm gonna be dead—dead and buried, just like most of my customers—by the time I ever get this shop rented."

Granny Po took off her floral smock and hung it on a wooden peg. She pulled on a taupe sweatshirt with fall harvest pumpkin appliqués on the front and turned to me, a sadness deep in her eyes. "At least tell me we haven't missed our show."

"Nope. You ready to get your butt kicked?"

Usually my threat to beat her at *Wheel of Fortune* got her revved up. But tonight Granny Po only nodded and looked out the window again, to the rusted white sign sitting ignored in the yard.

"Ah, heck with it," she said. "Maybe it's just as well. At least I'm giving that witch Loretta Scott a good laugh, since she thinks it's oh-so-funny how nobody wants to rent the place."

She turned the shop lights off, covering the seldom-used hair dryers in darkness.

I turned them back on.

"You know, Granny Po, that reminds me. Someone *did* stop by the shop. And . . . she left a card and everything. Her name is Gena Hopkins."

Granny Po took the card and reached into her smock pocket for her reading glasses. "Abbey! When was this?"

Lie or tell the truth . . . lie or tell the truth? Oh man, she'll find out as soon as she talks to Gena, so it might as well be truth. "Uh, last Saturday night."

"Saturday night?" Granny Po's eyes nearly bulged out of her head. She threw her hands in the air. "And you're just now remembering it? Why in the heck didn't you tell me then?"

"I don't know, I just . . ."

Tears welled in my eyes before I could finish my sentence, making me wish the lights were turned back off. There were reasons she just wouldn't understand, reasons I wasn't quite sure of myself.

Granny Po stared at me, making that face she always makes when she's trying to figure me out. She held the card up, rubbing a finger along the worn ends.

"I'm sorry, Granny Po. I should have given it to you right away."

She tapped the card against her palm. After a long deep sigh, Granny Po pulled me into a thick hug, her hair pungent from a recent dye job. "Abbey girl, it's all right. Don't you worry your pumpkin head about it anymore. It's not like someone's gonna swoop in and rent the shop after all this time. The woman probably just gave you the card to be polite."

"No," I pulled back, wiping my eyes. "That's just it. She seemed interested. Really interested."

Granny Po hesitated, pursing her lips. "Oh. She seemed interested? How old was she?"

"Thirty-one, thirty-two, maybe." Granny Po reached behind her and slowly sat down on the sofa arm as I told her everything about Gena's visit, how she lingered in the shop and told stories about her mother, and how she loved the back patio.

Granny Po's eyes seemed to cloud over as she listened. She put the card deep into her trouser pocket and glanced around at her shop. "Well, then, it's a good thing, right?"

"Right, a good thing."

"And it certainly would shut up that Loretta Scott."

I nodded. "That it would."

Granny Po's eyes came to rest on her collage of customer pictures from the last thirty years. In a faraway voice she said, "Right. Well, I guess I should call this Gena woman . . . tonight."

We stared at each other for a second.

"Yeah, I guess."

"*Wheel of Fortune*?" she asked.

"Absolutely."

It wasn't until the third puzzle, after I had solved one and let her think she solved the other, that Granny Po shot up in her seat and pointed at me. "Wait a minute! Abigail Lynn Garner, and just how *did* this Gena woman get to the patio? Oh, good Lord in heaven, please tell me, *tell me* she didn't see those messy back rooms."

Oh no. And here I was so close.

Gena walked through the shop door on Saturday, equipped with a digital camera, tape measure, and notepad. She greeted me warmly and introduced herself to Granny Po. "Thanks for calling this morning, Mrs. Randall. I was beginning to think the shop was rented to someone else."

Granny Po glanced at the sign outside, at the empty beautician chairs with no customers, and then back at Gena with a cynical look in her eyes. "No, Ms. Hopkins, I don't believe that's a problem."

For someone who's been trying to rent the shop for two years, Granny Po didn't seem very happy. She reluctantly accepted Gena's handshake and then acted like a Doberman on high alert while giving Gena a tour of the shop and discussing lease options. When Gena said she wanted to take measurements and some pictures, Granny Po looked at her strangely, as if she just asked to have her tongue waxed. "By all means, go right ahead," she quipped, "although I don't see why you'd need measurements. My great-granddaughter, here, will help you."

Granny Po pulled me aside before leaving. "Don't you dare let that woman in the back rooms, you hear?"

I hear. Especially after being reamed out for twenty minutes last night. Once Granny Po had left us, Gena brought out the tape measure, giving me one end. "Hold it against the front wall, will you?"

We were both silent as she measured the room—side to side, front to back, top to bottom—marking everything on her notepad. When she went to open the back door, I jumped forward. "You know what, I can measure them for you."

Her hand lingered on the door handle. "Ah, I understand. That's okay, I don't need them right now."

I made a show of folding towels as Gena crossed the room again, turning in a slow circle. She reminded me of a runway model, in her suede skirt and knee-high leather boots Kym would absolutely love. There were a few wrinkles around her eyes and mouth, but they looked as though they came from years of laughter. Not like my mother's face. Mom looked older than thirty-one when I saw her last spring, with a downcast frown locked in place, and worry lines etched on her forehead.

Gena caught me staring. "So, do you always help your great-grandmother like this, Abbey?"

She remembered my name. "Ah, yeah. I've been working for Granny Po since I was eleven—I mean twelve."

Gena nodded. "Wow. Since you were twelve, huh? So you must know a thing or two about what goes on."

I shrugged and said, "Pretty much. I hear all the gossip, unless Granny Po thinks it's inappropriate and makes me leave the room."

Gena laughed. "Well, I didn't mean gossip, although you can fill me in on everything later. I meant businesswise."

"Oh," I said. "Well, yeah, sure."

Gena ran a hand along the counter and picked up a picture of Granny Po with the other Gray Widows. "Good, I'll run my idea by you first."

She set the photo down, then walked to the middle of the room with her arms out wide. "I want to bring back this, the charm and warmth of the home beauty salon, where women gossip and drink too much coffee, where they come for more than a haircut. For friendship . . . but with all the modern conveniences of an elegant day spa. What do you think of that?"

My fingers fumbled with a towel, dropping it to the floor. I couldn't believe she was asking for my opinion, even though she hardly knew me. And a day spa? Here, at Polly's Parlor? No way; it was crazy. And totally screaming of bankruptcy and yet . . . brilliant.

"Well, I um, don't know. Maybe. But . . ."

"But what?" Gena asked.

I shifted my weight and went back to folding. It really wasn't my place to say anything.

"It's okay, Abbey. Go ahead." Her eyes were open and clear, as though she really wanted to know what I thought.

"All right. I was wondering . . . This is a duplex." I gestured at the outdated shop. "And it's two miles away from town, where most people go for hair appointments. I mean, Granny Po does okay, but she has few overhead expenses. You're talking remodeling expenses, rent, employee salaries, and that's just the beginning. Wouldn't this be a huge business risk?"

I really need to shut up now.

Gena crossed her arms, nodding slightly. "I could tell you're a smart girl. And you're right; it's a risky venture. Any time you open a business, there's always the possibility of failure. But I have a plan. A good one. Still think I'm crazy?"

I knew at that moment that I would do anything to see what that plan was. "No, I don't think you're crazy. But . . . I gotta warn you. Granny Po will."

Gena nodded, leaning toward me with a confident smile. "Well, then, I guess I'll just have to convince her otherwise, huh?"

Chapter Seven

And just what do you intend on turning my shop into, Miss Gena Hopkins? I didn't work for years, after being left penniless by my husband and forced to make my own living, for you to turn *my* beauty shop into some newfangled high-tech lounge."

Even though Kym and I were supposed to be studying our Spanish, we sat on bar stools by the kitchen counter, looking out the window to the scene on the patio. There was no way we'd miss this conversation, and neither would the other Gray Widows, sitting off to the side, collecting enough gossip material to last at least three days. Both Rosemary and Edith were giving Gena the cold shoulder, probably out of loyalty to Granny Po, although none of it made sense. You'd think they would be happy someone was interested in renting the shop.

Caddie, however, welcomed Gena with a warm hug, so either she'd missed getting the "boycott Gena" memo or chosen to ignore it.

Gena and Granny Po sat facing each other, a pitcher of

untouched pink lemonade between them. Granny Po's arms were folded over her stomach. The starched and pressed tablecloth she had me lay out fluttered in the breeze. Gena straightened a corner before speaking.

"Mrs. Randall, I wouldn't turn your shop into a space station. Just . . . give it a little makeover, so I could offer the same services as a day spa. Your house is the perfect location, right off the main highway but still private. It could be a wonderful place for a day of pampering and relaxing."

"A day spa? Pampering and relaxing? Good Lord. What on earth do women today need to relax for, Miss Hopkins? Hmm? Do they have to wash dishes by hand? No, there's dishwashers. Ever run clothes through a wringer and hang 'em on a line? Nope, washers and dryers. And cloth diapers? Now there's disposable ones. Pampering and relaxing, my foot."

Edith leaned forward, tapping a short fingernail on the table. "And I bet her generation never had to haul their rears out of a warm bed at five in the morning to milk a cow, huh."

"Edith, I don't need no help in this conversation, thank you."

I leaned forward and rested my elbows on the kitchen counter, watching Gena hold her ground.

"Mrs. Randall, things are easier with all of today's technology, but now there's even more expected from women and more stress. A day spa is where we put them back together."

Caddie inched her chair a bit closer, a dreamy smile on her round face. "Sounds heavenly."

Granny Po shot a "How dare you, traitor" look to Caddie as someone knocked twice on the front door, behind me.

Mitch walked in, with grass bits on his work boots and jeans from mowing the lawn. He reached in the fridge for a Coke, eyeing the leftover banana-cream pie. "So, what's the scoop? Did Granny Po say yes?"

Kym straightened to a more flattering position and brushed hair off her shoulder, even though it's been a long time since Mitch was on her top-ten list. "No, and it's been a while since I've seen her this worked up."

"Oh yeah," I added. "Like the time you accidentally pulled up her perennials."

"Ouch," Mitch said, leaning against the counter to look out the window.

Kym crossed her legs and looked at me. "But it would be totally cool if Gena opened a spa. Do you think I could get a discount on facials?"

Though Kym didn't mean anything, her interest in the spa bothered me. She never came to Polly's Parlor, because it was old-fashioned, so I couldn't help but feel defensive for Granny Po. I looked out the window, just as Gena told her about the remodeling to be done if she rented the shop.

Granny Po's eyes widened in aggravation. "Remodeling? What remodeling? The shop is available for rent, as is!"

Gena paused, reaching into her leather briefcase, her dark hair falling over one shoulder. "Well, your parlor is wonderful, but it doesn't exactly fit my needs . . . as it is. Here's a rough sketch of the floor plan I'm thinking of."

Once Gena had pulled out her plans, I forgot Granny Po's warning for me to stay out of the way. I hopped off the stool and walked through the patio door. "Can I see them?"

Gena put them on the table. "Sure, Abbey. There'll be

some minor renovation, like dividing the parlor with half and full walls, replacing the kitchen cabinets with three wet stations, and creating a separate area for the hair stylists, a manicurist, and the receptionist. The rooms in back will be modified for massages, body treatments, and an aesthetician."

"Este-who?" asked Edith.

Caddie's eyes shone bright and hopeful. "Facials, dear. Someone who does facials." Caddie turned back to Gena. "And paraffin treatments. Are you going to have them?"

"What the heck are they?" snapped Edith, reaching back to scratch a shoulder blade.

"They soak your hands in wax, dear." Caddie looked at her own hands, soft and plump. "I saw it on *The Martin Crouse Show* once. Most adorable bald man you ever saw. There's just something about bald men, with those little shiny dome heads."

But Granny Po wasn't amused. "For goodness sake, Caddie, do hush up! My gosh, you're as worthless as tits on a boar hog."

Gena turned her eyes to Caddie. "Of course I'll have paraffin treatments! And full-body seaweed wraps."

Caddie beamed with excitement. "Polly, this sounds divine! Why don't you consider it?"

I sat down slowly, watching Granny Po purse her lips. A crisp breeze picked up the corners of her dyed brown hair. She patted it back in place with a frown and exhaled loudly, as though she didn't want to say no but couldn't say yes.

Gena stood. For a second, I thought she was leaving, but she only excused herself, saying she'd be right back. Gena returned minutes later, holding the collage of all of Granny

Po's past customers that had been hanging on the wall. She pointed to the pictures. "This is what I want to bring back. Look at these ladies, and the friendship. You can't find that in a mall, where other people can walk by and see you with your hair covered with dye. There's something wonderfully intimate about going into someone's home; but yes, the shop will have to be updated, to bring in a modern edge, the best of both worlds."

Gena finished and sat back down. She looked so different from Granny Po in her faded work smock, and Rosemary in her prim heels, and ex-farm-queen Caddie eating a dough-nut, and Edith in jeans and boots. And . . . different from my mother. There was a feeling of purpose and hope surrounding Gena, things my mother lost a long time ago. Gena saw some-thing nobody else could in Polly's Parlor. She could see the *beauty* of the beauty shop.

Granny Po hesitated, staring at the collage and all her memories. But then she slapped a hand on the table. "No. My answer is no. A bunch of pounding around in my house? Good Lord. And what would I do with all that storage in the back rooms?"

My back stiffened when Granny Po shook her head. I wanted to plead with her as Gena slowly reached for her briefcase on the floor, and put her plans away. *Come on, Abbey, think of something!*

A thought crept into my head. I looked at Granny Po and nodded. "You know, you're probably right. It wouldn't be nice to mess with those back rooms. Disrespectful, even. I mean, that's where you store all my great-grandfather's stuff, right?"

Caddie caught on quick. "Riiight, Abigail darling," she said cunningly with a lifted eyebrow. "It would be a doggone sin to disturb them. And Lord knows, Polly doesn't want to do anything that may upset his memory, God rest his soul."

"God rest his soul," I repeated in faked remorse.

"Upset his memory? That man is too knee-deep in flames to notice what's going on up here. Leave me with nothing, will he. Let me tell you a story, Miss Hopkins. I was married to that son-of-a—"

"Polly!" Caddie nudged a thumb in my direction. "Little ears . . ."

"Fine. To that *man* for eighteen years. Then his car blows a tire and he's smashed by a semi to kingdom come. I find out he lied—there's no savings, no life insurance, nothing. I didn't have a pot to piss in or a window to throw it out of. Took me years to get back on my feet."

Granny Po sighed deeply and gazed at the shop door. Now I began to understand. The shop was her lifeline, her security for thirty years. Maybe she wasn't ready to let it go and retire after all. In a way, I felt the same. But still . . .

Please, Granny Po!

Finally, she nodded and looked at me as though she could read my thoughts. "Okay, Miss Hopkins, you can have your fancy spa."

Gena started to rise, holding her hand out for a handshake. "Great! Thank you, Mrs.—"

"*But,* only on two conditions. First, nobody's allowed in my private home area. That's strictly off limits. Second, you have to hire my Abbey. She can shampoo, sweep, or cut the hair of your uglier customers."

I spun my head toward Granny Po, seeing a hidden sparkle in her eyes.

Gena sat back down. "How old is she?"

"She'll be fifteen in November. But she works as hard as a church lady on fried-oyster night. And in case you've never been to church on fried-oyster night, that's pretty darn hard."

Gena hesitated. My breath stuck in my throat until she held a hand out to Granny Po. "Okay, Mrs. Randall. You've got yourself a deal."

Caddie jumped up from the table. "Finally! I've had to pee for the past twenty minutes."

Edith stood and swatted Granny Po on the shoulder. "Hey . . . Abbey cuts *my* hair. You saying I'm ugly?"

Granny Po ignored her and looked at me with a frown. "What are you grinning for? Why don't you make us some coffee, since you're so darn happy."

"Fine." At that point, I wouldn't care if she asked me to scrub toilets. I walked in the house just as Mitch was finishing the rest of the banana-cream pie.

"Hey," he said, with his mouth full, "looks like you've got yourself a new boss, Abbey."

Yes, I guess I do.

Mitch tossed his fork into the sink and grabbed a handful of candy from Granny Po's crystal bowl before heading for the door. He stopped, turning to face me. "Hey, by the way, you'll never believe what's playing at the Arts Council. *The Cowboys*. Remember that one? Do you want to check it out? My treat."

I remember that movie. I hated it because John Wayne died. But when we were younger, it was Mitch's favorite because the young boys his age killed all the bad guys in retaliation.

"Why doesn't the Arts Council play any decent movies, like a classic romance?" Kym said, grabbing her Spanish book from the counter. "What ever happened to culture?"

Mitch put on a goofy smile, slapping his leg. "Shoot, there ain't nuttin' wrong with cowboy culture."

I couldn't help but smile. Mitch grinned, confusing this as a yes. "So, you want to go then?"

My smile froze. Watching a movie with him may sound completely harmless, but what if he confused it as a date? Besides, that's how it started with my parents. For their first date, my father took Mom to a movie, cuddling in the dark and giving her his jacket when she got chilly. Five months later, she was pregnant.

I reached for Kym's bar stool, pushing it neatly under the counter. "Sorry, Mitch. I can't go."

Chapter Eight

Granny Po has three conditions, not just two.

The third is that once Gena's spa is up and running, none of the Widows can get any fancy treatments beyond hair, nails, and toes. No facials, back rubs, seaweed wraps . . . no paraffin treatments that Caddie was so excited about.

Totally unreasonable, yes. Bendable, no.

Granny Po laid down this law when Polly's Parlor had its official going-out-of-business sale on Saturday. She sat on the porch, her face hardened like cooled wax, as bargain hunters trickled up the driveway, offering insultingly low bids for her aged equipment that Gena wasn't interested in keeping. Her old-fashioned hair dryers, once lined up like proud soldiers, were carried out one by one, defeated and worn. And the television, once used daily for the soaps, went for a quick ten dollars. Every now and then, Rosemary reached over to rub Granny Po's hand while Edith bickered with the buyers for more money. Both of them agreed to Granny Po's unreasonable terms, saying that no fancy spa could *ever* be better than Polly's Parlor.

Only Caddie was crushed by the boycott. "Oh, Polly. No paraffin treatments?"

"Nope."

"Why in heavens not? I'm just *dying* to have one of those all-day beauty packages Gena says she'll be offering."

Granny Po looked away, her mouth in a tight line after the ancient cash register was loaded into a stranger's truck. "Just because, that's why."

Caddie shuffled over to sit by me on the porch swing. "No seaweed wraps," she whispered in my ear.

"Maybe she'll change her mind," I whispered back. *Right. And I'll grow that extra boob on my back.* But now I felt guilty for all those times I nagged Granny Po to replace that old register. We watched as the guy who bought it threw his truck in reverse, backing right into the FOR RENT sign in the front yard.

"Well, if that don't beat all," Granny Po said softly.

Edith stood and walked to the bent sign, pulling it out of the ground. It didn't hit me until I saw that bare, empty spot, how Polly's Parlor was gone forever. No more hanging out on Saturdays with the smell of Caddie's perm solution or Rosemary waddling across the room with cotton balls wedged between her toes. No more *Wheel of Fortune* sessions, with Edith trying to cover my eyes so she could solve the puzzle first. No wonder Granny Po was so quiet.

She waited until Edith returned, then said, "Well, now what am I gonna do?"

Caddie perked up. "Oh, I know! We can join that Red Hat Society! They wear the most adorable red and purple hats, even though that color combination reminds me of a bruise."

She stopped, noticing our stares. "What? Did I say something wrong?"

Music came from the highway as a black Jeep pulled in the driveway. Gena. She braked hard, noticing the sale at the last minute, but it was too late. She gave a shy wave and parked.

"Oh, for crying out loud," Granny Po muttered. "What's she doing here?"

Gena stepped awkwardly out of the Jeep, dodging a man carrying the old manicure table. She approached the porch and took off her sunglasses, looking as uncomfortable as Granny Po used to when she gave Amelia Presley's smelly feet a pedicure. Rosemary and Edith nodded a curt hello, but Caddie brought out the welcome wagon. "Nice to see you again, Gena! Iced tea, dear?"

Gena turned down her offer, probably knowing it wasn't a good idea. I gave her a quick wave, trying to put her at ease as a woman with thick glasses and a slight limp walked up, offering twenty dollars for a beautician's chair.

"No!" barked Edith and Granny Po at the same time.

Gena stepped back. "I'm sorry! I didn't know today was . . . I wouldn't have come."

"Hmph!" Granny Po snapped. "It makes no never mind to me whether you're here or not. You go do what you came to do."

"Uh, sure." Gena walked toward the shop door. "I'm just finalizing the floor plan. But let me know if you need help, like clearing out the back rooms. Or anything."

Granny Po put on a fake smile. "Thank you, Miss Hopkins, but I have everything under control."

No, she didn't. Those rooms were still jam-packed floor to ceiling with stuff. It would take a month to empty them. But when Gena shut the door, I found out what she meant. Granny Po turned to me. "Abigail Lynn Garner, I've got a proposition for you."

"Oh no, not me. I wouldn't know what to do with all that junk." Especially my great-grandfather's stuff. Going through a dead man's possessions would be downright creepy.

"How about for thirty bucks? And I don't give a rat's behind what you do with it, as long as I don't have to deal with it. Take it to the basement. Or better yet," Granny Po took a deep breath, "trash the whole stinking lot. I should have gotten rid of it years ago."

I hopped off the porch swing. "Okay, but you don't have to pay me."

"No, I insist," Granny Po said, her voice firm.

"Well, if you insist . . ."

My plan was simple. Decent clothes to charity, important papers filed in the basement, along with all salvageable items boxed for a yard sale in the spring. Might as well make a few dollars. But after one hour, "just trash it" was sounding better and better. I was surrounded by outdated receipts, appliance manuals, old photographs of caught fish, weathered *Farmer's Almanac*s, and closed bank-account statements. And the stupid deer trophies. What was I supposed to do with them?

Gena popped her head in before leaving, politely asking again if she could help.

"Um, thanks, Gena, but I'm okay. It looks worse than it really is." She nodded, accepting my lie.

But come to think of it, there was someone I could call. Who had a car . . .

Mitch came straight from Edith's farm, wearing a flannel shirt with horsehair flecked on it. He stopped short at the door, staring at the piles. "You've got to be kidding me."

I looked up, buried in hunting magazines. "Sorry. I know it's a lot, but these rooms need to be cleaned out and I'm desperate."

"Wow. Desperate makes me feel real special." He stood still, arms crossed over his stomach. "So, you won't go to the movies with me, but you'll ask for help, huh?"

"Well, I . . . yeah, that wasn't too cool of me. Sorry."

Mitch uncrossed his arms and walked in. "Okay, but here's the deal. I'll help you only if you agree to come to the game next Friday night. And wave a pom-pom."

"Forget it."

Mitch picked up a stuffed deer head and held its face close to mine. "*And* you have to kiss the deer. That's my final offer."

"There is no way I'm putting my lips anywhere near that disgusting thing," I said, pushing it away. "I'd rather kiss Bodie."

"So you'll come to the game at least?"

I threw the magazines into a trash bag and stood. "I refuse to wave a stupid pom-pom."

He grinned, putting the deer head under one arm and grabbing a trash bag with the other. "Okay, but you do have to yell at least five *go teams!*"

"Fine."

Two hours later, most of the trash had been loaded into Mitch's Chevy, ready to go to the dump. Sweat beaded on his forehead as he moved boxes to the center of the room for us to open. There was something I'd been meaning to ask him, and now seemed as good a time as ever.

"So . . . did you, ah, ask Amy Perkins to homecoming?"

"Not after the other night," he said. "I took her out for pizza, and she spent most of the time text-messaging to her friends. As if that wasn't bad enough, she kept relaying their conversation back to me. Stuff like how Macy's is having this huge, huge sale on boots."

"Really?" I asked. "How huge?"

Mitch shook his head. "Fifteen percent. Not so huge."

I went back to sorting through clothes while he cut open another box. "Hey, check out these photographs! Look at the funky pants on this guy."

I moved over beside him. A musty odor rose from the box filled with tarnished frames wrapped in yellowed newspaper. We unwrapped each one, propping them against an old humidifier. Some were of unknown strangers wearing ridiculous polyester suits, with forced smiles and frizzy hair. Others were of houses, fuzzy and out of focus, or of wood-paneled station wagons.

"Check out the hottie," Mitch said, giving a low whistle.

"Let me see."

My heart leaped to my throat. Mitch was looking at a teenage girl wearing a tight yellow shirt with a pointy white collar that was trimmed with small, embroidered flowers. Her long, straight hair was parted in the middle, and EVELYN GRACE 1973 was etched in gold letters at one corner.

I'd never seen her before. Granny Po had no pictures of her daughter anywhere, nor had she talked about her daughter's life. And she never, *ever* talked about her death.

"Who's that?" Mitch asked.

"She's . . . my grandmother."

That evening, I sat on my bed, looking at the photograph.

So this is what she looked like.

It was hard to believe that the pretty, smiling teenager would one day overdose on sleeping pills, ending her life at thirty-six. I searched her face for any clue, any sign of depression foreshadowing that one day her life would be unlivable. But there were none; her eyes were shiny and bright, like any other girl.

I wondered what my mother's high school photo looked like, before my father entered her life and she became pregnant. Guess I'll never know, since one day in a fit of rage, Mom threw away all of her old yearbooks.

Granny Po knocked twice and entered before I had time to hide the photo. She stopped short when she saw the picture of her daughter. "Abbey . . . w-where did you find that?"

Silence washed over the room, as though I'd violated a sacred taboo.

Granny Po put a hand to her mouth and then reached out to touch a corner of the frame. "It was in a box," I said. "We found it while cleaning out the rooms today."

"So that's where it was," she murmured, almost to herself. "I have others, in an album, but this . . . this picture was always my favorite."

Granny Po dropped her hand and cleared her throat. "Anyway, dinner's ready. If, ah, you're hungry."

I was hungry, but not for food. I wanted to know more about Evelyn Somers, other than what my mother told me. Like how Elton and Evelyn moved to a nearby city after they got married. And how my grandfather moved to Washington after my grandmother died, and never set foot in Winchester, Maryland, again, even though Evelyn was buried at Granite Hill Church. The bed creaked as I moved to one side, leaving room for Granny Po to sit. "Why is this your favorite?"

She hesitated, then sat, her weight causing me to shift. Granny Po took the photograph, then leaned back to rest her head on the headboard. She pointed to the tiny row of flowers along Evelyn's collar. "See those? She embroidered them herself. Back then, all the girls learned how to embroider. I think I still have an old pillowcase that she fancied up for me, somewhere . . ."

Granny Po took a deep breath, biting the inside of her cheek. "And that macramé bracelet; Lord, she loved that thing. She and her friend Maybien made them at our kitchen table and then wore them while swimming so they would shrink on their wrists."

Those facts were small, but it was like throwing drops of water on a very dry sponge. A start, but not enough. "What else did she do? What did she like?"

Granny Po kicked off her shoes, allowing them to drop to the floor. "She loved to watch *The Partridge Family* on TV, and she wore her hair just like Laurie Partridge did, even though some of her friends didn't think the show was cool. And Steve McQueen . . . Lord, that girl loved Steve

McQueen, despite the fact he was old enough to be her father."

Granny Po turned to me and nudged me with her shoulder. "Now, in my day, everyone watched the *Ed Sullivan Show* on Sunday nights. Ever hear of him? He'd start off by always saying 'We've got a really good *shew*,' not 'show,' but '*sshhheeww*.'"

I nodded, even though I didn't have a clue what she was talking about. Same with Steve McQueen, other than that Sheryl Crow wrote a song about him.

"Evelyn always did have a thing for older men, I suppose," Granny Po said, placing the picture back into my hands and looking out the window. Tears formed in her eyes and her voice grew tight. "She was only sixteen when she met Elton Somers, who was ten years older. No matter how hard I tried to stop it, she fell for him. Then, in nineteen seventy-four, *The Partridge Family* was canceled. Steve McQueen starred in his last good movie, *Towering Inferno,* Ed Sullivan died, and Evelyn got married."

She wiped her eyes and looked at me. "Funny, ain't it? How you can remember details like that?"

It was true. I can remember exactly what Mom wore the only time she took me to my grandmother's grave site. Faded black stirrup pants and an oversized brown sweater. I remember holding an autumn leaf up, noting how the color was the same as her sweater.

Granny Po slipped her legs over the side of the bed, bending down with a grunt to pick up her shoes. She walked slowly to the door, then turned around. "Well, come on. Dinner's getting cold."

"Wait," I said, sitting up. "The wedding, what was that like? Do you have any pictures?"

She gripped the door frame, as though for balance, her face pale.

"No, Abbey. I wasn't invited."

Chapter Nine

Sarah joined me in the library during study hall, wearing a new gold necklace with a heart pendant that looked rather heavy. It flopped against her chest when she sat down.

"Hey, when did you get that?" I asked, leaning forward to get a better look.

Sarah reached up and caressed the heart with her right hand. "Oh, isn't it beautiful? John gave it to me last night, for our eight-month anniversary. He even took me to Maria's for dinner and told me to order whatever I want, can you believe that?"

Sure I could believe it. John's parents probably fronted him the money for it. I mean, come on, his folks pay fifty bucks an hour for his batting lessons. Of *course* he can afford it.

Stop it. Don't be cynical. "That's great, Sarah. I'm happy for you."

"Thanks." She let go of her necklace and pulled a geometry book from her backpack. "So, what have you been up to all week, now that your evenings are free?"

"Not enough," I told her, before the study-hall monitor tapped on our table and reminded us study hall is for *studying*.

I doodled on my notebook, thinking of how empty the beauty shop was, except for a few nails on the wall, empty kitchen cabinets, and the antique cuckoo clock, which Gena had bought for fifty dollars. Granny Po was officially retired. And I was temporarily unemployed.

I don't like being unemployed. Even if only temporarily.

Edith, however, was loving it. After homework, I'd go to her farm to scrub water buckets, sweep away those awful cobwebs, and show Mr. Penny how to use the computer program. Horses were given extra-long grooming sessions, where all their nicks and scrapes were treated with Udder Balm. I cleaned saddles, and stacked hay bales with Mitch, who was more than happy to remind me that I promised to go to the football game next Friday night.

Granny Po claimed to be relieved by her newfound free time, saying she could finally get to those things she'd been putting off for years. Like the jigsaw puzzles her cousin Linda sends every Christmas. On Monday night, Granny Po dumped a thousand-piece Big Ben puzzle on the dining room table. I worked on the border, she the clock face. After one painful, boring hour, we swiped the stupid thing back into the box.

Tuesday night was knitting. Granny Po wanted to get a jump on Christmas presents, and I thought it'd be fun to learn, since a lot of celebrities knit to relax. Forty-five minutes later, my fingers ached from the whole knit-one-purl-two crap, and her scarf for Caddie looked deformed.

Wednesday night, we gave up and watched TV.

Every now and then, we'd catch a customer gazing in the parlor window at the empty shop. Granny Po would step out onto the porch and explain that yes, Polly's Parlor is indeed now closed.

"But just look at my nails," one older lady whined, wiggling her fingers in Granny Po's face. "These cuticles can't wait! And where am I gonna get my hair done until then? You know I can't drive into town and fit in them itty-bitty parking spaces!"

Granny Po assured her that the new owner would be opening a day spa soon, and if she wanted, she could come into the house right now and Granny Po would be *more* than happy to do her hair and nails.

The woman's eyes lit up. She clasped her hands together. "Oh my stars, a day spa, like on them makeover shows? You reckon they'll have paraffin treatments, Polly?"

It's a good thing Granny Po wasn't still holding the knitting needles.

Gena was at the empty shop every day, mostly when I was at school. By Wednesday, a SERENITY SPA, COMING SOON banner was hanging on the front porch rails. On Thursday, she pulled into the driveway seconds after I got off the bus, her face beaming with excitement.

"Awesome news, awesome news," she exclaimed, doing a little dance. "Somehow, by the grace of God, my permit will be ready to pick up tomorrow afternoon. So . . . we'll be ready to start remodeling this Saturday!"

"Saturday? As in *two days* from now?" Oh my gosh. We

just cleaned the shop out *last* Saturday. You would think stuff like this would take more time.

"And," Gena continued, "if all goes well, I should be set to open the weekend before Thanksgiving."

That's, what . . . four weeks from now? There's no way, *no way* the spa will be done by then. But Gena looked confident as she reached into her Jeep for a canvas tote. "Hey, you want to go inside and check out the final floor plan?"

Absolutely, and I wasn't the only one interested. Granny Po stalked through the shop door seconds after we walked in. Days before, she privately complained to me about the spa name. I could tell she hated the floor plans even more, only she wasn't all that private with her opinion this time.

"Nope, this won't work," Granny Po griped, her reading glasses perched low on her nose. "Any fool can tell you, Miss Hopkins, you can't have the styling chairs separated like this. Never, never, never. You gotta put the chairs in a row, so women can see each other."

I rather liked how Gena's design had individual, island-like stations, with a stylist on opposite sides. But instead of saying so, I watched Gena's face, waiting to see how she reacted to Granny Po's bluntness. Some people did not respond well to her candor. Others took it with a grain of salt.

Apparently, Gena had a shaker full. "Yes, but remember, since it's going to be a day spa, as well, there needs to be an element of privacy for the customers."

"Bull. Young lady, I have cut enough hair off the heads of women to stuff a couch, love seat, and matching recliners, and I say that women come to a beauty parlor to gossip with each other."

"True," said Gena, "but after owning a salon in Baltimore and styling several local celebrities, I found that sometimes women need privacy."

"Maybe a hoity-toity celebrity would." Granny Po huffed. "Or a person who lives in Baltimore with people up their butt night and day, but not in Winchester. Where're you going to find a celebrity around here? Unless you count Cheryl Jenkins, who was on *Jerry Springer* once after finding out her fiancé likes to stroll around in diapers at night."

By now, my salt shaker would be close to empty. But Gena only took back the plans, nodding her head. "You know, Mrs. Randall, changing the chairs is not a bad idea. Thank you, I'll consider your suggestion."

Huh? Did she just give in to Granny Po?

Granny Po seemed as unsure as I did, stepping back with a wary look on her face. "Well then, okay. Thank you. I, uh, have to go back to my . . . puzzle now."

Gena stuck the pencil behind her ear, calmly rolling up the floor plans and putting them back into her tote before catching my stare. "What?"

I quickly looked away and coiled my hair into a knot at the base of my neck in an attempt to look casual. "Oh, nothing."

Gena snapped her fingers and reached for a notepad in her tote. "Hey, while I've got you here, we can discuss your job responsibilities. But first, your salary."

Her tone of voice didn't sound promising. "Okay, sure."

Gena flipped through her notepad. "Mrs. Randall told me you made six dollars an hour, so why don't we start you at the same?"

Huh? Six dollars? No, I was only getting five before.

Granny Po must have . . . *oh my gosh*. That sneaky booger. *Six dollars an hour!* I can save more each week. And increase the monthly contribution to my mutual fund. My legs twitched, wanting to run to my computer and see what my projected savings would be with six dollars an hour.

". . . you can shampoo clients, but you won't be allowed to cut hair anymore because you don't have a cosmetology license." Gena closed her notepad, picked up her tote, and started walking toward the door. "Any questions so far?"

"Uh, no," I said, my mind still calculating.

"You'll also be in charge of washing towels, sweeping, keeping the display shelves stocked and magazines rotated. Eventually, you can help with inventory, if you can handle the workload."

"I'm sure I can handle everything, Gena."

Gena stopped at the door, holding her hand on the knob. "One more rule. I want to see all your report cards. If your grades drop, you don't work."

I nodded and followed her out on the porch. "My grades are always excellent."

"Great." She smiled and reached forward to wrap me in a big hug. "Then, I guess all I have to say is welcome to Serenity!"

For one brief moment, I closed my eyes and remembered hugging my mother on that rainy night she brought me here, standing right here on the porch. Except my mother never came back.

Gena will.

Two days later, construction of Serenity Spa officially began.

Gena's brother, Nick, and two of his workers showed up at

six thirty. I walked through the door at eight and stood open-mouthed at all the changes they had made. Gena put down her hammer and came over, her hair wrapped in a red bandanna. "Hey, isn't this great?"

Oh my gosh.

The old kitchen cabinets were removed and lying in a discarded heap by the front door. In the middle of the shop, a new wall to divide the room in two was already framed in. One guy was removing old wallpaper, and another used a circular saw to trim a two-by-four, spitting sawdust down to the hardwood floor.

Gena waved her hand at the mess. "Don't worry about the floor. I'm going to have it sanded down and refinished later on, anyway."

It was so overwhelming seeing Polly's Parlor like this, in a state of utter disarray. From behind me, there was a sharp gasp. Granny Po stood with a hand on her chest. She composed herself when I asked if she was okay, then started complaining about the loud noise from the electric nail guns, saws, and radio so early on a Saturday morning.

"Mrs. Randall, I apologize for the noise," Gena said, "but since my brother's doing the remodeling for me at cost, he'll have to work weekends and nights."

"*Hmph.* Fine, then," Granny Po said. She stared at a chunky worker standing on a ladder across the room, with pants hanging half-mast. His butt crack winked as he used a steamer to loosen and remove her faded wallpaper. "You just make sure no dust gets in my house, you hear? And tell Cracky over there to cover his ass before my great-granddaughter gets an education."

"Yes, ma'am," Gena said, watching her storm out and

slam the door behind her. Gena turned to me, unaffected by Granny Po's latest tirade. Nothing seemed to bother her, not the shop being a total wreck, not Granny Po's nonstop complaining or how the other Gray Widows still gave her the cold shoulder. Well, not Caddie. She was here before I was, with coffee and fresh muffins for the workers.

"So, Abbey," Gena said, "what are you up to today? Here to check the place out?"

I jerked my head up. "I . . . I thought you hired me."

Now it was her turn to look shocked. Gena's perfectly made-up eyes widened. "Oh. Yes, but for after the spa opens."

"Oh. Sure, that's fine," I said, burying my hands deep into my pockets.

Gena touched my arm. "Are you okay?"

I nodded, but inside, my heart had started to pound. Of *course* Gena had assumed I'd start after the spa opened—she had no idea how important this job was to me. But the spa won't open for *four weeks*. That's four weeks without a paycheck. Four weeks without making a deposit at the bank, and four weeks behind on my MBTF plan.

"Miss Hopkins," I said, my voice cracking, "is there anything I could do? Like clean up all this trash, or . . . or anything?"

Gena studied my face for a few seconds and then nodded. "Well, there *are* some things you could do to help out, so why not. You can start now. And call me Gena, okay?"

I let out my breath in relief. "Okay, and thanks, Gena. Just tell me what to do."

She looked around at the chaos surrounding her. "Like

you said, the trash can be picked up—anything to help speed the workers up. Oh, and you can help me next Saturday with the employee interviews. But for today"—Gena held out a scraper—"ever remove wallpaper before?"

No, I never took down wallpaper, but that didn't stop me from taking the scraper, anyway. Working with Cracky was a bit of a challenge, since his butt crack was impossible to ignore, like how a moth is drawn to a bug zapper, but it didn't matter. As long as I was working.

Chapter Ten

From then on, the shop was in a constant whirlwind, and every day there was something different when I got off the bus and checked in. New walls were framed and electrical wires run for the workstations. The plumber finished his rough-in, windows were replaced, and by that first Friday, the drywall was hung. When I walked into the shop that day, still in my school clothes, Nick was applying mud to the drywall seams. The rooms were littered with lumber scraps, sawdust, caulk guns, and open toolboxes, but in the middle of the chaos was Gena, who always seemed calm and in control no matter what.

Like when the permit inspector said the lighting outside didn't meet code. Or when the front door was on backorder, when the electrician came down with the flu, or when one of the delivered sinks had a crack in it. Stuff like this would make my head explode, but she just took it all in stride.

Tonight I was going to the football game with Sarah and Kym, but there was time to clean up some of this trash first. I told Gena I'd be back after changing, then stepped right into a large pile of goo—while in the good boots I planned on wearing to the game.

"Damn! How stupid can I possibly be!" I picked at the mess, which was twenty times worse than bubble gum. I slammed my hand on a windowsill. "They're ruined now."

Caddie scolded me as she walked in from Granny Po's with a tray of iced tea and sugar cookies. "Not proper language for a young lady, Abbey dear."

Gena looked at my boot and laid a hand lightly on my arm. "Hey, it's cool, hon. It's just construction adhesive. Here, give me it to me."

She reached into a tool belt for a metal scraper, then picked off most of the mess in even strokes. Gena then soaked a rag with mineral spirits and started wiping off what was left, just as a carpenter dropped a hammer on the hardwood floor.

Cracky. He cringed at the dent he caused and looked at Gena. "Miss Hopkins, I am so sorry."

Gena shrugged it off. "It's okay, Frank. Nothing a little wood filler can't fix."

I remember one time when Dad accidentally scratched the counter with his tool chest and my mother threw it out the window. Mom would have totally reamed Cracky, and Granny Po, oh my gosh. She would have found another use for those knitting needles if anyone dented her floor. And what about me? I flip out over soiled footwear.

Just like Mom would have.

An hour later, Kym knocked on the front door. She went straight to my closet, pulled out a red cashmere sweater, then held it against her chest. "Oh my gosh, you make me so sick! Where did you get this sweater?"

I stood beside her, selecting a pair of starched jeans and a wool sweater with a matching scarf, in an effort to stay warm tonight. "Rosemary gave it to me last Easter."

Rosemary has no children, so I'm her outlet for gift shopping. Kym pulled off her shirt and put on my sweater, modeling in front of the mirror with her hands on her hips. "Man, I wish I had a Rosemary. You are so lucky, Abbey."

If she only knew the whole truth. Kym and Sarah know that my parents are divorced and that my mom lives in another state; they just don't know why.

A honk came from the driveway. I pulled my curtains aside and looked out the window. "That's Sarah and her mom. We better hurry."

Granny Po was in the family room, resting in a recliner with her feet up and a sour look on her face. She flipped through the TV channels until she came to *Wheel of Fortune*. I walked over to say good-bye just as a new puzzle came on. Category: "thing." The first contestant correctly guessed a *c*. Then a *t*, an *r*, and he bought a vowel, an *o*.

"Constructive criticism!" I shouted.

Granny Po threw down the remote. "Dammit! You cheated!"

"Sore loser," I said, reaching down to give her a hug.

"Whatever," Granny Po said. "Be home by eleven."

It was beginning to worry me how depressed she seemed lately, especially when Caddie or Gena talked about the new spa. Maybe it was a mistake to give her Gena's card that evening weeks ago. Maybe she's not able to handle the change.

And maybe I should have let her solve the puzzle.

———

Sarah's mom told us to have fun when she dropped us off at the stadium. Yeah, fun. I'd rather bounce on a trampoline without a bra for two hours than go to a football game, but a promise is a promise. However, there's no way I'm calling out, "Go team, go," like Mitch wants me to.

Kym led the way through the gate, dodging people carrying hot dogs, hot chocolate, and popcorn to the stadium bleachers. Sarah saw John way at the top and waved. She's only been able to see him during school hours this week, since Mrs. Diehl thinks she's not spending enough time at home. Meaning, too much time with John, which, hey, she's got a point. Sarah turned to us with a hopeful grin. "You guys mind if I hang with John tonight?"

I lightly pushed her shoulder. "Go. Be free, young one."

Sarah hugged us and took the steps two at a time. So much for playing hard to get.

Kym linked her arm through mine. "It's just you and me, then. Let's do a couple laps, see who's here, and then find a place to sit, okay?"

"Okay," I said, like I do this kind of thing all the time. A brisk wind picked up, making me glad I brought along a heavy coat. Kym had to be freezing, wearing only a light jacket over her sweater because she didn't want to hide her outfit.

I looked up into the bleachers. The crowd was clearly segregated. On the top left side were the seniors, sitting in clumps, facing each other, not paying attention to the game even though Winchester was ahead seven points. In the middle section were all the parents, huddled in blankets and knit hats, watching their sons pile up on each other and screaming at the referees. Less popular kids were on the right front flank, somewhat popular kids on the left, and the band held court in the middle, holding instruments that looked amazingly cold.

Kym pointed to the varsity cheerleaders just as they finished a cheer, screaming out a mighty *Go, Wildcats, go!* "Man, I wish I'd made the varsity squad. Or even the fall JV squad instead of winter."

Nobody in the stadium seemed to be paying much attention to the cheerleaders, other than Kym and the parents, who politely applauded their enthusiastic efforts. I looked for Amy Perkins in the rows of black and yellow uniforms. Yes, there she was, her long hair streaked with all those "highlight things" Mitch mentioned. Oh my gosh, Granny Po would crap if she saw that dye job. Looks like a five-year-old did them with a paint roller. Amy did a superhigh kick at a Wildcat interception, causing me to oddly take comfort that I really did have legs much better than hers.

Just when I was trying to find Mitch among all the players on the football field, a deep voice came from behind me. "Hey, Abbey."

I whipped around to find Camden Mackintosh standing there. "Oh, hey."

Kym stepped behind him near the bleachers, smiling ear to ear, with both thumbs way up. *Don't leave,* I mouthed, but she was already going up the stairs. Camden shoved one hand halfway into his jeans pocket, and casually crossed his feet, like a model. "Good game, huh? Looks like Riverside High's winning streak might come to an end."

A group of girls wearing the same denim jackets walked by, staring at Camden as though he were a god, but he didn't take his eyes off me. I turned away and pointed to the field. "Yeah, well, Riverside made a huge mistake by throwing the ball on third down and one. They wouldn't have lost control by interception if they'd run it."

Camden took his hand out of his pocket and leaned against the fence. He gave me a lopsided grin. "A girl that digs football. Very cool."

Oops.

"No, there's no digging, *uh-uh,*" I said, waving my hands in front of me. "I just have . . . I mean, *had* a dad who talks, *talked* about football all the time, and you know, if you hear something for most of your childhood, some of it is bound to sink in, right?"

"Oh . . . right." Camden ran a hand through his dark hair, leaving perfect rake marks in the layers, and then noticed his friends waving at him from the concession stand. "Well, I gotta run, but look, some friends are coming over to my house later to play some pool, listen to tunes, you know. Hang out. Think you'd want to stop by?"

He was inviting me over? What, like a date? No, probably not a date. Camden kept his gaze on me as he held a hand up to his friends who were now calling out his name. "Well, what do you say, Abbey?"

"You know"—my voice sounded like a little girl's—"I can't. Interviews tomorrow, you know. Not my interviews, but I'm helping my boss, so I need to get up super early. But thanks, okay?"

"Sure," he said casually, as though it really was no big deal. "Maybe next time."

Camden trotted off to his friends, and Kym ran forward,

quickly replacing him along the fence. "'Next time'? What did he mean by that?"

"Oh, nothing," I lied, knowing that if Kym found out Camden Mackintosh invited me to a party, she'd drag me there herself. "You want to walk?"

"Absolutely. Man, have I got something to show you," Kym said, grabbing my arm and pulling me down the sidewalk to the midway point between the visitors' side and the home side. She stopped and pointed to a bunch of skaters. "Check that out."

Kym pointed to a tall guy wearing torn, baggy pants and a thin white tank despite the cold. He had a chain attached at his belt loop that led right up to the studded collar around his girlfriend's neck.

The sight was pathetic, enough to totally flush women's liberation straight down the toilet. "Oh my gosh, Kym, you have *got* to be kidding me. Is that girl serious? I would rather *choke* than have that thing around my neck."

Kym wrapped her thin jacket tighter and shushed me. "Stop! You want them to hear you? That girl could take the both of us. And besides, she's just having fun. You know, expressing herself and all."

"What?" I asked, keeping my voice down because that girl really could take us both down. "Expressing that she's an idiot? Telling the whole world her man is in control? Unbelievable."

Kym turned us around, away from the skaters and the dog-collared girl. "Honestly, Abbey, you sound like such a prude sometimes. An old-fashioned, outdated, mutilated prude."

"'Mutilated'?"

She shrugged. "It was the only thing I could think of that rhymed with outdated. But come on. Wouldn't you love to be chained up to Camden for a little while? I mean, really. From the way he looked at you, I bet you could totally get him to ask you out."

Too late for that. Before I could say anything, the crowd started screaming, getting to their feet. A Wildcat was running hard for a touchdown, dodging an opposing player who dove for his legs. Amy stood in front of the other cheerleaders, screaming, "Go, MITCH!"

That's Mitch. I laced my fingers in the wire fence, watching his arm pump with each stride, easily outrunning the linebacker who dived for his legs. He crossed the goal line with nobody around him, seconds before the first quarter ended. Kym pulled on my sleeve, but I was suddenly aware of how twenty-some years ago, my father *was* Mitch, the hero who high-fived his teammates, while cheerleaders shouted his name in the background.

"So, come on, why aren't you attracted to Camden?" Kym pressed.

I turned away from the field. "Just . . . because."

Chapter Eleven

Gena didn't need me on Saturday until nine thirty, so I left the house at seven to help Edith with the morning feedings. Mr. Penney had to drive the trailer to a riding stable accused of abusing their horses, and Mitch wouldn't be there until later, probably because he sleeps in the morning after a game.

I wondered if he went to Camden's party. Not that it mattered, or anything.

By the time I walked into the shop, Gena was waiting for me wearing a crisp white suit and black stilettos, even though the shop was in shambles. If Granny Po wasn't sulking in the kitchen with the other Widows, she'd knock Gena for wearing white after Labor Day, but I thought she looked amazing. Yesterday Gena had said it's imperative to dress fashionably in the beauty industry and to have a current hairstyle. So this morning, after getting out of my barn jeans, I had put on a black A-line skirt and a coral sweater. Gena nodded her approval and motioned me to the back patio.

"It's like Indian summer today," she said, "so let's hold the interviews outside, okay?"

On the patio, she handed me forms on clipboards for each applicant to fill out and instructed me to let her know when each person arrived. "Do you want me to bring them through Granny Po's side, so they don't have to walk through the messy shop?"

Gena paused and straightened her jacket's lapel. "No, that's probably not a good idea."

Yeah, as soon as the words left my lips, I knew it wasn't. I grabbed an extra chair so the waiting applicants had something to sit on but stopped at the door. She looked up at me. "Something wrong, Abbey?"

No. Yes. I set the chair back down. "I don't know . . . It's just, I've been wanting to ask you. Granny Po is fighting you on everything, like the spa name, and the plans. I mean, you changed your floor plans after she raised a fuss about how the chairs were placed."

Gena put down her schedule and walked over. "Abbey, Mrs. Randall isn't fighting me. She's just having a hard time letting go. And you know what, she was right about the chairs. Besides, there's a five-year policy that I read somewhere and I always follow."

"What five-year policy?"

Gena tapped her chest with a manicured nail. "Whenever I start to worry about something, I ask myself, will this matter in five years? Like where the chairs are placed, will that matter? The answer is no, it won't, so I'm not going to stress out over it. Everything will work out, you'll see."

"Oh," I said, nodding like I understood. But life can't be

that simple. Everything matters five years from now. Every move, every decision. Even the smallest yes or no makes all the difference. Just look at my mother.

Gena held the door open so I could carry the chair through. But before closing it, she stopped me. "Um, Abbey, there's something I've wanted to ask you, too. Is it really true what Mrs. Randall said about a woman in town going on *Jerry Springer* because her fiancé wore diapers?"

"Yep." I nodded. "Totally true. It's a visual I'd rather forget."

At first, the interviews were fun. A twentyish blond arrived promptly at ten, bounding up the sidewalk while straightening her skirt and picking between her front teeth. She flashed me a smile brighter than sunshine when I opened the door. "Hi! I'm here to interview for the receptionist position."

"Yes, hello. You're Rachel Clement?"

"Yeah . . . I mean, yes, that's me, Rachel Clement." She thrust her hand toward me for a handshake. I could have told her my butt wasn't the one she should be kissing, but instead let her think it might do some good. I felt important, carrying the clipboard with Rachel following behind, anxious as a dog at mealtime.

But by three o'clock . . . it was not fun. I was tired of the same list of questions, the same perky, ambitious expressions and exaggerated answers. I did love the one potential stylist, Paul Danehy, who kissed me on both cheeks. Gena planned on having four stylists for now, even though the front room was designed for six, and I really hoped he would be one of them.

"Who's left on the schedule for today?" Gena stretched her arms, raising them above her head with palms clasped together. "Hmm. I could use a yoga class right now."

Yoga. Kym, Sarah, and I rented a yoga tape once, since all the stars are doing it, and we wanted to see what the big whoop was. But I couldn't relax and let my mind "be still." We quit after the standing leg series, but right now, I'd rather torture myself with yoga than sit through one more interview. Five hours and eleven candidates were enough.

I looked at the schedule, trying to sound chipper. "Uh, two. Both for the receptionist position."

She groaned. "All right, let's get this over with." The fact that I wasn't the only one tired of interviews gave me an odd feeling of relief.

Louise Jenkins was nice, but her hair! It hung down well below her butt, like a black cape. I wondered if she ever got it stuck in a door. Or worse, down the toilet. She had two years of secretarial school, fifteen years experience at a salon, but I wasn't surprised when Gena crossed her name off the list two minutes after Louise left.

"Can you tell me why?" Gena asked, leaning back in her chair.

I tapped my pen on the table. "Because . . . employee hairstyles should be current? Not someone who hasn't had one in thirty years and trims her own split ends?"

"You got it."

The last interview was with a twenty-two-year-old named Brianna, who had the largest breasts I've ever seen in my entire life. And here I thought Cracky's rear end was hypnotic. It was impossible not to stare at those hummers, and it looked like I wasn't the only one fascinated by her bosom, since I caught Granny Po and the others peeking out the kitchen window. I also noticed how the window was open, so they could listen to every word.

After Brianna left, I gathered all the applications to file later, when Gena's office was finished. "Gena, do you want a cup of coffee? I'm going to make some for myself."

"Coffee? Aren't you a bit young for that?"

Young? I've been drinking coffee since I was eight. Sometimes it was the only thing Mom would make in the morning. Gena noticed my hesitation and said, "You know, I'm not much on coffee, but I'd love some tea."

My legs felt stiff from sitting. I opened the sliding glass door and saw Granny Po quickly resuming her task of spooning batter into muffin tins for bingo tonight. She looked at me with a sour expression, reaching for the streusel topping to sprinkle over the batter. The other Widows sat perched like crows on bar stools beside her, in perfect view of the patio. They tried to act nonchalant, munching on cookies and looking at the ceiling, but I knew what was up.

"Is this your only form of entertainment today, watching the interviews?" I teased.

"Heck no," Granny Po said, pointing at me with a crumb-crusted finger. "I'm making my cranberry-walnut muffins. Don't you think we all got better things to do than to watch Miss Hopkins out there?"

"She has a first name, you know. Gena. And you *were* watching."

"First names are for friends," she whispered. "And we *were not* watching."

I raised an eyebrow.

Edith shrugged. "Of course we were watching. Nothing else to do. Nowhere to go. Unless we sit around and watch the hair grow on Caddie's chin."

"There's no hair on my chin." Caddie raised a hand to her face. "Is there?"

"Made ya look."

I filled the teakettle with fresh water. "Well, that's the last one, so show's over. By the way, ladies, who did you put your money on?"

Rosemary put a hand to her silk blouse. "You don't think we'd bet on something as silly as that, do you, Abbey? We're much too sophisticated to worry about who Miss Hopkins hires."

"Oh please!" I giggled. "You four bet on everything from the weather to who'll clog the toilet next."

Edith pulled a wad of cash from her pocket, proving me right. "I put my money on that lady in the pink sweater, and Caddie here liked the Lady Godiva wannabe."

"The lady with long hair looked nice!" Caddie explained, still fingering her chin for that invisible hair. She must have missed Gena and me talking about Louise. Or her hearing aids were on the blink again.

Edith continued. "Polly didn't like any of them, and Rosemary here was for the Big Boob Queen at the end."

"All the good ones were taken." Rosemary shrugged.

Gena's voice came in through the open window. "Well, it's a good thing, because that's who I'm hiring." *Man, she has good ears.*

Granny Po stepped out on the patio, an annoyed glare in

her eyes. Rosemary followed, snatching the money from Edith's hand. "Thank you very much."

"The Big Boob Queen? BBQ? You're not really thinking of hiring her, are you?" Granny Po cupped her hands out in front of her chest. "Those knockers will put someone's eye out."

Gena pulled a mirror out of her purse and checked her reflection. "You can't judge a woman by her breast size. Brianna is smart, funny, and will work hard."

"Hmph. If her boobs don't get in the way." Granny Po took off her glasses. "I'd hire the scary-hair lady first. And what about that guy . . . Pete, or something. I'd never have a man working in *my* parlor. It would make the women feel self-conscious."

"His name is Paul Danehy. He's one of the best in town, so yes, I'm hiring him."

"And," I added, "male stylists on average attract more clients than women do."

Granny Po poked my shoulder. "What, you an expert now?"

She sat down, hiking her sleeves up and lifting her feet to a patio chair. But when loud blasts of an electric nail gun sounded from the spa, she gasped and clutched her chest. "Lord's sake, are they trying to give me a heart attack? Sounds like a bunch of gorillas in there."

The spa door opened. Nick walked out with a tool belt hitched low on his hips.

"Oh great," Granny Po mumbled under her breath. "And there's the head monkey."

Nick set a heavy canvas bag on the table, oblivious to Granny Po's comment. "Here's the paint samples you asked me to pick up for you, Gena. And three books of wallpaper samples. We'll be priming the walls by the end of next week."

Gena groaned, pulling out the paint samples and spreading them out like a fan. "Great. Now is when I wish I took that interior design course."

Rosemary's ears seemed to perk up. She looked at the bag like a curious child staring at a pile of wrapped presents.

Nick gave us a quick nod before walking toward the door, tool belt clanging with every stride. Caddie waved good-bye. "Nick, you tell the workers in there I'll bring some more cookies over later, all righty?"

Granny Po's angry stare made Caddie flinch.

"What did I do? I was just trying to be nice," Caddie said. She leaned closer and spoke in a dramatic whisper. "And I must admit something, although it's not very Christian-like. I just love a man in a tool belt. My heavens, even as portly as my dear Gary was, he looked awfully handsome in one, God rest his soul."

My mind flashed to Mitch and how one day he was doing odd repairs around the farm wearing Edith's old tool belt. I had to admit Caddie was right.

"God rest his soul," I repeated before I could stop myself. All the Widows stared as my face turned red. Time to change the subject. Quick. "What color are you going to pick, Gena?"

"I'm not sure. With everything else going on, I haven't given much thought to the decor." Gena sighed, fanning the color samples out again.

I could see an interested glow creep over the aloof, nonchalant look Rosemary normally wears around Gena.

She leaned in closer. "What kind of look are you going for?"

Gena sighed. "Well, there's the look I want and the look I can afford. I'd love it to be elegant and yet still have the charm of a home beauty salon."

"May I?" Rosemary took the samples from Gena. "Well, whatever you do, dear, don't skimp on paint quality or the draperies. Good paint lasts longer and cheap drapes are like tacky makeup."

Curiosity formed in Gena's eyes. "What color would you suggest?"

"Hmm . . . elegant and charming." Rosemary held a paint sample up. She cocked her head to the side, eyes narrowed as if she were seeing something no one else could.

"This olive is lovely. Classic and yet comforting. Pairing it with other earth-toned elements and texture for an intimate feel could be interesting, considering the layout of the spa, and *oooo!*" Rosemary waved her hand excitedly in the air. "You could put prints of old-time beauty products into gilded frames. I was watching this design show where they took these shabby wood frames and gilded them with . . ."

Rosemary stopped herself, put down the samples, and slowly picked up her coffee cup. "Oh, listen to me. Rambling on."

"Wow, Miss Rosemary," I said. "Sounds like you know what you're talking about."

"Well, I've tinkered around with design a bit."

Granny Po set her mug down with a bang. "Tinkered? Tinkered, my butt. You did more than tinker. Abbey, Rosemary here has a degree in interior design. Had her own business, too."

Rosemary nodded, her eyes glazing over as if seeing an image from the past. "Yes, I did. I loved it. Having people trust me with their home was such an honor. And to see the looks on their faces when I was done, well . . . let's just say I miss those days."

"But if you loved it so much, why did you stop?" I asked.

Rosemary hesitated, pulling on her earring. "Because I married Thomas and he needed help with his rental business, and Lord, things were too hectic so I, uh . . . closed my business."

It made no sense. How could she give up her passion? Sacrificing her happiness for a man, just like all the women of my family were convinced to do.

"But, Miss Rosemary, he died a long time ago," I said. "Why haven't you gone back?"

Rosemary took her napkin and neatly folded it in fourths. "Abbey, I . . . it was easier to . . . Thomas would have wanted me to continue the business."

But what about what Rosemary wanted?

"Well, here's a crazy thought," Gena said. "Since decorating was never my strong point, how would you feel about taking on the job? For pay, of course."

"Me? I don't . . . No. That's absurd. I'm much too old to start over."

"No, it's not absurd. You're never too old." Gena leaned forward, looking Rosemary in the eye. "It would really help me out, since I'm starting to get in over my head."

As much as I cared for Rosemary, I couldn't help but think Gena's offer was absurd. Gena has no idea what kind of decorator Rosemary would be and yet she's trusting her with something as important as this. With all that money invested? There's too much at stake.

Rosemary took a deep breath, fingers skimming the chain-link strap of her purse. "I don't know. There just isn't time. Unless I did hire a property management company . . ."

"Come on. I know you can do this," Gena urged.

"Well, I do have a few ideas . . . but . . ."

Edith threw her balled-up napkin at Rosemary. "*But, schmut.* You know you want to. Piss or get off the pot."

Rosemary looked around the table, her jawline tight. She glanced at Granny Po. "Polly?"

Granny Po was silent. I thought she'd freak at Rosemary for crossing enemy lines, but she only nodded, mumbling that it made no never mind to her. Rosemary pushed back her chair and stood, snatching up the samples. "I think I will. For free, of course. Taking money after all this time wouldn't feel proper."

Rosemary hesitated at the door. "And Gena . . . thanks."

"No, thank *you*, Rosemary. I really appreciate it."

There was something different about Rosemary when she left, muttering to herself about getting more wallpaper and fabric samples before the stores closed. And Gena's eyes sparkled as she put her jacket on. Funny, Gena didn't seem like the kind of person who got in over her head. Or who couldn't decorate. So why was she trusting Rosemary?

"Well, ladies," Gena said, "I'm going home and soaking in the tub for an hour. It will be a relief to stop working at four thirty for once."

"Four thirty!" Granny Po jumped up. "Forgot to put them darn muffins in the oven!"

"I'll help," Edith said, following her to the kitchen. Caddie left the table, giving Gena a little wink before ducking into the house. Gena winked back.

Oh my gosh . . . wait a minute.

"Did you know about Rosemary?" I asked. "About her decorating and all?"

Gena smiled, gathering her papers and placing them neatly into her briefcase. "Maybe."

No wonder Nick brought out all the samples. But none of it made any sense. What made her decide to offer the job to someone she hardly knew? I mean, come on. If there ever was a time when her five-year policy should be applied to a decision, it's now.

"I know what you're thinking," Gena said.

"You do?"

Gena nodded and stood, then placed her chair back neatly under the table at the sound of the oven door slamming inside the house. "You're wondering why I'm trusting someone I hardly know with the decorating."

"Well, yeah," I said. "What if you don't like it, after all the money is spent?"

"Abbey, hiring Rosemary might be taking a chance, but I'm willing to take it."

"Why?"

Gena rested her hands on the back of the chair. "Because you can't only worry about the bottom line. Sometimes it's the people that count. I have faith in Rosemary. She'll do a great job. If not, it's only money, Abbey, and money can disappear in a second. It's the person that matters. Trust me, I learned my lesson the hard way."

Part of me wanted so badly to believe her. But in my world, people disappear. Money doesn't. It's the one thing you can always count on. But as I crawled into bed that night, I thought back to that look on Rosemary's face. Maybe it wasn't crazy for Gena to hire her. Maybe it was . . . good.

Chapter Twelve

Hypothetical Question of the Week: If you were to be tortured for twenty-four hours, which technique would you find most painful? Being stuck in a room with fifty kindergartners in squeaky shoes, or with fifty obnoxiously loud eaters, or with twenty toddlers rubbing Styrofoam together?"

I thought for sure Granny Po would pick the eaters, since noisy eating drives her crazy, but she only glared at me over her cornflakes and morning coffee. Then the sound of something being dropped came through the wall from the shop.

"You know what's torture for me?" Granny Po pointed a finger at the wall. "That. *That* is torture for me."

I gave up trying to cheer her, and put the tabloid away. She grabbed a knife, jabbed it into the butter tub, and slapped it on her toast. Ever since Rosemary had agreed to do the decorating, almost two weeks ago, Granny Po's bad mood had doubled. And when Edith was the next to cross over—oh man. It tripled.

Caddie was the one who told me how Edith and Gena had struck up a conversation about art, of all things. Two days later, Edith was hanging wallpaper. For Gena. Of course, Edith tried to justify it by saying she was doing it only to help Rosemary, but Granny Po wouldn't budge.

After school yesterday, I found Granny Po sulking over her tea as Rosemary and Caddie covered the seats of salvaged dining room chairs with a dark patterned material. Rosemary squealed with excitement when she saw me. "Abbey, darling, look at these chairs! I practically stole them from a flea market for ten dollars each. Once they're reupholstered, they'll be *fabulous* for the reception area."

"Looks great, Miss Rosemary," I said.

"*'Looks great, Miss Rosemary,'*" Granny Po mocked. She rolled her eyes at Caddie, who flinched each time Rosemary used the staple gun.

"For heaven's sake, Caddie," Rosemary said. "Stop jumping, and hold the material taut! Trust me, I'm not going to staple your fingers."

"Oh sure, trust me . . . trust me. Isn't that what the witch said to Hansel and Gretel? *'Trust me,* children, come inside for some candy! I won't hurt you.'" Caddie flinched when Rosemary shot the stapler. "And what happened?"

"Oh please, Caddie. You'd follow anybody who offered you food. Now, hold still!"

Granny Po heaved herself from the chair, shaking her head when Caddie jumped again. Both of her knees popped as she knelt down, elbowing Caddie out of the way. "Oh, for Pete's sake, Caddie! Let me do that. My Lord, you're as—"

"I know, I know. Worthless as tits on a boar hog."

With only one week before Gena's grand opening, everyone had a job to do. Rosemary was finishing her fifties print project on the back lawn, by taking old wood frames and gilding them with an antique gold stain, gold foil, polyurethane, and white pickling paste. I was glad to be working far away from the fumes, planting shrubs around Gena's new SERENITY SPA sign out front.

Granny Po was busy inside, making a dessert for bingo: Edith was helping Rosemary; Caddie was getting in the way . . . and it was my birthday.

I really hate my birthday.

Gena tried to make me take the day off, but there's no way I'd turn down a full day's pay. I had shrubs and a box full of bulbs to plant, mulch to spread, and besides, I needed to dig. I needed to feel my muscles burn, anything to get my mind off this morning's phone call.

I had just stepped out of the shower and wrapped myself in a towel when the phone rang. Seconds later, Granny Po knocked and opened the bathroom door a crack, looking at the steam-covered mirror. "Stop using all the dang hot water. And here . . . the phone's for you."

Mom! She remembered my birthday!

"It's your father," she said.

Dad. Not my mother. My body chilled, even with the heat from the shower. *He* called before Mom did. "Tell him I'm busy, Granny Po."

She held out the phone, a firm look in her eyes. "Abbey, he's your father and he loves you. It wouldn't kill you to be nice to him."

"Fine." I reluctantly took the phone, moving as slowly as I could to sit on the toilet seat. I waited until I heard Granny Po walking to the kitchen before speaking. "Hey, Dad."

"Hey, sweetheart! I was getting worried there, thinking that Granny Po forgot me or something."

No, that's your job. Forgetting people.

"Got any great plans for today?" he asked.

"No. Just the same thing I do every weekend. Work." I pulled the towel off my head, fingering the knotty mess that fell to my shoulders.

"A birthday girl shouldn't be working! How about I pick you up, and we can spend the day together? There's a new restaurant near my house that serves the best shrimp in the world. It's your favorite, so—"

"I hate shrimp."

A pause hung in the air, interrupted by a drip from the faucet. "Oh. I thought you loved shrimp."

"You thought wrong."

Dad cleared his throat. "Okay, well they have other stuff, or we could go somewhere else, like to this new Japanese restaurant that makes your meal right in front of you. I can be there at around ten, and take you there later as a special birthday treat. What do you say?"

A thick ache spread in my chest, as it does whenever I try not to cry. God, I wish he'd just leave me alone and stop calling. He makes it too hard when he calls with that stupid eagerness in his voice. Every time I hear it, it reminds me how I always had to pick sides as a child, my mother or my father.

And I always chose my mother, even when she was wrong.

"Can't. Gotta work," I said, my words choked.

Dad paused. For a few seconds, he was silent, just the sound of static on the line. "Look, Abbey, for the past year I've been really trying, okay?"

I twisted a corner of my towel, watching a spider slowly crawl up the ceramic tile. Yes, he was trying. I'll give him that. But what about the two years I lived alone with Mom? He never called then—not on my birthday; not ever. He didn't even pay child support—like he just wanted to write me off like a bad debt.

"Abbey . . . are you there? Please, Abbey, I just want . . ."

I swallowed hard, trying to force the lump down my throat. "Look, stop making me feel terrible, as though it's my fault. You didn't want me, remember? When I was eleven and Mom left me here, you were too busy getting married. So now you come around just because Sharon divorced you and you have nobody left. But guess what, I don't want you."

"Abbey."

"Dad, please just let me hang up. Please."

He did.

Later, Granny Po pestered me with questions about our conversation, but I didn't give any details. What if she forced me to spend the day with him? Now I rammed the shovel into the dirt, my mind going into spin cycle. I get so tired sometimes. Tired of worrying about my mother, tired of having to be so angry at my father and wishing he would just leave me alone.

Please don't cry. Not today. Crying gives me headaches. And if I start, I may not be able to stop.

My thoughts were interrupted by a stereo blasting a Western twang. Mitch. He pulled into the driveway, parking beside Caddie's Cadillac and popping the trunk. He waved at me, but I ducked my head, trying to hide the tears in my eyes.

"Hey, Abbey! Happy birthday!"

God, even he remembered. Something inside me seemed to snap. "Why do you always have to play that stereo so damn loud? And what's with the stupid cowboy music?"

"Well, hello to you, too, sunshine. And yes, I'm doing well, thanks for asking."

Edith stepped out of the spa's newly installed door in time to hear my outburst. She gave me a disapproving look and then went to Mitch's trunk. "Don't mind her, Mitch. She's as pissy today as a starved pit bull. How was the football game last night?"

"It was close," Mitch said, "but we managed to get the winning touchdown with twenty-four seconds left in the fourth quarter."

Edith pulled a grocery bag from the trunk. "You tell that Coach Wilcox to tighten up the defensive line. I haven't seen it this weak since 2003."

"Yes, ma'am, I will."

Rosemary streaked out the door, running to Mitch's car. Rubber gloves covered her hands, disguising the fact that she hasn't bothered with a manicure in ages. Gone were the neat, tailored clothes. She had stocked up on cheap jeans and T-shirts, and the shock of seeing her like this still made me look twice.

"Mitch, you dear boy. Running errands for a bunch of old ladies. Did you get me more polyurethane? Ah, yes, here it is. Oh my goodness, the frames are going to be so amazing!" Rosemary dashed back inside, with Edith following.

As Mitch lifted the rest of the groceries out of the trunk, I made a show of digging a hole when he looked my way. There's nothing more irritating than someone who's cheery when you feel your world's a wreck. I was relieved when he finally took the bags into the house.

Thank God bingo was tonight. I'd have the house all to myself.

The shrubs looked scrawny and bare in the early November breeze, like children yanked from warm beds and left in the cold. I knelt down to touch a pointed leaf. Who knew if the roots would take and they'd survive the winter.

"Cool sign," Mitch said, stepping up beside me, munching a handful of candy left over from last week's Halloween stash. "And check Miss Rosemary out! In jeans with paint smears! Unbelievable."

I picked up a pitchfork and pierced a wheelbarrow load of mulch.

"Want some help? I have some extra time."

"No thanks. I'm fine."

"Sure? As a birthday treat?"

Birthday treat. That was exactly what my father said, as though going to a Japanese restaurant would erase everything that happened in the past.

"No, I said I'm *fine*." I yanked on the pitchfork, losing my balance and poking myself in the chest with the handle. "Ouch, *dammit!* Look, Mitch. If I wanted your stupid help, I'd ask for it. What—you don't think I'm capable of mulching?"

Mitch jerked back like I'd slapped him. His face hardened. "Man, what is your problem, Abbey? You don't need my help? Then, fine, I'm out of here. But hey . . . before I go, happy birthday."

His voice was icy. He held out a bouquet of flowers, which he'd hidden behind his back. *Oh my gosh, he brought me flowers.* My cheeks burned, but it was too late to take the words back as I reluctantly took them. "Mitch, I . . . you didn't have to do this."

"Yeah, I know. Next time, I won't. See you later, pit bull." He glared at the pitchfork, now lying on the ground, turned on a heel, and walked away.

Bluebells. My favorite. Although how he knew was beyond me. God, I felt horrible.

Mitch stopped at his car, resting his hand on the door handle. "Oh, and Abbey, I like this music because it reminds me of my grandfather and how we used to watch old movies together every Saturday. Until I was ten years old and *he died.*"

He slammed the door, his jaw clenched as he drove away. I felt low. Lower than the crap from a starved pit bull.

Rosemary blew away my cloud of guilt when she threw open a window. "Abbey—get in here, I need your opinion about these frames."

I trudged to the house, the small blue flowers bouncing like sleigh bells. I hoped Granny Po wouldn't say anything about them, but no such luck. She watched my every move as I walked into the kitchen and pulled a vase from the cabinet.

"Pretty flowers," she said, while using a melon baller to prod out round bits from a watermelon. The rind was already cut lengthwise in a zigzaggy pattern with a handle to make the watermelon look like a basket. Bowls of strawberries, grapes, and balled cantaloupe waited to be put in.

"Yeah, they're nice." I said. "Why are you going all out for bingo tonight? Why is it always such a competition for the most elaborate food?"

"Hey, I didn't start it. It's that snotty Loretta Scott, always bringing the fanciest food, trying to make the rest of us ladies look bad. Probably catered. I have to defend my honor, and don't you try to change the subject. That was real nice of Mitch to bring you flowers, and you nearly took his head off."

I glanced at the front window and saw the blinds were down. The sneak.

She noticed my frown. "Hey, it's my house. If I want to eavesdrop, I will. Now, go on. Rosemary needs you." She dug the baller into the watermelon, forming a piece that had a jagged corner, ruining the perfect round shape. That is, until she nibbled away at the imperfection.

"Granny Po! That's gross!"

"Well, you don't have to eat it, now, do you?"

She rolled her eyes at my exasperated look, popping the melon ball into her mouth. "There. Happy now?"

No, I was far from happy and didn't know what bothered me the most. My phone call from Dad. Mitch, or me biting his head off. Granny listening in, or how I had to help Rosemary with the smelly polyurethane.

But at ten o'clock that night, as I lay wide awake in bed feeling guilty about the surprise birthday party Granny Po threw for me instead of going to bingo, I realized what really bothered me the most.

All the Gray Widows had been there, showering me with presents, which ranged from a digital camera from Rosemary to a beautiful pink photo album from Caddie. Gena had left a gift for me to open, a cool leather wallet much like the one she had that I admired so much. Kym and Sarah were both there, after being dropped off at Edith's and sneaking to

Granny Po's through the pasture and, according to Kym, dodging many piles of poo. Mitch's flowers were the centerpiece. Even my father, of all people, called me first thing in the morning to wish me a happy birthday.

But my mother . . . the one person who should love me the most . . . never called.

Chapter Thirteen

I went back to my old habit of checking the mailbox every day after school, hoping there would be something from my mother. Anything that could prove she didn't forget her daughter's birthday after all. By Thursday, nothing had come. Maybe Mom was just swamped with a new job. Or maybe she did try to call last Saturday, and nobody heard the phone ringing.

Or maybe she forgot about me. Again.

No, I had to shake it off. I couldn't be stressed out about a missed birthday, not now. I had to focus, especially when the spa was opening in less than two days and Gena had asked me to organize the back storage room. I took a deep breath before opening the spa door. *Just shake it off.* But inside was a frenzied atmosphere, which made it impossible to shake anything.

Rock music played as footsteps pounded back and forth on the now-polished wood floor. Most of Gena's new employees were here, rushing to get their workstations ready. Brianna Dalton gave me a brief smile before going back to organizing the reception desk, her sweater pulled tightly over those enormous boobs. Paul Danehy opened the front door, giving me a wink before helping Gena's product distributor, Eric Winters, carry in supplies. Nick was hanging a light fixture for Samantha Klein, the second stylist to be hired. Gena originally planned on having four stylists, including herself, but decided to keep it at three for now.

As I tried to dodge Cracky, who was hanging pictures for Rosemary, I glanced at Samantha's reflection in the mirror. She was beyond trendy and polished, with perfect makeup and hair, and outfits that never wrinkled. I, on the other hand, looked like a rumpled student at exam time, with limp hair, and worry lines creased down my forehead.

I walked past the manicurist, who had nails that put Caddie's to shame, and the rest of Gena's staff, who were preparing their private rooms. She had hired an aesthetician for facials, waxing, and body wraps, and a masseuse, who was rumored to give the best massages in town.

But I bet even she couldn't calm me.

Especially after I walked into the back room that Gena was using for storage, employee breaks, and her office. Boxes of merchandise Eric had delivered were piled on the floor, full of shampoos, conditioners, leave-in treatments, finishing creams, hair sprays, gels, and all of it had to be sorted. Then there were the many containers of hair dye, permanent-wave rods, application bottles, tint brushes, neck strips, cotton tubes, gloves, bottles, and more bottles. I ran a hand through my hair, starting to feel as overwhelmed as when I first walked into my great-grandfather's storage rooms. Except this time, I couldn't call on Mitch to bail me out. He had been ignoring me all week, since I took his head off.

Why did I do that?

Gena came into the room, carrying more boxes, with a cool, relaxed smile. "Everything okay in here?"

How could she be so calm? Didn't she realize there would be customers here on Saturday? I waved a hand at the disorder. "I don't know where to start. Why was this stuff delivered so late, anyway? There's so much to do, and there's no way we'll be ready to open!"

Gena put her boxes down, then leaned against the table. "Abbey, relax. Everything will be okay."

"But if we're not ready?" I bit down on a thumbnail, trying hard not to cry.

"Then we'll open on Monday, and the world won't come to an end." Gena took my hand. "Come on. Caddie said Granny Po's taking a nap, so I'll make tea and we'll drink it in her kitchen where it's quieter, okay? We'll get to all of this later."

I felt calmer sitting at the kitchen table with the sun streaming in through the window. Gena handed me a cup of mud-colored tea, the scent of vanilla and cinnamon rising in the steam.

"What's this?" I asked. "Chai tea?"

"Vanilla chai." She picked up her mug, holding it to her mouth. "You doing okay, Abbey? You seemed a little stressed out there."

That was an understatement. My father calling, my mother *not* calling, Granny Po being so bummed out, Kym calling me a prude today because Camden said hello and I only waved back, and the horrible guilt I felt whenever I saw Mitch. "Um, it's nothing. I'm fine."

Gena took a sip. "In other words, stuff that I wouldn't understand."

I stirred my tea, clanging the sides of the mug with my spoon. "Sort of. I guess. I mean, you're always so positive, like nothing ever goes wrong. Everything just falls into place for you, like your new business here."

She almost choked. "What? Yeah, I'm positive, but a lot has gone wrong in my life, Abbey. I guarantee it."

"Like what?"

"No," she said. "This is not about me. I don't want to lay out my story and have you think I'm trying to belittle yours. When I was a teenager, I hated when adults did that."

I rested my elbows on the table and leaned toward her. If Gena had flaws, then I had to hear about them. It would make me feel . . . human. "No, I really want to know."

Gena hesitated, set down her mug, and uncrossed her legs. "Okay, how about we start with this. I'm divorced."

"Divorced? I didn't know you were married."

Gena brushed her hair back, the pain in her face obvious. "Yeah, I married Rick when I was twenty-four, but neither one of us was ready. We moved to Baltimore, where I had just opened a salon and was in way over my head. Rick was still paying off college loans, and things were so stressful that we grew apart. Then, after four years of marriage . . . I came home early from work and caught him with one of my friends."

My mouth hung open. "Oh my gosh, you're kidding! I swear, men are such pigs."

Gena put a hand on my arm. "Not all men, sweetheart, but yes, Rick was a pig. But you know, as crazy as it may sound, he actually did me a favor."

"A favor?" How could cheating on somebody be referred to as a favor?

"Oh yeah. I hated living in Baltimore, and the salon was killing me. I was so far in debt, and every day there was a new crisis. But I was afraid to do anything about it, thinking it was too late. Rick's cheating forced me to take a hard look at myself."

"And . . . what did you see?"

"That I wasn't happy. My chest was constantly tight with anxiety. It was time to give up, give God the reins, and make some changes. So I filed for bankruptcy, sold my business and furniture to help pay off some of my debt, and moved back here."

"Bankruptcy? You filed for *bankruptcy*?" No way. Not someone as smart as she was.

Gena must have read my thoughts. "Hey, you don't have to look so shocked. It wasn't exactly my proudest moment."

"Sorry, I didn't mean it that way. I was just surprised," I said.

"That's okay." Gena traced a finger over Granny Po's autumn place mats and picked her mug back up. "And trust me, it wasn't easy. Filing for bankruptcy was beyond humiliating, but sometimes bad things happen. If they didn't, then I wouldn't be here, building my dream spa, with some help from my brother, of course. So I'm thankful."

"Even though you lost everything?"

She nodded. "Yep. That road hit a serious dead end. But sweetie, sometimes it's the dead ends in life that put you on the right path, and that path brought me here. And who knows, maybe I'll even fall in love again."

Out of all she said, this I found the most shocking, that she could ever trust a man again.

"Can I ask you another question?"

Gena nodded. "Absolutely. Fire away."

I told Gena about the girl at the football game who was chained to her boyfriend. For some reason, I had to get her opinion. "So . . . do you think I'm a prude for thinking that was totally stupid?"

Gena drummed her fingers on the table. "Hmm, okay . . . she was wearing a collar. Well, I don't like to judge, and she was probably only doing it for attention, but . . . I have to say that if I saw you with a collar, I'd rip it off with my own bare hands."

Thank God.

Gena took her empty mug to the sink. "Well, I better get back before Polly wakes up and catches me here in her kitchen."

"I'm sorry Granny Po isn't nicer to you."

Gena laughed, pretending to strike a pose. "Don't worry, one day she'll fall victim to my charms."

The spa door opened. Rosemary's head poked out. "Abbey! You better get in here quick, sweetheart. We have a situation in the spa. The weasel's in the henhouse!"

I jumped to my feet.

"What? What weasel?" Gena asked.

Rosemary ignored Gena's questions. "Abbey, will you—"

"I'll wake up Granny Po."

Rosemary wheeled on her sneakers, motioning for Gena to follow her, before she hightailed it back to the spa. Gena stared at me for an answer.

"Well, Gena, you're about to meet the she-devil. Loretta Scott is here."

I followed Granny Po as she walked stiffly to the spa, like someone had poured cold water down her back. "Who does that old bat think she is, snooping around here? Did she ever come to *my* parlor? Nooo, only one time in the past thirty-some years, just to be nosy. Now she's interested because there's some young girly-girl running the place? To heck with both of them."

Oh, boy. This oughta be good.

We passed through the shop door in time to see Gena shaking Loretta's hand.

"Look at Miss Hopkins, kissing that bat's rear end," Granny Po mumbled, embers sparking out of her eyes. There are certain rules around here: You don't take the last of the coffee without making more; you don't take a magazine from the bathroom when it's turned to a certain page for future reading; and you never, *ever* cavort with any enemy of the Gray Widows.

Loretta Scott stood primly, her beige hair teased and prodded to a high bouffant in an attempt to hide her thinning hair. A heavily starched linen suit hung on her short, wiry frame. Granny Po stepped forward, hands on her hips. "Well, Loretta. What in Sam Hill could possibly bring you to this place?"

Loretta smiled, her false teeth looking like plastic corn. "Polly Randall! How nice to see you, dear. I was simply in the neighborhood and thought I'd drop by . . . since it's under *new* ownership. Oh and, Polly, that was a wonderful German chocolate cake you had at bingo a few weeks ago. A bit flamboyant, however, since it's *only* a church function."

Maybe I should tell her how one of the layers was dropped on the floor. And put back.

Granny Po murmured, "I'll flamboyant you, all right, you conceited old flake."

Loretta Scott put a hand behind her ear. "Beg pardon?"

"I said, you could overeat on cake."

"Right, ah . . . I guess you could." Loretta Scott pursed her lips, wrinkles darting from her mouth. She turned on her scuff-free tan heels, smiling a catlike grin while her beady eyes took in the newly decorated walls. "I must say, major improvements have been made to this place. I hardly recognize it. Quite stunning, Miss Hopkins, quite stunning."

"Thank you, Mrs. Scott," Gena said, "but it's Rosemary who deserves the credit for the interior design. She did a fabulous job."

It *was* amazing what Rosemary had done, and with so little time. The wallpaper was beautiful, matching the custom-made draperies hanging from brass curtain rods.

I loved the reupholstered chairs and how each styling station had a large mirror mounted in frames Rosemary gilded, making them look like expensive antiques. Even the posters promoting the latest hairstyles and product lines were in gilded frames, and on the half walls, philodendron and Swedish ivy plants were draped in gentle swirls around antique perfume bottles.

I could see Rosemary's pride that Gena acknowledged her hard work. But hearing it was Rosemary who decorated the spa caused Loretta's impressed smile to morph into disdain, as if the textured walls suddenly transformed into plaid wallpaper with polka-dotted trim. "Mmm. I thought it was a bit excessive."

"Oh, up your ass," Granny Po muttered.

"Beg pardon, Polly?"

Granny Po smiled through clenched teeth. "I said, 'upper-class,' Loretta. I think Rosemary's decorations are very upper-class."

I snorted, then saw Gena glance at Granny Po with a knowing look, as though an unspoken understanding passed between them. Gena pointed to her watch. "Gosh, Mrs. Scott, it has been a pleasure, but I'm afraid I need to get back to work. Big opening on Saturday and all. So, if we're done here . . ."

"Well, actually, Miss Hopkins, *I* have another engagement as well," said Loretta, clutching her purse in front of her stomach. "Best of luck with your opening. Perhaps this establishment will actually turn a profit for once."

Granny Po fumed, her mouth in a tight line. I could see the steam rising from her head. Gena narrowed her eyes and crossed the room with her shoulders back and chest lifted, stopping to stand protectively beside Granny Po. "Actually, Mrs. Scott, that would be complimenting Mrs. Randall as well. She has offered invaluable input on all the decisions made regarding the spa, everything from the floor plan to who I hired. Isn't that right, Mrs. Randall?"

Granny Po stood stunned for only a moment. "That would be correct, Miss Hopkins."

Loretta stepped back and huffed with an indignant frown. "Well . . . I—"

Gena cut her off. "Mrs. Scott, this has been truly enjoyable, but I'm afraid I'm now late for an appointment."

From the corner of my eye, I could see Rosemary and Caddie joining Granny Po in a united front on the right. Edith gasped, looking at her watch. "Lord Almighty, Gena, I do believe you're right! Look at the time! We're late for that bikini wax you promised to give me!"

Edith looked down at Mrs. Scott with a wink. "Got me a Pap smear scheduled tomorrow and I want the doctor to be able to find the darn thing. Sorry I have to cut your conversation short. Or—you know what?—why don't you come back with us and we can chatter all you want. Maybe even get one yourself. Would that be okay, Gena?"

Loretta arched her mouth in disgust.

Gena opened her eyes wide and pressed a finger to her cheek. "That's not a half-bad idea, Edith. I could even offer a special: Wax one; wax the other half price." Gena leaned toward Loretta. "I could even give you a Brazilian wax. You've heard of them, right? *Everything* goes. Even your butt cheeks are spread to get what's in between."

Loretta recoiled at the notion of waxed butt cracks. Her face burned red, just like the rouge dotted on her cheeks. "Miss Hopkins, I do believe that was quite unnecessary. Perhaps I have misjudged your character."

The room was silent after the door slammed shut, Loretta shuffling loudly on the wood porch. We all stood still, holding our breath until Edith exploded with laughter, slapping a hand to her thigh. "Good God Almighty, that was fun!"

"'Misjudged your character.'" Rosemary chuckled. "That woman!"

"Oh heavens, I nearly peed myself!" Caddie dabbed her eyes with a tissue. "But those Brazilians sound quite sensible. I'll have to try one someday."

"Miss Caddie? You serious?" I asked. She gave me a wink.

"Gena," Granny Po said, peeking out the window to see Loretta's car barreling down the driveway, "I do believe you've just officially made an enemy out of Loretta Scott."

I stood back, watching Gena's face, vibrant with laughter. Yes, Gena sure did make an enemy out of Loretta Scott. But she did something else, equally important.

She got Granny Po to finally call her Gena. *First names are for friends.*

Chapter Fourteen

I want to thank everyone for your hard work. For me, Serenity Spa is a blessing, and I'm truly grateful for finding such a wonderful staff. So here's to you!"

Each of us raised our champagne glasses at Gena's toast late Friday night. Nick, the Widows, Paul, Samantha, and the rest of her staff. The spa would open tomorrow, despite my doubts. Gena set down her glass and pulled a box out from behind her chair, filled with gifts wrapped in gold paper.

"These are tokens of my appreciation." She turned to Rosemary, handing her a present. "Rosemary, I can't even begin to thank you for the amazing decorating job you did."

Rosemary blushed, unwrapping a beautiful leather organizer with tabbed sections for a calendar, addresses, and notes. "Goodness, Gena, this is lovely!"

"It's for the appointments you're going to book once people see your work. Especially now that you hired a management company to take care of all those rental properties."

For hanging the wallpaper, Gena gave Edith a glossy hardcover book of art. I thought it was a rather odd present for Edith, but her worn hands stroked it lovingly. Caddie got a book of coupons for the local car wash, to help keep her Cadillac shiny for months. "Now, aren't you the dear! Why, I go there at least once a week. How did you know that?"

"Oh, I heard it through the grapevine," Gena said, before giving me a thick leather journal with a red ribbon to tie it shut and a blue fountain pen. "I thought you might like to try journaling, Abbey. It always helps me stay centered. Now, open it up."

Inside the journal were coupons for five massages and a note saying, "Use when you want to chill out." Cool.

Granny Po's present was shaped like a book, but wasn't. It was her framed cosmetology license. "What in the world . . ."

Gena walked to Granny Po's side. "I never did hire a fourth stylist. There's only one person who really belongs in this place."

Granny Po brought a hand to her lips. "Gena! Oh my gracious. I don't know . . ."

"Wait! Don't answer yet."

Gena ducked into the closet, bringing out a larger gift. Granny Po slowly tore off the wrapping paper, then put a hand to her chest, the threat of a tear in her eye. "A portable television! Oh my heavens, Gena! It's too much."

Gena touched her shoulder. "I knew you'd only work for me if I let you watch your soaps. What do you say?"

I cheered when Granny Po said yes, feeling a warmth spread in my heart. Gena caught my eye, raising her glass in my direction. So that's what she meant when she said things will be okay for Granny Po. I smiled back, raising my own glass.

Here's to tomorrow.

At exactly nine on Saturday morning, Gena turned the sign on the front door to OPEN and stood back. "Let's do it!"

She winked at me and nodded her head toward Granny Po, who stood ready at her new styling station. She had stayed up late last night taping photographs of me and the Widows around the gilded mirror frame and decorating the countertop to her liking. Her small corner of the spa looked just like her old parlor, and it soothed me like a warm caress to see Granny Po and her new TV, armed with scissors and out of retirement.

There were a few snags, but Gena took them in stride. The college student Gena hired to help me wash hair on Saturdays called in sick. Permanently. So Caddie rolled her sleeves up and sidled toward me at the wet station, saying she didn't have anything else to do. She accidentally got shampoo in the sheriff's wife's eyes, and Paul's first customer canceled, making him fear it was a bad omen. But his client's daughter was giving birth, so we convinced him it was a very good excuse.

All the other appointments came, including five walk-ins, two of which came because of the free shampoo offer announced on the radio. The other three were attracted by the balloons and plastic streamers Mitch and I had placed around the sign this morning.

He had shown up early, at seven o'clock, with a steaming coffee in his hand. Edith had told him to come here, instead of the farm, to help set up, so he asked Gena what to do.

"Hmm, why don't you help Abbey hang these streamers in the front yard? It's really a two-man job." Gena handed me the streamers and motioned us outside, making me wonder if she knew we'd fought.

Mitch frowned, giving me a sidelong glance. Not that I blamed him for being apprehensive. We'd barely spoken since my birthday meltdown, and I guessed he was waiting for an apology.

And I guessed I owed him one.

After Mitch and I walked outside, he took one end of the plastic streamer, holding it steady while I unrolled the other end. I cleared my throat, thinking of how to begin. "Um, you know, the other day . . . I didn't mean to be such a jerk. I mean, I had a lot on my mind and—"

"Hey, it's fine. Whatever," Mitch said. "Let's just get this done, okay?"

"All right." The anger in his voice surprised me. My hands fumbled with the streamer, making it hard to tie one end to Gena's sign. Maybe I deserved it; all he did was bring me flowers . . . and pick up the groceries for *my* party.

"Mitch, look." I dropped the streamer and stepped in front of him. "I really am sorry for giving you such a hard time. Maybe I can . . . I don't know, buy you lunch or something."

"Lunch?" His voice was edged with sarcasm. "Abbey, come on. You don't have to buy me lunch."

It wasn't that I felt obligated to buy him lunch. It's just that after talking with Gena, maybe seeing that John Wayne movie wouldn't have been all that bad. I took a deep breath, squaring my shoulders to face him. "Okay, then how about dinner. Maybe like a . . ."

He hesitated, then leaned in close, the smell of warm coffee on his breath. "Like a what?"

It was crystal clear he was going to make me say it, even though I had no clue what "it" was, or what I was doing, other than stammering like a complete idiot. "I don't know, just . . . you know, me and you eating food. And maybe seeing a movie or something, that's all."

Mitch nodded. "Ah, you mean like a date."

"No! I didn't say anything about a date."

He watched my face, a trace of a smile playing on his lips. Why does he have to label it? But . . . maybe it wouldn't hurt. My heartbeat quickened as he stared at me, the wind picking up his now longer hair. *Crap.*

Okay, I give. "How about dinner and a movie. And you can call it what you want to."

"Fine. Just say it. It's a date."

I grabbed the streamer from the ground. "Look, do you want to go or not?"

"I'll pick you up at seven."

Oh God. Kym is going to have a heart attack.

At four o'clock, my new shoes were killing me but I hardly noticed. I took a break from sweeping the floor around Samantha's station to look at the streamers fluttering in the crisp breeze outside the window.

"You okay, Abbey?" Gena asked, handing a cup of coffee to Granny Po and hot tea to a customer.

Things were good. Better than good. For the first time in weeks, I felt settled. The spa was open and the Widows spent the entire day hanging around, just like old times. Mitch and

I were speaking, and tonight might be fun after all. I wanted to grab Gena by the elbow, pull her into the storage room, and tell her about our plans. But I still had to ask Granny Po for permission first, and the last thing I wanted to do was have everyone find out. Their teasing could be ruthless.

"Yeah, I'm okay. Absolutely."

Edith tossed me a tabloid, then sat back down on the deep olive love seat Rosemary had reupholstered. "Good, then why don't you do the honors and really break this place in."

"My pleasure." I flipped through the pages and called for everyone's attention, causing some of the new clients to look at each other in confusion. "Okay, here we go. Hypothetical question of the week: If you were forced to smell only one thing for the rest of your life, what would you want it to be?"

Gena returned to her workstation and picked up clippers to trim a man's sideburns. "Daffodils. I love the smell of daffodils."

"New leather," Edith said. "There's nothing like walking into a tack store and smelling all them new saddles."

Granny Po raised her scissors. "Pumpkin pie."

"You do know, Polly dear, that pumpkin is an aphrodisiac for men, don't ya?" Caddie called from the shampoo sink. "That and doughnuts."

Paul said that he loves the "new car" smell, and his client got into the groove by picking cocoa butter.

Samantha said, "Olive juice," which got a few odd looks. I was tempted to open a jar from Granny Po's refrigerator and give it a whiff.

"What about you?" Gena asked me. I thought of a few answers, like fresh-cut grass in June and peanut butter when it's first opened. But an image of Bodie, just after he was abandoned at Edith's horse rescue a year ago, flashed into my mind, and how Mitch and I played with him in the barnyard.

"Puppy breath. There's nothing sweeter than the smell of puppy breath."

"Oh, that's nasty." Granny Po made a face. "Puppy breath. My Lord."

"Have you ever smelled puppy breath before?"

"No, and I've lived many good years without doing so." She returned to her client, shaking her head.

I went to the receptionist desk, where Gena now has her own basket of lollipops, and grabbed two, handing one to Gena. "So, has anyone scheduled any of those spa packages you're offering?"

"No, no packages yet," Gena said, peeling off the wrapper. "But we've scheduled several facials and massages. Oh, and some body wraps, as well."

Poor Caddie. At the mention of body wraps, she let out an exaggerated sigh while drying her hands, pouting like a tortured victim from Granny Po's *Thou shall not have spa treatments* policy. Enough to drive Granny Po to surrender.

"Oh, good Lord in heaven, Caddie Daniels. Go get your facial and your seaweed wrap and para-whatever and have the boogers sucked out of your nose. Just stop that pouting!"

Caddie nearly ran to Brianna, scheduling "the works" for next Tuesday morning. I laughed when Rosemary handed Edith a ten. Edith smirked at Granny Po's sulking grimace. "Don't you go being all crabby, Polly-O. I was betting you wouldn't be a stubborn goat too much longer."

Edith gave me a high five as the phone on Granny Po's

counter rang. "I'll goat you all right," Granny Po said, reaching for the phone. "Now hush that fool giggling so I can hear."

But the laughter in her eyes faded when she answered the phone. Granny Po looked to me. "Abbey . . . it's your mom."

I stopped laughing, too.

Pressing the mouthpiece against my chest, I felt guilt jolt through my arms, as though Mom caught me having fun. "I'll take this in my room."

Granny Po nodded, her sidelong glance sullen as she picked up her scissors.

I walked slowly to my room, feeling angry and resentful at Mom for not calling for so long. There were a thousand questions filed in my brain, just waiting for the moment I talked to her next. Questions like How could you forget my birthday? How could you make me wait all day, praying and hoping you would call? And don't you care about me starting tenth grade? It's been three months since school started and you never wondered how I'm doing?

But the second I held the phone against my ear, my throat clenched shut and tears erupted from my eyes. "Mom . . ."

"Sweetheart! It's so good to hear your voice!"

I was so thirsty for the sound of her voice that my planned speech washed away. "Oh, Mom, I miss you so much."

"I know, darling, I miss you, too! And your birthday. Abbey, honey, I'm so sorry I missed it, but things were crazy and you know how it gets, don't you, sweetheart?"

"That's okay, Mom. Really, don't worry about it," I said, meaning every word. It does seem silly now, how I got so upset about her not calling. She's calling now.

I could hear her breathe a sigh of relief. "Thanks, sweetheart. Was it a nice birthday?"

"Not the greatest, not the worst." I quickly began to fill her in on everything that had happened since we last spoke. There was so much to say! I wanted to tell her every single detail. About Polly's Parlor being transformed into a dazzling spa, and how I was taking on so many new responsibilities. How Rosemary hasn't worn one of her prissy suits in weeks, and she now has three interior-decorating jobs. I told her about Caddie pouting about beauty treatments, how Edith bought a '76 Dodge pickup that she calls a classic, and how Loretta Scott came to the spa.

"You should have seen her, Mom, snooping around with her nose in the air."

She gave a polite *uh-huh* while I continued, telling her all about the foal at Edith's that has to be bottle-fed, how Granny Po was telling everyone she was dying to retire but now is so happy to be working, and of course . . . I told her all about Gena. How I answered the door that night and everything that's happened since.

Mom had fallen silent as I gave her all the details. Then she spoke slowly. "My, isn't that nice. And she's only thirty-two, opening a spa like that?"

"Yeah, and in just five weeks! You should have seen how busy we were, Mom. I thought I was going to go out of my mind. But Gena really knows a lot about business."

Mom cleared her throat, her voice dry. "Well, then. I suppose I'm happy for her success, but things do come easy for some people, don't they?"

"Oh."

I could feel my heart fall down to my knees. Why did I have to go on like that? I should have known better than to run my mouth. First time I've spoken to her since June and I'm blowing it. "I'm sorry, Mom. I'm being rude."

"That's okay, sweetheart! Don't you worry none about me. I just love to hear your voice. Tell me more."

I paused, thinking about my date with Mitch. Or whatever you want to call it. Talking about Mitch would take her mind off Gena. I learned a long time ago that Mom loved it when people asked for her advice. It made her feel needed, worthy. "Well, there is this guy . . ."

I could hear the click of a lighter in the background and the exhale of smoke as I told her everything about Mitch. "He's a football player? What, the big man on campus? Oh, you've got to be kidding me, Abbey."

No, she had it wrong about Mitch. I mean, yeah, he's popular in the sense that most people like him. But he doesn't get into that whole snotty A-list scene, the kind of popularity that Kym craves so much. "Mom, he's not like that."

She snorted. "Yeah, right. For now he isn't. But if you have any brains, you'd stay away from all guys. Wish I would of. My life could have been so much better if I wasn't so damn stupid in high school. Maybe then I'd have my own business, like this Gena person you keep talking about. But instead, I let some stupid asshole ruin everything for me."

Why did I bring up Gena? I *knew* better!

She sighed deeply. Even though she was miles away, I could feel her bitterness wash over me like a hot wind. I slowly sat down on my bed, holding a pillow tightly to my chest.

"Abbey, are you still there?"

My skin felt rigid from the severity of her voice. In a matter of seconds, all the excitement I had felt about Mitch and the spa seemed torn to shreds.

"Abbey?"

"Yeah, Mom. I'm sorry."

"No, I'm sorry. Here I'm wasting time talking about that when I have some wonderful news to tell you!"

I pushed my chin into the pillow, trying to sound enthusiastic, anything to guide the conversation to a safer subject. "Really?"

"Really!" Her voice rose with excitement. "There's so much happening! I'm living at Dewey Beach, about twenty-five miles from Ocean City. Remember your father taking us there once? When he actually bothered to take us on a vacation. You probably don't remember. Well, it's like a dream come true for me. I can see the ocean every day, and you know how I've always loved the beach. The people here are amazing. Most of the locals don't like the tourists, but I love them. Every day, everybody is on vacation. You'll love it here."

I sat up straight, my back ramrod stiff. What did that mean, I'll love it there? With her?

"Look, Abbey, I'm going to tell you something, but I don't want you to get your hopes up, okay? I'm gonna try to buy a house here. A real house of my very own, not just renting some old dump. There's this guy who's been coming into the bar lately, a mortgage broker, named Tony Adams. Or Adamson, something like that. Anyway, he told me about all these different options for single mothers with low income, like me. Ain't that something? Nobody ever bothered to tell me about them."

I sat speechless, thinking how Tony was probably more interested in his different options to get her into bed and she was too blind to see it.

". . . so Tony's going to help me find something. Isn't that exciting? He says I just need to save up some money for a down payment. It'll be tough, since the season is over and there are fewer tourists, but maybe we'll be together soon!"

Together, with my mom. She said it so casually, as though she assumed I'd been sitting around waiting for those words for the past four years. I didn't know what to say or think. There's no way I'd want to leave, but deep down, there's still that eleven-year-old girl watching out the window, waiting for her mom to return.

"Well, say something!" Mom said impatiently.

"That's . . . that's great, Mom. Sounds awesome." What else could I say? She's never stayed at one place for more than six months, so this sounded like another one of her wild schemes. Like the time she used our savings for secretarial school only to drop out after half a semester.

"And here's the best news. I'm coming to see you Thursday, for Thanksgiving dinner! A friend is going to loan me her car, since the transmission went out on mine. What do you think about that?"

"Are you serious? Oh my gosh, I think that's awesome!" Mom here for Thanksgiving? That would be so incredible, but a flash of doubt stopped my excitement. "Does, um, Granny Po know about this?"

"Well, no," Mom said, her voice growing hesitant. "But you can tell her, right? It's not like the woman doesn't make enough food, or anything. You don't think she would mind me being there, do you?"

No, Granny Po wouldn't mind. But she *did* mind when Mom promised to be here for Thanksgiving dinner two years ago and never showed up. Granny Po was furious, but I couldn't tell Mom that. It would only make her mad. "Granny Po will love to see you, but not more than me. And if there's not enough turkey, we'll go out to eat. There's this one place that has the best pizza burgers in the world; you'll love them."

"Deal. I'll see you then, baby." She paused. "I love you, Abbey."

My voice choked with emotion. "I love you, too, Mom. And . . . do you promise you're coming?"

"Of course. I swear, Abbey."

Chapter Fifteen

Granny Po didn't ask about Mom, and I never volunteered any information. This was the way we dealt with the topic of my mother. We just didn't. It was safer to keep Mom's promise to visit to myself for now, anyway. I didn't want to hear Granny Po's doubts, or to have her remind me how upset I was the last time Mom said she was coming and never did.

But even though Granny Po was furious at Mom two years ago, I still remember something she said. It was the oddest thing. "Don't hate your mother, sweetie. It's okay to be angry . . . but don't hate her for what she did."

And I never could. For some reason, I always feel bonded to my mother, despite all that's happened. She needs me to defend and protect her because nobody else will. I'm all she has, even if she doesn't realize it.

Because of this, I canceled my dinner plans with Mitch.

"Why?" Mitch asked. "Did something come up?"

I pressed the phone against my ear. "Yeah, I, uh . . . my mom called today. She's coming to visit for the holidays, and . . . there's so much that needs to be done. I need to clean, and find a place for her to sleep—"

"Abbey, Thanksgiving is next Thursday. It's only Saturday night."

Why am I doing this? I tried to think of something to say. But my mother's words kept swirling dizzy circles in my head, the same words I heard over and over when we lived together. And just like my knowledge of football from my father's constant talk, if you hear something for most of your childhood, some of it is bound to sink in.

Mitch broke the silence. "Forget it, Abbey. It was a dumb idea, anyway. I thought there was a chance, but obviously not. I'll see you Monday."

With that, he hung up, and I didn't call him back. I had to get ready for my mom.

By late Wednesday night, the duplex was scrubbed from top to bottom. Whenever I wasn't working in the spa or doing homework, I cleaned. The floors were polished, windows washed, carpets vacuumed—even underneath the sofa—and Granny Po's aged furniture was glowing from beeswax polish.

Outside, I wiped the bird poop off the porch rails, swept the wood floor, and hung a harvest wreath on the front door. A few times, Granny Po peeked out the window, her brow all furrowed and mouth pinched tight.

Still, she never questioned me once, even when I asked Rosemary to drive me to town. Signs and flyers announcing a huge Black Friday sale welcomed us at Wal-Mart, where I used my own money to buy fresh candles in autumn colors, a tablecloth, linen napkins, and pumpkins for the centerpiece.

Thanksgiving morning, Caddie came over early to peel potatoes while I crammed stuffing into the turkey and sewed up its butt. She limped around the kitchen, like a crooked wishbone, from her first bikini wax at the spa. I gave her a sympathetic grin while making a centerpiece of fallen oak leaves, Indian corn, and small pumpkins.

Granny Po's china was arranged perfectly according to Rosemary's etiquette rules, and the candles were lit, filling the house with the warm scent of nutmeg and cinnamon. Rosemary couldn't stay for dinner and Edith was spending Thanksgiving with relatives, so I set Granny Po's small dining table for three, hiding an extra plate and silverware in a nearby basket to yank out the moment I heard the doorbell ring.

Everything was perfect . . . except for one thing.

When the carved turkey was placed on the table, flanked by mashed potatoes, string beans, and creamed corn casserole, when Caddie led the prayer and forks were raised . . . one seat was still empty.

Mom's.

Now I know why I didn't tell Granny Po and hid Mom's plate and silverware. Deep down, I knew she wouldn't come.

The turkey felt like rubber in my mouth as I forced myself to eat it, landing in the cold, hard pit in my stomach. Caddie and Granny Po kept glancing at me and then at each other, regardless of how many times I assured them nothing was wrong. *Don't cry . . . don't cry. Not now.* But that stupid empty chair seemed to scream out to me.

I took a small bite of casserole and tried to look festive. "Your creamed corn is excellent, the best you've ever made, Miss Caddie."

She gave me a hesitant smile back, saying, "Thank you, it's an old family recipe from my mother's side."

Mother.

Tears threatened my eyes. "Will you excuse me?" I said, setting down my fork and pushing back my chair.

"Oh, Abbey, honey . . ." Caddie rose from her seat, her face crumpled with tears. "Please tell us what's wrong!"

Granny Po placed a hand on her arm. "Let her go, Caddie. Just let her go."

My room was perfectly neat for Mom's visit. The bed was made up with crisp hospital corners, and a small bouquet of fresh flowers sat on the nightstand. The bookshelves were organized, and in the corner by the window, two fuzzy pink chairs that Caddie had bought me at Target last year were placed facing each other, so Mom and I would have a quiet place to talk.

And Mitch. I had canceled my plans with Mitch.

I kicked the chairs over and collapsed on my bed, ruining the hospital corners and wrapping myself in a comforter. All that work, all that money. Hurting Mitch's feelings. For nothing. A familiar ache swelled in my head, telling me that once again I was the fool.

How could a mother do this? How could she open the door wide, only to slam it in my face?

The journal Gena gave me lay next to the flowers on my nightstand, still untouched. I hadn't written in it once since Gena gave it to me last Friday, since each and every spare moment of my week had been devoted to *her*. It would stay empty, because there were no words to express my emotions.

She had done it again. Like she'd done a thousand times before.

I would get a phone call, or maybe a letter, saying she was coming back. She'd give me a small thread of hope to cling to, pulling me close with her vague promises. And then she'd let go . . . leaving me with nothing but blank, empty pages.

Hours later, Granny Po softly knocked, bringing in a tray of food. She glanced at the knocked-over chairs and sat down on my bed, wearing a sweatshirt with a turkey appliqué sewn on by a neighbor.

"So, what's the best thing about Thanksgiving, hmm?" She didn't wait for an answer. "Leftover turkey sandwiches on white bread, with mayonnaise and just a touch of salt and pepper, am I right?"

Leftovers. That's all I am to my mother. Some kid she got stuck with in high school. A leftover from her wrecked marriage, wrecked life, something to throw out, like she did four years ago by leaving me here.

Granny Po nudged me with the tray, trying to act casual, but I could see the concern in her eyes. She and Caddie had probably been worrying about me all afternoon. Especially Caddie, because I hardly ate and she swears I'll die of malnutrition if I happen to miss breakfast. It really wasn't fair to make them worry. At least they cared, unlike my liar mother who probably hasn't given me a second thought.

I sat up in bed, taking the tray even though I wasn't hungry. "It's only the best thing if there happens to be leftover pumpkin pie with that sandwich."

"That's my girl." Granny Po pointed to a huge slice with whipped topping mounded on top, just how I like it. Before she left, she stopped at my door. "You going Black Friday shopping with Rosemary and me tomorrow? We may need you as a distraction again."

Right, like last year, when I screamed out in pain, doubled over, and held my stomach so Granny Po could snatch the last set of kitchen knives at 50 percent off.

"No, think I'll pass this year. Sleep in a bit."

Granny Po looked disappointed but didn't say anything. She tapped her fingers against the door trim and nodded. "Okay, next year then, all right?"

"All right."

"And Abbey?"

"Yeah, Granny Po?"

"Don't hate her, sweetie. She's your mother."

I bolted upright, almost dumping the tray. "You knew all along, didn't you? Why didn't you say something?"

Granny Po grabbed the doorknob, starting to pull it shut behind her. "For the same reason you didn't."

Sometimes I do hate her.

And I love her. Miss her. Want to protect and defend her and yet get her out of my life at the same time. I feel sorry for Mom, for everything she's been through, and yet I also blame her. For bringing it on herself.

As Black Friday morning wore on, those same excuses, those nagging feelings of hope crept back into my mind, trying to explain why she never came. Like maybe Mom was still upset over the way I talked about Gena. Or she couldn't borrow the car and the transmission on hers still wasn't repaired. Maybe she couldn't get off work, or she was sick. Maybe she'll call any second now and explain what happened.

The phone never rang.

Maybe it's easier to cling to hope than admit you've been rejected. Again.

Granny Po returned at eleven, dark circles under her eyes from waking at three. She was sporting an ugly purple bruise on her left elbow. Rosemary walked in, gave me a hug, and told me how Granny Po collided with another customer while making a mad dash for the last half-priced seven-speed deluxe hand mixer.

"Did you get it?" I asked, starting to feel left out from sitting in my room all morning depressed while they were out having fun.

"You insult me, girl." Granny Po pulled the mixer out of her bag, as well as a pair of cute gloves she bought me and three new movies that I've been wanting to see. She held one up, looking at the back copy. "See, I saw this and thought it sounded like the dumbest movie ever. So I thought for sure you'd love it. Why don't you invite Sarah or Kym over to watch it? How about that?"

That *did* sound like a really great idea.

Sarah answered on the third ring.

"Hey," I said. "How was your Thanksgiving?"

"All right, I guess," she said with a sigh. "I saw John last night, but he had to help his folks pack all weekend. His mother wants to move into the new house before Christmas."

"Oh, bummer." I hesitated, waiting to see if she would bring up anything about Mitch. I didn't tell anyone about making plans with him . . . and breaking them hours later. Obviously, neither did Mitch. Sarah and Kym would have both been all over me if they knew. "So, Granny Po bought me some new movies. You want to come over and watch them?

Sarah paused. "Only if you promise not to give me a hard time for missing John."

"Promise," I said, really meaning it. Because right now, I was missing Mitch.

By the time Sarah and I had finished the movies and she was conked out on my bed, my mind was made up. I'll never again play the fool by believing my mother's empty promises. The cycle was over and not one more second of my life would be wasted being depressed. I was going to apologize to Mitch and somehow make it up to him. I was going to shake off this crappy mood and get into the holiday spirit.

In the family room, Granny Po was crashed on her recliner, with Christmas magazines lying in a heap by her feet. I pulled an afghan up over her shoulders, wishing I could have witnessed her fighting over a mixer. In the fridge was a plate full of turkey sandwiches on white bread.

I ate three.

Saturday morning I was up before Granny Po and in the kitchen brewing coffee with a Christmas CD playing. We always follow a strict routine after Thanksgiving every year. Friday morning it's Black Friday shopping, followed by an afternoon nap, and in the evening, we leaf through Christmas magazines, bookmarking new recipes and decorating ideas. On Saturday we decorate, stopping only if Granny Po has a customer. And when I say decorate, I mean a total holiday assault that blows the fuses each year without fail and looks as though someone spewed red and green everywhere. *That* kind of decorating.

Yesterday, I had missed out on the shopping, napping,

and planning because of my mother. But I refused to miss out on one more thing.

Granny Po walked in, now dressed in a festive Christmas sweatshirt made by the same neighbor. She saw me by the counter and looked at me with apprehension. "Abbey! You're awake. Ah, how are you feeling?"

I handed her a mug. "Absolutely fabulous. You ready to decorate?"

She took the coffee and snorted. "Heck, yeah. You better lace up them tennis shoes. There's over twenty boxes full of decorations to carry up from the basement."

Sarah stumbled in from the hallway, rubbing her eyes. "Oh my gosh, are you serious? It's five thirty in the morning! You're going to start decorating *now*?"

Granny Po put her arm around Sarah and gave her a gentle shake. "Got to get as much as we can done before the spa opens, so come on, buck up, girl! You gotta be tough to hang around here, am I right, Abbey?"

Tough. If Granny Po was tough enough to open Polly's Parlor after my great-grandfather died, and if Gena was tough enough to bounce back after her bankruptcy, then I could be tough enough to forget how my mother blew me off like a forgotten dental appointment.

"Yep," I said. "You got that right."

By late Sunday morning, my mood was so fantastic I knew karma was rewarding me for making the right decision with my mother. Caddie took me to her church's early service, and when I got home, the house looked amazing, *smelled* amazing from the new banana bread recipe Granny Po was trying out. Gena had offered to pay me cash if I decorated while the spa was closed today, and cash is always a good thing. Only one thing left to make me feel better. I had to apologize to Mitch.

I slipped on a pair of Edith's old coveralls, which were stained beyond belief but warm. I planned on being at the horse rescue at eleven, just when Mitch normally arrived to clean out the stalls. But instead of Mitch pushing the wheel-barrow, it was Mr. Penney.

"Abbey! Darned pleased to see ya!" Mr. Penney smiled broadly, a black knit hat pressed onto his head and auburn strands poking out at the sides. Bodie saw me and ran over.

"Hey, Mr. Penney," I said, pulling a biscuit from my pocket for Bodie. "I've got some fresh banana bread for you, without nuts. It's a new recipe."

Mr. Penney clucked his tongue and made a show of patting his stomach. "Oh, that Polly Randall, she is a miracle in the kitchen, I tell ya! Let me have a crack at it."

Mr. Penney knows the routine by now, how Granny Po always needs a report on the taste of any new recipes. I waited while he took a huge bite, rolling his eyes in joy.

"Yes, ma'am, it's another miracle. You be sure to tell her so, will ya?"

I nodded and rewrapped the bread for him, placing it on a hay bale. "Hey, Mr. Penney, is, ah . . . Mitch here by any chance?"

Mr. Penney pulled up on the wheelbarrow handles. "No, he's not feeling well and it's a darn shame. Edith had some 4-H'ers come over to help yesterday and darned if one of them gave alfalfa hay to the wrong horses. I haven't seen horses with diarrhea so bad in my entire life. You think you could give me a hand?"

Karma. She rewards . . . and punishes.

Mitch wasn't at his locker Monday morning. Or in homeroom. During his lunch hour, I roamed the crowded cafeteria with a bathroom pass hidden in my pocket. I spied him at a table with his friends, but ducked behind a tall guy before he could see me, knowing now was not the time to talk.

I worried for the rest of the day about what to say to Mitch. The more time that passed, the more desperate I was to see him, to apologize and make things right. Dodging the crowd after the final bell rang, I ran out to the side parking lot, where he usually parked. There he was, unlocking his car door.

Okay, be cool.

I slowed to a walk and reached up to straighten my bangs. A cold, damp breeze that felt like approaching rain messed them up again, but I focused my eyes on Mitch. There was reservation in his eyes, when he noticed me.

"Hey," I gushed, my breath still quick and unsteady from running.

"Hey." Mitch opened the car door, standing with one foot inside as if he wanted to leave.

"Did you, um, have a good weekend?" I asked.

"Yeah, it was fine. How was your Thanksgiving, and your *mother*?"

His voice was edged with sarcasm, as if he knew she hadn't shown up. But that was impossible. Granny Po is usually the first in line to spread gossip, but not about me. I scuffed the pavement with my heel, feeling tears well up in my eyes. "It wasn't good. Not good at all. Look, Mitch, I really owe you an—"

"Mitch, hey! How are you?"

I turned around to see the student council secretary for our sophomore class walking toward us, wearing a long leather coat with brown fur around the collar. *Oh God, why now?*

"Hey, Paulina." Mitch smiled, stepping away from his car and shutting the door, as if he'd decided not to leave after all. I grabbed my sunglasses from my purse, jabbing my cheek as I quickly put them on. Mitch turned to me. "Abbey, you know Paulina Richards, right?"

Of course I knew her. Everyone and their mother knew Paulina Richards. "Yeah, hi."

She acknowledged me with a brief nod and then turned to Mitch. "Congratulations on winning that away game at North Branch. I heard you scored a few runs."

Runs? Try touchdowns, moron.

Mitch thanked Paulina, not bothering to correct her blunder. She gave him a flirtatious wave. "I'll see you later, okay?"

"Sure," Mitch said, watching her get into her friend's BMW and pull away. He then leaned against his car, crossing his arms. "So, Abbey, you were saying?"

I paused, trying not to think of Paulina's coy "see you later." Mitch cleared his throat. It was obvious by the way he glanced at his watch that his guard was firmly up. I wanted it to be like before, when we were comfortable with each other. When we could just be ourselves.

"Mitch, I just wanted to apologize for canceling out on you at the last minute and everything."

He just stood there. "You already apologized. It's fine, really."

I took my sunglasses off, set my backpack on the ground, and pulled out a gift wrapped in gold craft paper. "No, it's not fine. Look, I really want to make things up to you, so here, let me start with this."

Mitch hesitated, then took the present from my hands. He ripped it open, and a slow smile spread across his face at the DVD he was holding. "Oh man! *The Cowboys*! My favorite John Wayne movie."

"Yeah, I know. I miss the days when we'd watch movies on Saturday mornings."

"Me, too," Mitch said.

"So, am I forgiven? And before you answer, I should let you know that I spent two hours cleaning diarrhea-covered stalls with Mr. Penney after you called in sick yesterday."

He laughed at that and put the movie into his jacket pocket. "Yeah, you're forgiven. And I mean that, Abbey. You're one of my closest friends."

Friends. I was hoping he'd say we could watch it together. That's why I bought it . . . but I guess being only friends with Mitch was for the best, anyway.

Mitch opened his car door and pointed at the road in front of the school. "And, seeing how that's your bus driving away, it looks as though I'm going to have to drive my friend home."

All the emotions I tried to keep in check before seemed to peak as I walked around his car and got into the passenger side. Mitch started the engine, and said, "How is your mother, anyway?"

That was all it took. I looked out his window and started to cry.

"Abbey? Whoa, what's wrong? Man, did I say something?"

Something inside me broke. "No, you didn't. It's just . . . my mother never came."

Mitch pulled the car into an empty lot and turned to face me, the concern etched deep into his face. "Okay. Okay, why don't you tell me all about it."

And so I did. I told him everything. All the cleaning, making everything perfect. Only to stare at her empty chair, for the past four years. And then he held me as I cried, saying everything was going to be fine, just fine. But I just couldn't believe him.

Chapter Sixteen

Christmas at Granny Po's is never ordinary.

It's extraordinary. The Gray Widows always go overboard for me at the holidays. Maybe they think the busier I am, the less time I have to miss my parents, and for the most part, it worked. Sometimes thoughts of Mom would creep up, killing whatever good mood I was in, but it would be quickly dismissed by our jam-packed schedule of shopping, wrapping, and baking.

And the food. Oh my gosh, the food.

Granny Po and I baked almost every evening when we weren't working. Breads, pies, new recipes, old family favorites, you name it. We handed out goodies to our neighbors, clients at the spa, Mr. Penney, and Gena's distributor, Eric Winters, who stopped by quite often. And making cookies is always a full-blown event. Granny Po even allowed Kym, Sarah, and me full use of her double oven one night to crank out enough cookies for three families and a nearby nursing home. I took a container of Mitch's favorite peanut-butter cookies to school as a surprise, and tried not to be annoyed when I saw him share one with Paulina.

The spa was hectic, as well. Gena's appointment book was always full, with both Granny Po's regulars and new customers, and my weekly deposits at the bank were looking sweet with the huge number of tips I'd received. People loved how the spa still had the charm of a home beauty salon, but with big-city flair. When I mentioned this to Gena while picking up my paycheck, she warned me not to get too confident.

"It could be because of the holidays and the novelty of the new spa. The truth will lie in whether they return in the new year," Gena said, leaning back in her chair and propping her feet up on her desk.

"No way," I said. "Look at these surveys; they love the place! Listen to this one. 'I especially loved hearing about deep-fried fritters while getting a shampoo before my superb haircut by Paul.'"

That would be Caddie talking about the fritters. Gena had offered her a job shampooing and Caddie gladly accepted, saying again she had nothing else to do. But I knew it was because it gave her a reason to hang out at the spa all day . . . and an employee discount.

"I hope you're right," Gena said. "By the way, Granny Po invited me to Christmas dinner. Looks like I did win her over with my charm."

"Really? Granny Po invited you?" I sat up, excited about Gena sharing the holidays with us. "Are you going to come?"

Gena rubbed her temples, her eyes tired from working so many hours. "I don't know. Usually I visit my brother on Christmas evening."

Oh. Of course. Christmas is the time to be with family. "That's okay; I understand."

Gena rested her head in one hand, studying my face. "Hmm. Is the food any good? Nothing low-fat or anything. Christmas is the one time of the year I forget all about healthy eating."

"*Please.* Do you really gotta ask that question?"

She smiled. "Okay. Then, I'll go to my brother's in the morning and your house in the evening. But on one condition. I need help with my shopping. Think you can go to the mall and help me pick out presents?"

Shopping with Gena? Absolutely. "When?"

She kicked her feet off the desk, reaching into a drawer for her purse. "Now. Go tell the boss you're calling in sick."

They say those who don't *have* don't know what they're missing. Like a man born deaf doesn't miss the sound of rain. An only child doesn't miss having siblings. But for me, walking in the mall with Gena made me acutely aware of what I've been without for the past four years. Her tall, good looks brought attention from nearly everyone, and shopping was different with her than it was with my friends or the Gray Widows. Granny Po would balk at all the trendy stores, complaining about their high prices for such little material. Kym would want to spend most of the time following some cute guy. But with Gena, it was different. She was young enough to wear cool clothes and yet old enough . . . old enough to be my mother.

"Are you sure the Widows will be getting me presents?" Gena asked, while paying for a silk scarf for Rosemary. "I don't want to embarrass them by showing up with gifts when they didn't buy any for me."

"Trust me," I said, holding up a hand. "If you're invited, then you're on the gift list."

"Then you gotta help me with Edith," she said, taking her bag from the cashier.

I stopped at the entrance of the bookstore. "How about something to read?"

Gena picked up a mystery, then put it back down. "No, I gave her an art book already."

"Okay, then follow me." We headed toward a store that sold the Western-cut shirts Edith loved. Gena linked her arm through mine, then stopped to gaze into a boutique I'd never shopped at before.

"Oh!" Gena pulled me inside and almost danced to a rack of blouses. She reached for a gorgeous sheer one with beaded velvet trim, and held it up to her chest. "Tell me the truth . . . is this even half as fabulous as I think it is?"

"No, it's *full* fabulous." I felt the fabric. It was light and silky in my hands. I flipped the price tag. "And 40 percent off!"

Gena looked in the mirror, posing like a model. "Then, this baby is mine! It's perfect for New Year's Eve. Sexy, and yet not revealing. Don't want to give the wrong impression."

"To whom?" I asked. "Are you going on a date?"

Gena hesitated, a faint blush rising on her cheeks. "Okay. I'll answer only if you swear to not repeat it. To anyone, meaning any of the Gray Widows. Am I clear?"

"Clear," I said, since I'm not one to turn down a juicy tidbit, even if it can't be repeated.

"And if you do tell," Gena continued, "then I will be forced to make you work with Bridget when she gives bikini waxes, and trust me, you don't want to do that."

"Okay, okay, no one will know but me, promise."

Gena leaned forward. "I have a date with Eric."

I almost dropped the beige turtleneck in my hand. "The distributor guy? No way!"

She started walking toward the cashier, looking at me over her shoulder. "Yes, way, and don't look so surprised! Eric is sweet, and not just because he has great taste in shampoos."

It wasn't whom she was dating that surprised me, even though it explained Eric's frequent visits. It was her wanting to date at all after what happened with her ex-husband. But I couldn't help but admire Gena and how she is always willing to take that risk.

"No, I think it's great, Gena. Really. And . . . I hope you're getting a discount on those products he sells you."

Gena pulled out her wallet with a mischievous grin. "I am."

After shopping, Gena bought us some iced tea and we sat at the only empty table in the food court. I found out she had the same habit I did of analyzing everything we purchased, before leaving, in case we had a change of heart and wanted to return anything.

"I love those earrings you bought Kym," Gena said. "She is one dynamic girl. Bridget said she talked the entire time during her facial."

That I would believe. I pulled out the leather journal Gena helped me pick out for Sarah, when I noticed a familiar face coming toward us, dodging the throngs. "Oh my gosh," I hissed, holding the journal up to the side of my face.

"What?" Gena looked around, trying to see whom I was hiding from.

I ducked down in my chair. "Stop! I think he saw me."

"Who?" Gena whispered.

"Camden!"

"Oh." She peeked to the left. "Abbey, honey, put down the book, okay?"

"Why?"

A voice came from above me. "Because I'm standing right here."

I looked up, to see Camden giving me a sly grin. *Oh great. He catches me hiding behind a journal like a moron.* "Hey, Camden. Um, what's up? What are you doing here?"

Camden held up a bag. "Christmas shopping, for my mom."

Right. Stupid question, Abbey. Camden glanced at Gena and then back to me. I sat there and said absolutely nothing until he motioned to Gena. "Is this your mother?"

"Yes, I mean, *no,* she's not my mother, or anything," I rambled, my tongue suddenly deadweight in my mouth.

"Hi, I'm Gena, Abbey's friend," Gena said, holding out her hand. Camden shook it, still watching me out of the corner of his eye. Gena picked up her purse and reached for our cups. "How about I get us more tea, okay?"

She walked away, leaving us in awkward silence. *Great. Now what do I do?*

Camden stood with his hands looped casually into his back pockets, rocking back on his heels once. Sunglasses hung on the front of his thick sweater, and his hair looked freshly cut. And cut well, too, since both of his sideburns were perfectly even.

"So," I said, feeling stupid for staring at his sideburns. "Do you, ah, want to sit down?"

Camden looked at the chair and shrugged, placing his shopping bag on the table. He sat down and pointed at my head. "Hey, I like your hair. You do something different?"

Different was an understatement. Paul had grabbed me one night after closing and begged me to let him do something with my hair. He cut it right above my shoulders, and then gave me a side part to make the front hang slightly over one eye, swearing it made me look divine.

Maybe it did . . . and it *was* kind of flattering that Camden noticed.

"Thanks," I stammered, reaching up to touch the ends. "Um, Paul—a stylist from the salon—cut the sides along a diagonal forward-moving line, so that's why it looks thicker. And, um, to give it shape, he sliced the long pieces framing my face on an angle and—"

I stopped, realizing that Camden probably didn't care about haircuts. Why can't I just be myself around this guy and not ramble on like an idiot?

"So," Camden said, tapping his palms on the table like a drummer and then glancing at his watch. "I have to get going, but hey, you wanna come to my house for New Year's Eve? My parents throw a huge shindig every year, and I get to have a party in the basement."

Oh my gosh. Even *I* knew about Camden's New Year's Eve parties. Everyone talks about them at school, and nearly every student wants to be invited.

"Well, what do you say?" Camden asked again. "Will you be my date?"

"I . . . uh, I don't know." Oh no, he's asking me to be his date, and isn't just inviting me to the party to be nice, like, as a friend. *Say no, say no.*

"Oh, come on," he said, leaning his head to the side and hooking an arm on the back of his chair. "There's going to be good music, good food . . . a pool table. I bet you're an awesome pool player, judging from the way it seems you're always analyzing everything, like right now. And you can bring a friend, in case you're scared, or anything."

My body tensed. Yes, I was terrified. And analyzing. Here's one of the most popular guys at school sitting at my table, and asking *me* to a party. If Kym were here, she would clothesline me if she even *thought* I wasn't tempted. Which I was, only a little. "I'm not scared. Not at all. It's just that . . . my great-grandmother . . . she may not let me go."

Which wasn't a total lie. This seemed to satisfy Camden. "Tell you what. You ask her and then call me." He asked a nearby shopper for a pen, reached forward to take my hand, then wrote his phone number on my palm.

With that, he gave my hand a squeeze, then stood and walked away. I didn't look at my palm until he had rounded a corner, gone from my sight.

"Wow, he's a cutie," Gena said, coming up to me and breaking the spell. She waved her hand in front of my blank face. "Hello, Earth to Abbey. Man, have you got it bad!"

I blinked hard, shaking my head. "Got it bad? No, of course I don't. Not at all, and there's no way I'm going to go to his party."

Gena poked a straw into her tea and took a sip. "So he asked you to a party, huh? What did you say?"

I had no clue. Something incoherent, I'm sure. She turned my hand over, to see the phone number. "Do you like him?"

"No," I blurted, loud enough to catch other shoppers'

attention. I lowered my voice. "I hardly know him, that's all. I mean, it's cool he invited me to his party. What do you think?"

Gena pulled the wrapper off a straw and handed it to me. "Well, I guess it depends on whether or not you *want* to get to know him, Abbey. If you do, then go! And if you don't, then stay home. It's just a party."

Of course her statement was so casual; Gena didn't understand my family history. But as we drank our tea, I had to acknowledge Gena had a point. It was just a party. Camden wasn't trying to walk me down the aisle, and besides, it wouldn't hurt to go to a party for once in my life. And Kym and Sarah would go—well, maybe not Sarah, but definitely Kym, and maybe then she'd lay off with the prude accusations.

I took a deep breath and let it out slowly. "So, Gena, what's good to wear at a New Year's Eve party?"

She grinned and pointed to the bag that held her new blouse. "They have another in your size! It'd be perfect with jeans to keep it casual, heels to make it dressy, *and* a *very* conservative tank underneath, of course. Since you are fifteen, and otherwise Granny Po would have a heart attack."

Oh no. Granny Po. What will she say?

Camden waved at me in the hallway a few days later, just as I began my daily battle with my locker. *Please open, please open.* If Camden came over to help, I'd have to give him an answer. Thankfully, I popped it open just as Kym bounded to my side, with Sarah following behind her.

"Just finished it this morning," Kym exclaimed, holding up her latest, greatest top ten. "You'll never guess who's at the top this week."

I glanced back to Camden, who was about to pass through the stairwell door. He held his thumb and pinky up to his head like a phone, a gesture that Kym was able to see. She wheeled around and grabbed my arm. "Girl, you better tell me right now what that was all about!"

I bit my lip and then took both of her hands. "Okay, promise me you won't say anything yet, okay? Or I'll have to make you do bikini waxes with Bridget."

"Huh?" Kym gave me a confused look.

"Nothing, just kidding." I leaned forward to whisper. "Don't freak out, but Camden asked me to his New Year's Eve party."

She freaked out.

"What? Are you kidding me? Camden Mackintosh invited you to his party, and you didn't tell us? What the . . . Abbey, please tell me you're going. Please tell me you said yes and that he said you could bring a friend."

"Well, he did but . . ."

Kym pressed her hands together in prayer. "Oh please, please don't prude out on me now, Abbey, and say yes, so I can go, too. His parties are the absolute coolest. They are the social extravaganza of the year, and I've been *dying* to go forever. Please, please, please?"

I looked at Sarah, but she shook her head. "Don't look at me. John and I are going to a party one of his baseball teammates is throwing."

Kym pulled my sleeve. "Come on, Abbey, you are such a boob sometimes! It's not like someone's going to kidnap us and force us into prostitution. It's just a party!"

Just a party, just a party. How many times have I heard that lately?

I turned from Kym's desperate gaze and saw Mitch coming down the hall, with Paulina talking a mile a minute by his side. She was wearing this low-cut top that would make a minister reach for his cross, and couldn't possibly meet the school's dress code. Mitch waved, and for a second, I thought he was going to stop at my locker. But he kept going, listening to whatever Paulina had to say.

Kym snapped her fingers in front of my face. "Hello, Abbey? Come on, just say yes. For me, okay?"

I could feel my resolve slipping away.

"Okay."

Chapter Seventeen

On Christmas Eve, Granny Po and I were working in the kitchen, the counters loaded with ingredients, and a note with Camden's address and phone number in my left pocket. A twenty-pound turkey was defrosting in one side of the double sink, and a colander full of apples waited to be peeled in the other. A pie for our neighbor was in the oven and Granny Po was making an elaborate chocolate Yule log, something she saw in a magazine and wanted to try. She handed me a knife, pointing at the apples.

I groaned. "Christmas Eve and you're giving me the crappiest job?"

She turned on the radio to a station playing carols non-stop. "Well, whatever we get done tonight, we won't have to do tomorrow. Besides, you're the piggy who eats half the bowl of apple fritters, aren't you?"

"Guilty. I love 'em so much I could wear 'em behind my ears." Granny Po laughed, but as soon as I'd said it, my hands froze. Mom always said that about lemonade . . . how she could wear it behind her ears. The one person I swore never to be like and yet I find myself saying the same things she did. The knife handle dug into my palm. What else have I inherited from Mom? Or from my grandmother?

"You want some dinner?" Granny Po asked.

"Uh, sure." I shook off my anxiety, carefully cutting out the core of an apple.

Granny Po opened the fridge, taking out a handful of cheesecake cookies we'd made this morning and popped one into my mouth.

"Thanks." *Good dinner.*

She went back to her Yule log, sifting confectioners' sugar on a towel, and then she carefully flipped the baked chocolate cake onto it. With weathered fingers, she peeled off the waxed paper, gently rolling the cake up in the sugar-covered towel. I watched her hands work, patient and steady. So many times I've thought of Granny Po as my grandmother instead of great-grandmother. She looks like the grandparents of kids my age. If my real grandmother Evelyn was alive, she'd only be forty-eight.

Granny Po placed the Yule log aside to cool before starting the cream filling. She looked up and caught me staring.

"What? Something on my face? Confectioners' sugar?"

There was sugar on her face, but that wasn't what I was looking at. My present for Granny Po this year was Evelyn's picture, beautifully reframed at a photo shop. I was afraid of the picture dredging up bad memories, almost as much as I was afraid of bringing up the party. But seeing how I had already told Camden yes, I had to ask her sooner or later. "Granny Po, can we talk about something?"

She got the whipping cream out of the fridge. "Oh no, not another one of those 'period talks.' I can't bake and talk about *that* at the same time."

"No . . . not that. I was invited to a party. By a guy. For New Year's Eve."

She hesitated before shutting the refrigerator door, her back rigid. "Well . . . I, uh, Abbey, what did you tell him?"

"That I had to ask you first. But if you don't want me to go, then just say the word." Maybe that would be the best thing, if she said no.

Granny Po set down the whipping cream and picked up a dish towel, rubbing her hands even though they were bone dry. Her face paled as she twirled the towel into a tight knot. "A party . . . on New Year's Eve? And just where does this 'guy' live?"

I reached into my pocket for the slip of paper and handed it to her. She put on her reading glasses and squinted at it. "Hmm, Mackintosh, on Rolling Hill Drive. That's about five miles south of here, no major intersections. I guess Edith could . . ."

Her voice drifted off. The radio station shifted to a commercial break, the loud squawk of a car dealership's ad. Her mouth seemed tight, as though it physically pained her to speak. "No, Abigail Lynn. I'm not crazy about the idea."

For a moment, a wave of relief spread through me. But it would be totally humiliating to tell Camden that I wasn't allowed. And Kym would blow a gasket. "Granny Po, I never ask for anything like this, and you know how responsible I am. Don't you trust me? And I'm not going alone. Kym would go with me, too."

The timer rang for the pie, but she didn't move. Granny Po reached for the silver chain around her neck and looked deep into my eyes. "Yes, I know you're a good girl . . . and I do trust you. But it's just . . . I'm not ready for all this."

"I know, and I'm sorry."

Granny Po sighed. "No, nothing to be sorry about. I guess you're just growing up."

Minutes seemed to pass before she finally spoke again. "Okay, Abbey. But I'm calling his parents first, to make sure the party will be strictly chaperoned, you hear?"

"Thanks, Granny Po." I guess.

"Fine, now that we're done, I need to finish this Yule log and the fritters, and one of us needs to deliver that pie to Miss Callis, since she's taking it to church tonight. Lord, I hope it cools in time."

"Wait, there's one more thing, Granny Po." I walked to my room, bringing back her wrapped present while she got the pie out of the oven. She saw the gift and frowned.

"You know the rules, no gifts are opened before Christmas."

I pushed the present into her hands. "I know, but this one is . . . I want you to open this in private, now, okay?"

"Well, if I must." She sighed, carefully tearing off the wrapping paper at the seams to save for later. But the paper fell to a careless heap on the floor when she saw her daughter's face staring back at her.

"W-What, this is . . . ," Granny Po said weakly.

"I thought you'd like it reframed, you know, since it's your favorite picture of my grandmother. And . . . since there's no pictures of her on the walls or anything."

Granny Po held the frame tightly in both hands and then traced a finger along the polished wood. "Well, sometimes we don't like to be reminded of our mistakes," she said softly.

There were so many burning questions I wanted to ask her, so much that I didn't know, that my mother kept from me. Maybe instead of accepting their silence, I needed to learn how to ask.

"Granny Po, how was the relationship between my mom and grandmother? Did they ever get along?"

The question caught her off guard. She set the picture on the table and strode to the Yule log, keeping her head down while measuring the heavy whipping cream. "Get along? Well, not exactly. Maybe when Grace was very young, but as a teenager, no. They didn't."

"Why?"

Granny Po glanced at me, then put the cream back into the refrigerator. "I wouldn't know. Evelyn and I . . . didn't exactly communicate, not after she got married."

I pulled over two bar stools, inviting Granny Po to sit with me. "Why weren't you invited to the wedding?"

Granny Po declined the bar stool and reached up to rub her temples. "Lord, Abbey, you have some timing. I didn't approve of her marrying a man ten years older than her. But Evelyn was so determined . . . they eloped. She got pregnant two months later. Evelyn brought Grace by occasionally to visit, but I think Evelyn grew to resent Grace as she got older. When she saw Grace, she saw all the things she never got to be. Popular. A cheerleader. Then Grace became pregnant with you, and my Evelyn gave her two choices. Have an abortion, or leave."

"Oh my God." Mom never told me this. So . . . she had a choice. *And she chose me.*

Granny Po dug in the cabinets for her mixer. "Well, we still have a ton of work to do—"

"Wait," I said, louder than I expected. "Please don't stop now. There's so much I need to know. Like why did my grandmother kill herself? And how did Mom react when she found out? Did she even go to the funeral?"

The color drained from her face, telling me that I'd gone too far. But it was too late, the question was out there, hanging between us. Granny Po shut the cabinet door, then gripped the counter's edge. "No, Abbey, she didn't, and . . . this really is a bad time to have this conversation."

My heart pounded as I walked toward her. "Granny Po, I'm fifteen. I want to know why she was so depressed. Was it because of my mother? Or me? You must know how hard it is, having a grandmother kill herself and then my own mother try to do the same. What if . . . what if I turn out just like them?"

Granny Po pulled me close, enveloping me in her arms. "Don't you ever talk like that, girl. You hear me? That's not going to happen to you. Ever. I won't make the same mistakes this time."

Mistakes? I was about to ask what she meant, but Granny Po held up a hand, her voice trembling. "Not now, Abbey. Please. For the love of God and all that is great, *please* don't ask me to talk about this anymore. Not tonight, not on Christmas Eve."

She reached for the sugar bowl. I pretended not to notice how she dabbed at her eyes with the dish towel, and went back to peeling apples.

Later that night, a light snow blanketed the ground. I watched it fall from my window as Mrs. Callis, the woman responsible for all of Granny Po's appliquéd sweatshirts, came back late from church. She was bundled to the max and carrying the empty pie pan in her gloved hands. It would have been nice to go to church, maybe even put flowers on my grandmother's grave sometime over the holidays, but I knew better than to bring that up with Granny Po.

Granny Po woke me Christmas morning for coffee and muffins. We sat by the fire in our flannel pajamas, watching a sappy but sweet Hallmark movie on TV after opening a few presents. The phone calls started at nine, the Widows each wishing us Merry Christmas, saying they'd see us at six. Mr. Penney, who thanked me again for all my help at the farm and for the wonderful cookies I'd left for him a few days ago. Sarah called, my father called, and so did a few of Granny Po's faithful customers.

But nothing from my mom.

"Who's sewing the turkey's butt?" Granny Po asked, as we began to cook dinner.

"I did it at Thanksgiving, remember?"

Granny Po frowned. "Oh shoot. That's right. Well, get me a needle, girl."

"I'm going to die." Granny Po leaned back in the chair, holding her stomach with her hands. "I have committed one of the seven deadly sins. Gluttony."

Christmas dinner, as usual, was a success.

"Mashed potatoes are going to seep out of my nose any

minute now." Rosemary pushed away her plate, staring at the table full of nearly empty bowls, dishes, and plates with a guilty expression. "Abbey, my girl, I'll give you a dollar if you get me some coffee."

"Two dollars."

"Fine. Don't forget the cream."

"Anybody else want some while I'm up?" Four hands rose. Granny Po, Caddie, Edith, and Gena—the diehard tea lover—who'd come over after spending the day with her brother.

My family of mismatched ladies.

From the kitchen, I looked at each of them in turn. Rosemary, who was checking her lipstick with her compact, Caddie attacking the rest of the apple fritters. Granny Po decked out in her most elaborate holiday sweatshirt yet, and Edith, who burped quietly into a napkin, but not quietly enough for Caddie. "Good heavens, Edith! Is that necessary?"

"Yep. Had to make room for those coconut macaroons you brought."

Caddie looked at Granny Po in confusion. "Is that a compliment?"

"It's the holidays. Just take it as one," Granny Po said, her brown hair stylish and quite lovely from the new cut Gena'd given her.

"In China, it *is* a compliment," Gena added.

I really was blessed. Too blessed to waste any time worrying about my mother and how the holidays always upset her so much. Especially when she would sit on her rocker, flipping through magazines that showed the perfect families enjoying their Christmastime together.

Later, we moved to the family room, leaving the heap of

dirty dishes. A fire was still softly flickering in the fireplace as Granny Po took her spot by the tree to hand out presents. Caddie's gift to me was a swollen goody-bag filled with all sorts of things, since Caddie likes to give a lot of little presents rather than one big gift. Cologne. Barrettes. Nail files, nail polish, lip gloss, colored gel pens. Scented lotions, foot cream, magazines, cotton underwear, and a pack of toe rings, among other things. I tried on a toe ring while Caddie opened her present from me, a collection of gospel music I ordered from a TV commercial.

"Oh my stars, honey, you know I *love* my gospel music," Caddie said. "Nobody can sing the Lord's praises like a gospel choir."

Edith gave me a new set of winter coveralls for the barn that were thinner and a better quality than my old pair. Rosemary surprised me with small diamond earrings.

My mouth dropped. "Miss Rosemary! This is too much!"

She reached out to tuck a strand of hair behind my ear. "Nonsense. I have no children. No grandchildren. Just you. You work hard and you deserve it."

"What the heck are these, Abbey?" Edith held up one of my gifts to her, two dome-shaped plastic cups with leather straps. She held them over her breasts like a bra. "Is this what you young folk are wearing now?"

I almost spit out my coffee. "No! They're knee pads. For gardening."

"I know that!" she said, throwing a ball of wadded wrapping paper at me. "Girl, I didn't fall off the turnip wagon yesterday."

Rosemary *coo*ed when she opened the silk scarf Gena

had chosen for her. "This is simply divine, Gena! It can go with my suits or my jeans."

Gena pointed to the scarf tied around her own neck. "Look! I got one, too. And if you don't like that color, you can exchange it for another. They had quite a selection."

"Everything has a wider selection these days," Edith said, draining her mug with a gulp.

"Lord, isn't that the truth!" Caddie said.

Edith wiped her mouth. "Yep, from tennis shoes to maxi-pads. Just the other day, my daughter-in-law asked me to pick up some maxi-pads, since she just had the baby and you know how you bleed like a stuck pig after delivery. Anyway, I must have stood in the aisle for an hour, looking at all the pads on the market now. Long, short, plus-size, regular-size. Heavy, medium, light. Wings, no wings. Quilted. Rippled. Dimpled. And if that don't end all, they even have a thong style. Don't get me started on thongs."

"What's wrong with thongs?" asked Gena. "I mean, you're going to get a wedgy, anyway, with regular underwear. At least with thongs there's no panty lines. Besides, how did the conversation go from scarves to maxi-pads? You all are twisted."

"And this you just noticed?" Rosemary laughed, tying the scarf around her neck. "As twisted as those awful perms we got in the seventies. Remember them, Polly? Lord, it's a wonder our hair didn't fall out."

The doorbell rang. I stood up to answer it.

Granny Po grabbed my pant leg. Her face was pink with laughter. "Twisted as Caddie's underwear the last time that television evangelist Raymond Parker came to town. Remember that, Abbey? How she made me tease her hair all poufed and perfect?"

"Yes!" I laughed at the memory of Caddie, dolled up and perfumed, hoping to get personally saved by him. "And then it rained and the tent . . ."

"The tent stakes came loose." Granny Po snorted.

The doorbell rang again.

I walked to the door, trying to suppress my laughter. I reached for the doorknob. "Trapping poor Caddie under . . ."

It was *her* waiting on the porch.

Mom.

Chapter Eighteen

Surprise!"

I stood clutching the open door, cold air freezing my bare feet. My heart skipped a beat as I stared in disbelief.

"Aren't you going to give your mom a hug?"

Too many thoughts coursed through my brain. I wanted to be angry at her for not coming at Thanksgiving. I wanted to give her the cold shoulder and let her see how it feels. But instead, tears welled in my eyes as I stepped out and wrapped my arms around her neck, the smell of cigarettes and a tinge of salt air coming from her leather coat.

All the anger, all the pain, melted away like ice in hot soup as my mother's arms folded around me. "Oh, baby, I missed you, too. Don't cry, Abbey, or I'll start crying."

She pulled back, holding my arms out to the sides. "Look at you! Such a dazzler you are, all grown up." Her eyes drank me in from top to bottom. She reached forward and touched my hair. "And your hair is shorter. I love it."

She's really here.

Footsteps came from behind me. I turned to see Granny Po at the door, her brow furrowed. "Abbey, come in before you catch a cold. Your feet must be freezing."

Mom dropped her arms and raised her eyes to Granny Po, her head cocked remorsefully to the side. "I guess I should have called first, huh?"

I held my breath, mentally pleading with Granny Po not to criticize Mom for Thanksgiving or for showing up like this. Not now. But instead of yelling, Granny Po's eyes softened. She stretched her arms out, pulling Mom to her chest. "Nonsense. You're always welcome."

Mom walked in, clutching her overstuffed purse with both hands. The Widows and Gena stared at us from their seats, the festive humor we shared moments ago disappearing like smoke up the chimney. They all smiled politely as my two worlds collided. The mother I've missed for so long and the women who replaced her, which left me in between, not sure of what to say or think.

Caddie rose from her seat, stepping forward to break the ice. "Now, doesn't this just make our Christmas complete, having Abbey's momma home? Praise the Lord. Can I get you anything, dear? Coffee? Hot chocolate? Coconut macaroon?"

Thank you, Caddie.

Mom walked awkwardly to the family room. "Ah, sure. Coffee would be great. Thanks."

Edith moved to sit by the fire, pointing Mom and me to the sofa. "Sit down, Grace. You must have had quite a drive. We were just talking about . . . about . . ."

"The spa." Gena extended her hand. "Hi, I'm Gena Hopkins. I'm renting the beauty shop."

"Yes, the famous Gena. Abbey told me all about you." There was more than a wisp of resentment in Mom's tone as she shook Gena's hand. I *knew* I shouldn't have run my mouth so much. Mom sat down and reached for my hand, rubbing my knuckles with cold fingers.

Gena smiled, not able to say in return she'd heard a lot about Mom. "Well, I'm happy to finally meet Abbey's mother. I can see where she gets her good looks."

"Thank you."

Caddie brought a tray of coffee, setting it on the table and glancing at me with worried eyes. She wasn't the only one. Although Rosemary acted polite, I could feel her scrutiny as she examined my mother's appearance. Granny Po sat down in her chair and exchanged an uneasy glance with Edith.

Mom thanked Caddie and leaned forward to put two teaspoons of sugar in her coffee, her movements tense. Her hair looked as though she curled it with a curling iron, and her makeup was carefully applied, like she wanted to look her best. But the heavy makeup only made her look more tired. I smiled gently, to put her at ease, and felt sorry for her, almost defensive, despite everything she'd done.

Edith cleared her throat. "So, Grace." *Please, Edith, don't bring up maxi-pads!* "We hear you're living in Dewey Beach."

"Yeah, but I work in Ocean City. It's the town right beside Dewey Beach."

Edith nodded. "Yes, I know."

"Oh, right," Mom said.

More silence.

"Where do you work, Grace?" Gena asked.

Mom placed her purse on the floor, almost spilling her coffee. "Um, I used to work at this one nightclub where the college students hang out, but that didn't work out, since they all saw me as their mother. The trick is to always work where the customers are older than you, not younger. The place I'm bartending at now serves the elderly crowd over fifty, so I'm making good money."

I winced, wishing Mom hadn't said that. Maybe she's too nervous to realize that all the women here are over sixty except for Gena. Granny Po's lips tightened and Rosemary looked away, pulling on her new scarf. Only the cracks and pops from the fireplace broke the silence.

Mom looked at me and smiled weakly. She slowly nibbled on a cookie as though she'd realized her mistake. I squeezed her hand.

"Oh, Abbey! I almost forgot. I brought you a present." Mom reached into her purse, pulling out a brown paper bag. "Sorry. I didn't have any wrapping paper."

Gena excused herself and Granny Po quickly followed. I held the gift in my hand. A Christmas present . . . from Mom. It had been so long since my mother had handed me a gift that I held it in my lap for a few moments with Mom anxiously waiting.

I opened the bag and found teenage romance novels with smiling blonds on the covers.

"Do you like them, Abbey? I'm always seeing girls reading stuff like that."

I nodded, trying to look excited. "Yeah, sure! These are great. Thanks, Mom."

Mom looked at the hardback books on financial planning that Rosemary had given me. "Those aren't yours, are they?"

I waved my hand. "Yeah, but I love reading all kinds of books. Really. I do."

Mom nodded and leaned back in her seat. Her eyes scanned the torn wrapping paper and presents stacked by everyone's feet. She slowly raised her coffee cup to her mouth, shifting her gaze as though disappointed none of them were for her. It wasn't like we knew she was coming; she shouldn't be upset. But still . . . maybe I should have gotten her something. Just in case.

Gena lingered at the doorway, catching my eye and motioning me with a slight tilt of her head. I excused myself and went into the kitchen.

"Here, this is for your mom." Granny Po watched as Gena handed me a present wrapped in the same gold foil as the earrings she'd given me earlier.

"How did you know I—"

Gena turned me toward the family room. "I just did."

Mom's face brightened when I handed her the present. It was a gold locket, with my school picture fitted inside. I didn't realize until later it was Gena's present for Granny Po.

"Wow, this is some room," Mom said, as she kicked off her shoes, threw her jacket and purse on the floor, and flopped onto my bed. She loosened the knit scarf around her neck and tossed it on the headboard. "Man, I never had a room like this when I was young."

Mom propped a pillow under her neck and tilted her head to look at all the books neatly stacked on my bookshelf. Seeing Mom's stuff sprawled out on the floor reminded me of how it was in our apartment: clothes spilling out of the hamper, dirty dishes piled in the sink, and a garbage can that overflowed. For a second I was tempted to hang her jacket up in the closet to keep my room neat. "Um, thank you."

Mom rolled over on my bed, fingering the gold locket that looked oddly out of place with her sweater and jeans. "Yeah, guess some people are meant to have nice things."

Our conversation had to be turned around, far away from me and all that I had. "So, Mom, tell me about Dewey Beach."

She flipped to her stomach, propping herself up on her elbows. "Oh, it's such a beautiful town, about twenty-five miles from Ocean City. Did I tell you that before? I can't remember. Anyway, even now, with most of the shops boarded up, it's still beautiful and peaceful."

Mom was more relaxed now that we were alone, away from the Widows and Gena. I reminded myself to not mention a word about Thanksgiving, the spa, or Gena. Nothing that could upset her. "I'm glad you like it, Mom."

I could easily imagine Mom living in a small beach town, with the ocean so near, living each day like summer vacation. No wonder she loves it so much and would want to buy a home there, unless that idea has already been long abandoned. "So . . . any news from . . . what was his name?"

She squinted for a second and then sat up straight. "Oh, right! Tony, about buying a house. Well, he wasn't much help, but I did meet a real estate lady who was real nice. Maxine's divorced from a jerk herself, so she really wants to help. She showed me this small rancher with blue shutters that the owners have been trying to sell. For years college kids have been renting it over the summer, so it looks like a dump now. But there's a porch, and a pizza parlor called Big B's Pizza just down the street! I even know how I'd decorate it. Pastel greens on the walls, seashells everywhere, and wicker furniture. It's amazing what you can get away with in a beach house."

I nodded, trying to look interested, but I knew this house of hers couldn't be anything more than a pipe dream, another one of Mom's changing plans.

"And the bay . . . you can see the bay from the porch," she exclaimed. "You can walk down to the water and watch the seagulls. You and I could even get a boat. Wouldn't that be amazing, Abbey? Cruising along the water . . ."

She scooted over, tapping the bed beside her. I hesitated, then lay down next to her. Mom slid her arm under my neck and pressed her head to mine. For a second, I closed my eyes, remembering how we would lie together when I was a child, listening to her favorite Aerosmith tapes where Steven Tyler sang about sweet emotions.

"But," she drawled, "you probably wouldn't want to live with me, anyway. You'd probably want to stay here with Polly and that Gena woman."

I swallowed hard. No, I didn't want to go back to chaos, to always walking on eggshells, trying not to upset her. But no matter what has happened in the past, she's my mother and I'll always miss her, especially now, when we're lying close, knowing that soon she'll be gone again. "No, of course not, Mom. Don't be silly."

Mom rolled her head toward me. "Thank you, baby. And I want nothing more than to be with you, Abbey. You know that, right?"

Even though I couldn't see her eyes, I could feel their penetrating gaze. "Sure, Mom, I know that."

"Thank you, baby." She relaxed and put her head back down, but the arm underneath my neck still felt tense. "By the way, have you heard from your dad?"

I knew it was just a matter of time before the topic of my father came up. Each time we speak, no matter how long it's been or how short the call, she grills me about Dad. When's the last time I spoke to him, what's he doing now, and does he ever ask about her?

I thought about what she would want to hear. "Well, he asked if I wanted to spend the holidays with him, but I said no, so there's really not much to tell." *Except for the hundred-dollar check he sent me last week, with a card.*

Her muscles relaxed. "Good for you. To hell with him. You know what I should do? I should sue the bastard for all the back child support he never paid. Then I could have my down payment for the house, and get something for myself, for once."

The anger in her voice worried me. Mom stared at the wall, curling a lock of hair around her finger. The sleeve of her sweater edged down, exposing the faint scars that lined her wrists like a tattoo. No wonder she was depressed. The holidays are always hard on her, and she probably felt like a complete stranger, walking into the house in the middle of our happy celebration.

"I tell you what, Mom. Why don't we get into our pajamas, I'll make popcorn, and we'll watch *Miracle on 34th Street,* the one with Natalie Wood. You love her, remember?"

She hesitated and then smiled. "You mean where the postal clerks deliver bags of letters to Santa, dumping them on the judge's desk? I haven't seen that in ages."

"Great," I said, pointing to the shelves in my closet. "You get something comfy on, and I'll make the popcorn, okay?"

I dashed out of my room before Mom had a chance to answer, past the Widows playing Michigan Rummy, to where the microwave popcorn was stored. Granny Po called out over her shoulder, "Hey, Gena said good-bye and Merry Christmas."

"Cool." I ripped open the package, setting the popcorn in the microwave. Too bad Granny Po didn't have any beer in the house. Mom might relax more with a beer. I set the kettle on for tea instead. Or maybe hot chocolate. I'll make both.

With the tray loaded, I went back to my room. When I opened the door, Mom was facing me, holding up the sheer blouse with the tags still on. "What is this doing in your closet?"

I gripped the tray. The blouse. I forgot all about that.

"Answer me, Abbey. Since when do you wear clothes like this? You can see right through it." She grabbed the tag, almost ripping it from the seam. *"Fifty-five dollars?* And here I worry about paying *rent."*

"No, Mom." My voice was a weak croak. "It was 40 percent off. And it's not all that inappropriate. I'm going to wear it with a tank top underneath."

There was no way I'd tell her that Gena bought it for me. Not with her standing with a hand on her hip, holding the blouse up like it was a cheap bikini top. "And just where do you plan on wearing this?"

"A . . . party."

"'A party,'" Mom repeated, with a disgusted tone. "Whose party?"

She had no right to grill me and criticize the top Gena picked out. But I felt obligated to answer, since she is my mother. "Camden Mackintosh. His parents are having a New Year's Eve party and he's having friends hang out in the basement. That's all, it really isn't a big deal."

Mom threw the blouse on the bed and turned to me. "That boy you were talking about last time?"

"No, that was Mitch," I said, praying she wouldn't ask me about him.

"Okay, whatever. So now it's Camden. What, is this a first date or something?"

"Well, sort of, maybe," I muttered. "I don't know."

She shook her head, with a condescending glare, crossing her arms across her stomach. "And your first date is a New Year's Eve party. Don't you find that a little weird? First dates are movies, or bowling. But a party is totally inappropriate, and so is that shirt. What kind of a statement are you trying to make, Abbey? This is something no fourteen-year-old should wear."

My cheeks burned. How dare she question *Gena's* judgment? *Mom's* the one who got pregnant at sixteen, not Gena. I slammed the tray down on the nightstand, spilling tea. "Gena got me the top. And I'm fifteen, Mom. Fifteen! Remember that birthday of mine that you forgot?"

She stepped back as though I'd slapped her, her lips drawn in a tight line and tears threatening the corners of her eyes. I knew right away that I'd gone too far. "Mom, I'm sorry. I didn't mean that. Not at all."

Mom took a shaky breath and knelt for her purse like she was leaving.

"Mom, don't go! I really am sorry; it just popped out."

She pulled out a pack of cigarettes and a lighter. "That's fine, Abbey. I guess I deserved that. And it's obvious you're older now and want to make your own decisions, so do as you please and have a *great* time. I'm going out for a smoke."

We didn't talk anymore about the party that night. After I

followed her out to the porch, I turned the conversation back around to the little house with blue shutters, anything to keep her from leaving.

But at twelve thirty, after the movie ended and Santa Claus won his court case, she got ready to leave, despite my pleas for her to stay. "Mom, please don't be angry about what I said. Spend the night. We can go out for breakfast, anywhere you want. My treat."

"I'm sorry, honey. Maybe next time."

While she packed her things, I slipped to the kitchen to make her coffee for the road, using a travel mug that I hoped Granny Po wouldn't miss. When Mom and I walked out to the porch, she took my chin in one hand and kissed my cheek. "I'm sorry for getting upset, honey. Just think about what I said, okay? And if you still go to the party, be smart. Don't make the same mistakes I did. Call me on New Year's Day, you promise? I left my new number on your desk while you were making coffee."

I promised, then stood on the porch as she drove away. Again.

At one thirty, my eyes were still wide open, staring at the knitted scarf she'd left behind on my headboard. I slid from the bed, stepping out into the hall, where the smell of food, cinnamon, and evergreen lingered in the air. Granny Po had wished us both good night hours ago, saying not to mind the mess, she'd clean up in the morning, but I grimaced at the disorder. Dirty dishes covered the table and counters, and the food-crusted pans sitting in stale dishwater made me cringe. I reached for the trash bags under the sink.

Starting in the family room, I filled two bags with crumpled wrapping paper and neatly stacked the gifts under the tree. I carried dishes to the kitchen, loaded the dishwasher to bursting, and washed the rest by hand. The floor was swept and counters scrubbed clean, but no amount of order brought to the house could settle my thoughts. Maybe going to the party was a stupid idea. And the blouse that Gena and I absolutely gushed over . . . was all wrong. Maybe I shouldn't go. Forget the whole thing. But to do so would be admitting that my mom was right . . . and Gena was wrong.

I grabbed a bucket from the closet, my mind set on scrubbing the floor. Hot water flowed into the bucket as I rested my arms on the sink, thinking of how Mom said she was worried about me. Usually I was the one who worried about her: where she was, whom she was with, what she was doing. Now Mom's concern pulled me in two directions: Gena, the person I want most to be like, or my mother, the woman who needs me the most.

The floor was nearly done when Granny Po stumbled into the kitchen, her hair a frizzed cloud of brown and her eyes squinting from the light. She stood with her hands on her hips, staring down at me scrubbing the vinyl floor. "Lord sakes, what in Sam Hill are you doing, Abbey?"

I stared at her feet, afraid to meet her eyes. "Your hairy toes need a pedicure."

She huffed. "Girl, all of me needs a cure. And watch what you say about hairy toes. They could run in the family. Now answer my question."

"I . . . uh, I'm cleaning."

"Yeah, smart pants, I know that. And normally, if you had

the itch to clean, I'd never stop you, but it's almost three in the morning. Something other than dust bunnies is keeping you up. Fess up, girl. Tell me what's wrong so I can go back to sleep."

I stood up to empty the bucket, staring as the dirty water swirled down the drain. "Sorry to wake you, there was just so much today, you know, with Christmas . . . and my mom. I couldn't sleep."

Granny Po sighed. Either she believed my lie or was too worn out from the holidays to push it. She took the bucket, set it back in the closet, and pulled me toward the family room. "Yeah, I know, toots. Come on, you got me up now, so we might as well watch a movie. *Miracle on 34th Street?*"

I flipped off the kitchen lights. "No. Anything but that."

Chapter Nineteen

The day after Christmas, Granny Po and I always do nothing. Absolutely nothing, except eat leftovers and watch too much TV.

By the twenty-seventh we're both tired of Christmas. We can't wait to take down the now-dusty decorations and get ready for the new year with all its possibilities. This year, I really needed a fresh start, but I was beginning to doubt if Camden's party was the right way to go about it.

As I was stuffing the artificial tree back into its box, Camden called, wanting to know if I was still coming. Here was my chance. I could just tell him something came up, forget the whole party thing, and go back to playing it safe. But Kym would kill me. And my mother . . . she would think I did it only because of her.

"Yeah, sure, eight o'clock, right?"

So much for playing it safe.

By Saturday morning, I needed air. Lots of air. I put on my new coveralls, snuck a handful of sugar cubes from the pantry, and told Granny Po I was going to the farm.

"Do you have—," she started.

"Yes, I have my cell phone. And I peed and pooed, too," I said, giving her a smile before ducking out the patio door.

Just as I climbed the fence, Kym called my cell for the third time today, because she couldn't decide between two different outfits. One was a cute fitted blazer with a matching skirt and heeled boots that ended just below her knees. The other, a more casual ensemble of low-rider jeans and a cardigan sweater set. "What do you think the other girls will wear tonight?"

Like I had a clue. Going to parties isn't exactly a habit for me, but Kym will worry all day if she doesn't decide soon. "Okay . . . how about the blazer with the jeans and boots? And your long silver earrings?"

Kym seemed satisfied with this. For now. I shoved the phone deep into my coat pocket and headed up the barn path. Music came from inside, sounding like Mitch's favorite Sons of the Pioneers tape. We hadn't been alone together since my breakdown in his car weeks ago, other than passing each other in the hallways. It was totally stupid to feel awkward around Mitch, and yet I hesitated before opening the barn door. But it's like he said, we're friends. And good friends shouldn't feel awkward.

I opened the door and went straight for Lena's stall, a new arrival that was in quarantine for two weeks. She was a bay quarter horse about two hundred pounds underweight, with welts on her flanks and a dull coat. Her face was still beautiful though. She greeted me with a nicker and pushed against her stall door, knowing there were sugar cubes hidden in my pocket. I was amazed by Lena's trust and sweet disposition even though she had been horribly abused.

The side door opened and Mitch stepped in, carrying full water buckets with both hands. He saw me just as Lena sniffed out the sugar with her muzzle. "Edith would flip if she caught you feeding her junk."

I gave the sugar to Lena on my flat palm and glanced at Mitch as he went to hang one of the buckets in an empty stall. There was no awkwardness on his end. He was acting like the same old Mitch I've known for the past three years. Well, if he can be like that, so can I. "No, Edith wouldn't flip. I caught her doing the same two days ago."

"Yeah, and I caught her earlier this morning," Mitch said. He strode over with the other bucket and scratched Lena behind the ears. A piece of hay clung to a strand of his hair. I almost reached over to pick it off, but stopped when he turned back to me. "So, Abbey, you gearing up for the marathon tonight? Who won last year?"

"What? Oh, right. That." Sometimes it shocked me how well he knew my life. Granny Po's Monopoly Marathon was a tradition every year on New Year's Eve. Usually, Caddie is broke by nine, and Edith gets bored by nine thirty. It always comes down to Rosemary, Granny Po, and me, and Rosemary's knowledge of rentals and investments gets us every time. "Uh, Rosemary did. But I'm not going to be there this year. I, ah, have other plans."

"Really?" Mitch asked. "Where are you going?"

"To a party."

"Whose?"

I hesitated, looking down at my barn boots. "Camden Mackintosh's."

Mitch spun around to face me. "Camden Mackintosh, are

you serious? Why are you going to *his* party? The guy's a total jerk."

"He . . . asked me to be his date, and I don't know, he seems okay."

"So you're dating him. *Him?*" Mitch stared at me for a second, then looked away, shaking his head. "Whatever. Have a great time, Abbey."

It looked as though he was going to walk away, but I didn't want him to. I didn't want to end the year on a bad note with Mitch. "Well, hey, what are you doing tonight?"

He opened Lena's stall door, pushing on her chest so he could fill her water bucket. "I have plans."

"Oh. Cool," I said, trying to sound casual. "With who?"

"Paulina."

I shouldn't have asked.

After taking a long shower, I went to work at Gena's to help with a rush of clients getting their hair and makeup perfected for New Year's Eve. One lady tipped me double, saying she loved the way I shampooed her hair. Which, yeah, I *am* rather good at. I always used the pads of my fingers to gently massage the client's scalp, with no stabbing fingernails, no jerking their head in the basin, and no harsh knot pulling while their conditioner sets in.

After I did my share of shampoos, put away all the laundered towels, and even rotated the magazines to more current issues, Gena called me to the front.

"Did you need me?" I asked Gena.

"Yeah," she said, while studying her appointment book. "We have an important guest arriving and I wanted to make sure she's completely taken care of."

"Who?"

"You!" Gena smiled and grabbed my hand. She led me back to where her masseuse, Jodie, was waiting for me, with candles lit and a robe lying on her massage table.

"Gena, are you serious?"

"As a heart attack." She handed me the robe. "You're getting a massage, a facial, and a manicure, which, judging by your nails, you are in dire need of. Are you ready?"

Oh my gosh, was she kidding me? Of course I was ready.

Three hours later, I could not believe how fabulous I felt. My skin glowed and all the tension from the week had been massaged away by Jodie's capable hands. Gena did my makeup and, after I thanked everyone at least twenty times, walked with me to the door.

"Abbey, you're beautiful," she gushed. "And I want you to call me tomorrow with all the juicy details, promise?"

I did feel beautiful and amazing, like this was all going to work out. Going to the party was no big deal, and Kym and I would have fun. Her parents dropped her off at seven thirty, and Kym's jaw dropped when she saw my new blouse. She couldn't believe my hair, which cascaded down in soft waves.

"Paul did it," I said.

"I love Paul." Kym sighed.

The Gray Widows had already started their first Monopoly game when we were ready to leave, but they put it on hold so Edith could drive us to Camden's in her old pickup. Granny Po looked like she was about to cry when she hugged me. I squeezed her extra hard, telling her not to worry, I wouldn't stay out one minute over the twelve-thirty curfew we argued about for days.

"Darn right you won't, or I'll have Edith, here, go to the party and find you," she said, holding me tight for a few seconds before finally letting go. "You remember who you are, girl, and don't do anything stupid, you hear?"

"I hear, Granny Po. And don't worry, okay?"

Kym tugged on my sleeve. "Come on, Abbey! There's fashionably late and then there's just *late* late!"

We piled into Edith's truck, with Kym talking nonstop the entire way. "I cannot believe we're going to Camden Mackintosh's party! I wonder how many sophomores are going to be there. Candice Blackburn said that any freshmen who try to get in are totally thrown out. Are you sure I look okay in this? Geez, Miss Edith, can this truck go any faster?"

The more she talked, the more my stomach knotted up in fear. *No. Stop it.* I'm making too much out of all this. Tonight is just a party. Normal teenagers go to parties all the time. This is no big deal; I'll just walk in with Kym, and if things are horrible, I'll call Edith and she'll come get me. No problem. No big deal.

But when Camden's house loomed into view, my anxiety grew and everything Mom said came crashing back. His house was trimmed with lights, and evergreen garland was wrapped around the elegant columns. A man and woman walked arm in arm to the front door, dressed in evening wear and carrying a bottle of wine. As they rang the doorbell, a cluster of girls got out of the minivan behind us. They followed the string of blue lights that led to the basement entrance, where Camden's party was.

"Oh my gosh, did you see who that was? Mindy Sible, head cheerleader on the varsity squad." Kym unbuckled her seat belt and grabbed a compact from her purse, to check her reflection. "Maybe I should have worn my jeans. Are you sure this outfit is okay?"

"It's fine, Kym. Great." I went to unbuckle my seat belt, gripping hard on the canvas strap. Mindy Sible? Varsity cheerleaders? Who am I kidding? I don't belong in there, no matter how much Paul curled my hair. This was nothing but a huge, terrible mistake.

"Abbey, you okay?" Kym asked, smearing on more lip gloss.

You remember who you are, girl.

Mom was right. Agreeing to go to this party was stupid. I'm the girl who works hard, the one with a strict plan, who swore to be smarter than the women in my family, and yet I accepted an invitation from a guy I know almost nothing about.

And why did Mitch look that way when I told him about Camden?

"Abbey! Come on," Kym said, opening the truck door and stepping down to the sidewalk.

I stayed glued to my seat, not able to move a muscle. "Kym, I . . . I . . ."

She rolled her eyes. "Oh my gosh, don't tell me that you're wussing out on me."

Tears began to stream down my face, probably ruining Gena's wonderful makeup job. After all she did for me to get to the party and now I'm sitting in the truck, too petrified to go in. "Kym, I'm sorry, but—"

Kym stomped her foot. "No! No *but*s! I can't believe you, Abbey. We finally get invited to the hottest party of the year and you're backing out on me! What is *wrong* with you?"

I went to open my mouth, but there was no way to explain. How could I make her understand the bad feeling I had about this whole idea? Edith put a hand on my shoulder. For a second I thought she was going to side with Kym, since she's always the one who thinks I need to act more like a teenager. But her wrinkled eyes were soft and patient. "You want to drive around the block for a while? Think things through?"

"No," Kym said, her breath coming out in angry bursts as she spoke. "The party has already started and I don't want to miss one more minute. Abbey, are you coming or not?"

"Kym, I can't. Please try to understand—"

She whipped open her purse for her cell phone. "Forget it. I should have known you would pull this stunt. But if you think I'm going to miss the party because you pruded out, you can just forget it. I'll go hang out with Candice."

Kym called her parents, asking them to pick her up, and then slapped her phone shut.

"Kym, wait," I said. "Please, just tell Camden I'm sick, okay? Please?"

She narrowed her eyes, looking away for a second. "Fine. Whatever. But thanks a lot, Abbey. For bailing."

And with that, Kym was off, stomping down the hill to Camden's basement door without looking back.

Edith put the truck in drive and was quiet for the first two miles. She cleared her throat and glanced at me. "Hey, how about tomorrow you come over to the farm and I'll have Ragman and Splash tacked up. We'll go for a nice trail ride, walking only. How about it?"

She was trying to make me feel better, but the last thing that could possibly do that was riding a horse. I shook my head.

"Okay," she said, "then how about Monopoly? I'll even let you cheat, anything to beat that hag Rosemary."

No, I wasn't in the mood to play games, either. My life already felt like one big fat game. And I was losing.

Granny Po tapped on my bedroom door Sunday morning, and brought in the phone. She never questioned why I backed out of the party last night. If anything, she seemed relieved. "Morning, Abbey. Phone's for you."

Please let it be Kym. I had been lying awake most of the night, wondering how Camden reacted to my no-show. Gena's voice was cheerful and energetic. "Hey, sweetheart! How did it go last night?"

Gena, not Kym. She sounded so positive, so optimistic. Now I had to let her know that her beauty treatments yesterday were a total waste. "Um . . . I didn't go, Gena."

"Didn't go? Why? Did something happen?"

"No, nothing happened, just . . . a change of heart. But I'm so sorry, after all that you did for me yesterday."

"Oh honey, don't you worry about that for one second," Gena said. "*You* are my only concern. Are you okay?"

I don't know. And I won't be until Kym calls and tells me how Camden reacted. I had to switch the subject. "Yeah, it's all good. So, how was your date with Eric?"

Gena sucked in her breath. "Abbey . . . please tell me Polly was nowhere around when you said that."

I leaned out of bed and peeked out my open door. Granny Po was standing in front of the bathroom mirror, combing her hair, and from the look on her face in the reflection, she'd heard every word. "Well . . ."

"Oh no." Gena sighed. "Consider yourself on wax duty."

By Sunday evening, I was tired of Granny Po pestering me for all the gossip about Gena and Eric, and Kym never did call despite the messages I left for her. I thought about calling Camden to apologize, but what if he really didn't care if I came to his party or not? I'd just sound stupid. Then I thought about calling Mom, who made me promise to phone on New Year's Day. She would feel victorious if she knew I didn't go.

And I just didn't want to give her that.

Chapter Twenty

I was the last to step off the school bus Monday morning. My stomach churned at the thought of seeing Camden. And Kym. Two cheerleaders walked past me, looking back with an odd expression. Or maybe I was just being paranoid.

The hair on the back of my neck stood straight up while I walked down the hallway. Even though I knew I was being totally stupid, it felt as though every student stared at me. I stopped at my locker, the menacing piece of junk that existed only to torture me.

"For the love of God, please open today."

It did. Without an ounce of fight. But Kym slammed it shut when she appeared by my side. Sarah joined us from the other direction, looking at me with concern.

"Kym," I stammered. "I tried to reach you all day yesterday."

My turtleneck tightened around my neck under her harsh glare. Kym put a hand on her hip. "Do you have any idea how embarrassing it was, walking into the party by myself?"

"Kym, I'm so sorry for not going, okay? I just . . . panicked."

She leaned against the locker, wearing a new outfit that looked very similar to what Mindy Sible was wearing Saturday night. Kym sighed, looking at me from under her fringe of bangs. "Well, I guess I can forgive you, especially since I had a fabulous time. Candice and I hung out all night, and Mindy even said she loved my boots. Oh, and Amy Perkins and I talked about cheerleading. Can you believe it?"

Amy Perkins, as in the girl we made fun of for text-messaging during Mitch's date? Now Kym and Amy are discussing cheerleading?

"And," Kym crooned, "I danced with this super hot junior from the wrestling team. He is number one on my list!"

"Great," I said, feeling relieved that Kym wasn't mad at me, though she wouldn't have been able to go if I hadn't been invited in the first place. But what I really needed to hear was about Camden. "What did, ah, Camden say when you told him I was sick?"

"Oh, that," Kym drawled. "Nothing. He was fine, whatever."

It didn't sound fine. A couple of Camden's friends from the lacrosse team walked by, whispering to each other when they saw me. My entire body tensed as they both smirked. Now I knew I was *not* being paranoid when those two cheerleaders had looked funny at me earlier. "Kym . . . what is going on?"

Kym glanced at Sarah and shifted her weight. A prickly sensation went up my spine as Kym then looked at her nails and started to chip at her thumb. "Nothing, Abbey. Well, nothing big, or anything. And, uh, you know . . . I forgot that Candice wants to meet before first bell, so I'll talk to you guys later, okay?"

Kym tried to take off, but Sarah grabbed her sweater sleeve. "You need to tell her!"

"Tell me what?" My voice rose. "Sarah? Kym? What's going on?"

First bell echoed through the hall. Kym bit her lip and brushed her hair off her shoulder. "Look, it's not as bad as it seems. It's silly, really. Camden was just a little drunk, and nobody will believe it, anyway."

"Believe what?" I shrieked.

Kym pulled us both into a huddle. "Okay, don't freak, but I told Camden you were sick, right? And later on, one of the guys cracked on him because you didn't show . . . and Camden said you couldn't come . . . because of a case of genital warts."

It felt as though someone just slammed into my stomach. "What?"

"Genital warts," Kym repeated.

"I heard you the first time," I said. "Warts? He told everyone I had warts?"

Kym shrugged. "Yeah, but don't worry. Not everybody heard."

A math whiz walked by, the kind who was obviously not in with Camden's crowd, but even he looked at me funny. I pointed at him. "Did you see that?"

Kym paused. "Well, then, okay, maybe just a few people heard."

I sank back to my locker, pressing my back against the

cold metal. "I can't believe this. I've never even had sex with a guy, and now everyone thinks I have genital warts? How do they think I got it, through 'Immaculate Wart-ception,' or something?"

Kym looked confused. "'Immaculate Wart-ception?'"

"Oh, never mind," I said, feeling my blood pressure about to explode.

The second bell rang. Great. Now we were late. Sarah put an arm around my shoulder and led me down the hall. "Don't worry, Abbey. This is one of those over-the-top rumors that nobody will truly believe, okay?"

Who cares if anyone believed what Camden said or not. It was bad enough that they were talking about it. I couldn't even look at Camden in chemistry class, but I heard him slap hands with another one of his butthead friends, as if he was proud of his accomplishment. I cannot believe how stupid I was, even thinking of accepting an invitation from a guy like that. Especially when I saw him in the cafeteria flirting with another naive sophomore.

Sarah sat down beside me and then motioned to another table, where Kym was setting her tray down, right beside Candice Blackburn. Great. I guess Kym thinks sitting with the Wart Woman would damage her newfound friendship with the elite A-listers.

But at least I had Sarah, who only rolled her eyes when a dorky freshman pointed at me. "Good God, people, do you believe all the crap you hear?" she shouted.

I didn't see Mitch until the end of the day. The look on his face when he saw me said it all. He had heard the gossip, and knowing that made my disaster of a day even more miserable. Mitch stopped in front of me, jamming his hands into his jacket pockets. "So, hear any good rumors lately?"

I knew he was only trying to make light of the situation, but Mitch was the one who said Camden was a jerk. He must have known something like this was bound to happen.

"Mitch," I said, looking down at his shoes, which were double-knotted and worn. "Please don't say it."

"Abbey, I—"

"And don't tell me nobody believes the rumor." My gaze drifted to the row of lockers, one of them dented in the middle as though someone kicked it. "I just don't want to hear it."

Mitch stopped me by touching my elbow. "Abbey, I just wanted to see if you were okay. That's all."

Oh.

"Seriously, Abbey. This will all blow over," he said, giving me a crooked grin. "And it could be worse, you know. Your name could be Harry Peters."

This got a smile out of me. Mitch nudged me with his arm and laughed as we started down the hallway. "There you go. And look, you gotta understand guys like that. Camden probably only made that comment to save face."

I stopped in my tracks, almost getting rear-ended by a student aide before turning to face him. "So . . . this is my fault?"

"No," Mitch said, shaking his head. "I never said that. But, come on, Abbey. You did stand him up, and all his friends knew that. Yeah, it was totally obnoxious what he said, but you gotta understand male pride. Guys don't like to be stood up . . . or when girls cancel dates at the last minute."

Mitch didn't say any more. He didn't have to. The undertone of hurt in his voice said it all.

I got on the bus feeling angry at myself for being so stupid about Camden. Angry for not being more supportive of Sarah's problems with John, when she was the one who stood up for me. Angry at listening to Gena, who was wrong—it wasn't just a party that was no big deal—and I should have known better.

I should have done what my mother always told me to do. Say no in the first place.

Granny Po wasn't home when I stepped off the bus. She had left a note on the counter saying she was grocery shopping with Edith. One hour later, the phone rang.

"Abbey? You never called me yesterday and I was getting worried."

Mom. For the first time all day, I began to cry.

"Baby? Are you okay? No, you're not. Oh my gosh, tell me what happened!"

It took me forever to finally get the story out, all the while praying for her not to laugh. Hoping she wouldn't say she told me so. Mom didn't, not once. She said all the things I needed to hear, how high school guys are jerks and how she wishes she could knock that Camden senseless. It meant the world to hear her take my side, to hear how she wanted to protect me.

"Would you feel better if I came for another visit, Abbey?" Mom asked. "We really didn't get to spend too much time together last time. And right now, you sound as though you really need a hug."

Yes. I needed her hug. "That'd be great, Mom."

"This weekend I'm earning some extra cash waitressing for a wedding," Mom said. "How about next weekend? I'll treat you to those pizza burgers, okay?"

"Okay," I said, not asking her to promise this time.

"And Abbey"—Mom paused, her voice softening—"I won't tell you not to worry and how everything's going to be okay, because right now, I know how devastated you feel. When people gossiped about me being pregnant, I wanted to die. But I held my head up high and got through it. So will you, sweetheart. Soon people will have something else to talk about, okay?"

"Okay . . . and Mom? Thanks for calling. It means the world to me."

And it did.

This time, I didn't clean the house to perfection after she promised to visit. Even though part of me desperately wanted to believe her, I couldn't allow myself to get excited, sitting around like an anxious child waiting for her arrival. But she was right about something. After a few days, people got bored with my story, and the gossip mill shifted to a junior volleyball player who cheated on an exam. In some selfish way, I was grateful to be out of the spotlight, but every time I saw Camden, his cocky smile would bring back my shame. It was a reminder of exactly what happens the second you let your guard down . . . with anybody.

So, two weeks later, when I was shampooing a client and listening to Granny Po nag Gena to death about her third date with Eric, I could not believe my eyes. There was Mom, pulling in the driveway in her Ford Escort.

She's here. For me. Mom's really here for me.

I walked quickly to the window, pulling the curtains aside, and could see Mom checking her hair in the rearview mirror. I went to the coloring station, where Gena was brushing blond dye onto the strands of a brunet and then folding it up in aluminum foil. A twinge of guilt hit as I remembered her saying how busy we would be tonight. "Gena, um, is there any way I can take off tonight? My mom's here for a surprise visit."

Gena rinsed her hands, drying them on a white towel that had the initials SS embroidered by Caddie in the lower right-hand corner. "Sure, that's no problem, but, honey, do you think you could rinse the customer first?"

Oh no. Gena's client was waiting, looking impatient, with her head back on the sink, shampoo dripping down by her ears. "Oh my gosh, I'm sorry, Gena."

Gena tossed her towel into a laundry basket and then walked to my side, putting an arm around my shoulder. "I'll take care of her. Now go, have a good time with your mom. I'll see you tomorrow, then."

I didn't want to say that it depended on whether my mom was staying the night or not.

Mom felt thin and frail when I hugged her in the driveway, thinner than she had at Christmas, or maybe that was only my imagination. She stroked the back of my head with her gloved hands. "Are you happy to see me?"

"You have no idea."

She embraced me again. "Good. Then let's get out of here. Are you hungry?"

"Starved."

At the restaurant, a waitress brought us coffee as Mom lit a cigarette, making sure the smoke was blowing away from us. "How are things at school? Getting any better?"

"Yeah, a little," I said, handing back the menu to the waitress right away, since we knew exactly what to order. Mom flicked ashes into the ashtray, her nails looking ragged, as though she'd been chewing them. "Man, what happened to your nails, Mom?"

She frowned and held them out in front. "Oh, you know. Just . . . no time to fuss with them, I guess. So, what's going on with Condom or Camden, whatever his name is."

I laughed at her joke but couldn't take my eyes off her hands. Mom used to spend hours on her nails. The small kitchen table in the apartment we shared would be littered with polish, acrylic tips, and tiny little decals she'd glue on. She loved the way her nails would *tap, tap, tap* on the table. But just like the parties she used to have, the manicures stopped when her depression grew worse.

"Well, forget about Camden," Mom said, snuffing out her cigarette and blowing smoke out the side of her mouth. "Men are pigs, Abbey. It's best you learn that lesson now and stay away from all relationships. While you're young, at least."

"That's my plan," I said, thinking that she was preaching to the choir here, but I was still distracted by her hands. *Not only are her nails a mess, but she's lost weight.* "But you know what, he's nothing. Let's not talk about him. Tell me what's going on with you."

She watched as the waitress refilled her mug. "No, I came for you, Abbey. Besides, there's not a whole lot to talk about. I'm . . . great! So, how are things with your job?"

"Fine, but are you sure you're okay?"

Mom shivered, pulling her coat over her shoulders. "Yeah. Guess I've been tired lately, that's all. From working so many hours."

No, she was more than tired. There was a nervous twitch in her eyes that reminded me of a frightened animal backed into a corner. Something was wrong, just as I thought at Christmas, when we talked in my room.

About the house.

Our food arrived, but she only picked at her pizza burger. What was she saying at Christmas? I can't believe I wasn't paying closer attention. "So, Mom, what about that house you were talking about, a rancher, right?"

She stopped chewing and wiped her mouth. Mom took a deep breath and reached for her coffee. "Yeah, it was a rancher. With blue shutters. But . . . I couldn't get my loan, so forget about it. Things didn't work out."

"Oh," I whispered, not knowing what else to say. We ate in silence for a few minutes and then I reached over to take her hand, my problems with Camden now pale in comparison. "I'm real sorry about that, Mom."

She placed her other hand on top of mine. "So am I, baby. So am I. The house was going to bring us together again, and I tried so hard to get a big enough down payment. You don't know how heartbroken I've been without you with me. I miss you so much. I miss *this*."

Mom let go of my hands and gestured her arms out wide. "Just hanging out with my daughter, eating junk food."

Tears welled in my eyes. Sometimes I miss it, too.

Mom picked up her fork, absentmindedly jabbing what was left of her burger. "But maybe it's for the best. You've got a life now, and it wouldn't be fair to take you away from it, so I guess it's just something I'll try to live with."

Try to live with?

One o'clock in the morning and my eyes were wide open. I slid from the bed and pulled the covers over my mother's shoulders. In sleep, she looked so peaceful, her face relaxed, a fist curled at her cheek. So different from the troubled look she had at dinner.

I've seen that look before. Many times in the last year we lived together.

I was such an idiot back then, missing the warning signs, the desperate SOS that said her ship was sinking. But I didn't know what to do, especially on the day when the FedEx guy knocked on the apartment door and handed Mom a white envelope. I sat breathless at the small kitchen table, fork poised over a TV dinner, watching her slowly open the envelope and read its contents with shaky hands.

Mom threw the papers across the room. I tucked my legs underneath me on the chair, watching her cry as she sucked on a paper cut. She pressed her back to the wall and slid to the floor.

"Mom, what's wrong? What happened?"

"Your father wants to finalize the divorce," she said. "So he can marry another woman. Nice, huh?"

I didn't know what to say. She had left him two years ago; I thought they were already divorced, but I nodded like I understood.

"He doesn't want either one of us, Abbey. He'd probably be happier if we were both dead." *Dead.* Mom started shaking her head faster and faster, then jerked up from the floor and stumbled to the bathroom, slamming the door behind her. I followed, afraid to have her out of my sight, and knocked. Her voice low and weak. "Go away, Abbey."

"Mom . . . please—"

"I said *go away*!"

My knees felt weak as I sank to the burgundy carpet, which was threadbare and worn to a dull beige in the middle. "Mom? Do you want a beer or anything? Please say something . . . I'm so sorry."

I leaned my head back and shut my eyes, waiting for the storm to pass. But with each passing minute, my heart beat faster. I pressed my ear to the door, desperate for a sound. A drawer opening. Anything. An icy finger traced the length of my spine. "Mom? You're scaring me, Mom . . . please say something!"

I stood up. Holding the doorknob with a trembling hand, I turned it hard. The cheap wood rattled in the loose frame but would not budge. "Mom! Please, let me in!"

Panic rose in my throat.

Stop it. You're just being paranoid. Stupid.

A small moan came from the bathroom.

The key. I needed the key.

I ran to the kitchen, grabbing a chair from the cheap kitchenette set. My legs buckled as I stood on it, feeling above the bathroom door frame for the key. None there.

Mom? Hold on, Mom . . . I'm coming.

None above my room. Found it, over Mom's door. I picked at the lock, dropping the key to the carpet. *Mom . . . say something! Oh God.*

The lock finally clicked. I closed my hand over the knob, turning slowly. Mom was on the toilet, her hair falling forward in a tangled mass over her face, looking at the stained razor blade between her fingers.

A red bloody path, along her wrists, over her hands, trickled to the ceramic floor.

If I had only paid attention back then. If I wasn't so absorbed with my own life, I would have noticed the hopelessness, the way the light dimmed in her eyes. The same way her eyes looked tonight. The house. The house was the lifeboat she'd been scrambling for, so she could be with me, and now that dream was lost.

Mom might have come this weekend to console me, but it's always been my job to protect her, no matter what. I turned my head away from the window, looking at my desk. To the small drawer that held my savings account book.

Chapter Twenty-one

She woke slowly, stretching out her arms and legs, black mascara smudged beneath her eyes. I sat in my chair, waiting for her to get up. She looked in my direction and smiled.

"Mom, I have something for you." My words were labored, but I had already made my decision. I put a check in her hand. Postdated ten days so I had time to sell the shares from my mutual fund and transfer all my savings to my checking account.

She rubbed her eyes, straining to focus. Once Mom understood the check in her hand, she bolted upright. "Holy crap, Abbey! Where did you get this money? Did you steal it?"

The question knocked me back. I have never stolen anything in my life. The accusation stung, but she did just wake up, and probably wasn't thinking clearly. "No, Mom. It's my life's savings . . . my life. I've worked almost every day for years, and now it's yours, *ours*. For the deposit on the house."

Mom lowered her legs to the floor. "I had no idea you . . .

this is . . . such a shock! Holy crap, seventy-five hundred dollars? I can't take this, Abbey!"

"But I want you to take it. For the house. *Our* house."

Mom stared at the check. She held my life, my hopes for the future, everything, all in that one slip of paper. I saved that money to keep me from living a life like my mother's. But now I had no choice but to give it to her.

"Oh my God, Abbey. I don't know what to say. Are you sure about this?"

I forced my head to nod yes, ignoring the burning ache in my heart. *This is what I have to do, no matter how much it hurts.*

"Abbey, you don't know what this means to me." Mom reached up and hugged me hard. When I saw the tears flowing down her face, I knew I'd done the right thing. For once. She got out of bed, wiped her eyes, and stripped out of her pajamas to her underwear. "Oh my gosh, I can't believe this is happening! Let's see, I need to make another appointment with the loan officer. Wait till you see this house! It's the most darling place ever."

I moved to sit on my bed, wrapping an arm around the bedpost as Mom pulled on her jeans. "Oh, and I better call the real estate agent. As soon as I get home."

Mom put on the sweater she'd worn last night, then placed her purse on the bed. I explained why she had to wait ten days before cashing the check, while Mom looked into a mirror, licked her finger, and rubbed away the mascara smudges. She put the check into her wallet and slipped her car keys into the pocket of her jeans. "Well, I better get going, then, shouldn't I? My coat is in the hall closet, right?"

"W-What . . . you're leaving?" I stared in disbelief.

She tilted her head toward me, putting on an earring. "Well, yeah, honey."

"But it's early. Can't you even stay for breakfast?" My lower lip trembled as she ran a comb through her hair. "You know, talk about the house?"

She paused, dropping her arms to her sides, then sat beside me and took both my hands in hers. "Oh, Abbey. I'm sorry, honey. I guess I'm too excited, thinking about how we're going to be together again soon. You can't blame me for that, can you, sweetheart?"

I swallowed hard as she reached up to brush hair out of my eyes. "I guess not."

"I tell you what," Mom said, hopping off my bed and picking up her purse. "Once you join me at the beach, I'll take you to the best places for breakfast. There's this one restaurant, called Cooper's Café, that serves the most amazing crepes. You'll love it, sweetheart!"

I nodded and took her outstretched hand so she could pull me off the bed. We walked shoulder to shoulder down the hall, hearing Granny Po singing off-key in the bathroom. I thought Mom would wait until Granny Po was done with her shower, but she opened the closet door and took out her leather coat.

"Well, I guess I got everything," she said, pulling me to her for a hug. "I love you so much, Abbey."

My voice cracked as I said, "I love you, too, Mom."

She stepped away and put one hand on the doorknob. "Abbey, you don't know how much this money means to me. One of the saddest moments in my life was leaving you here, so I'll be counting the days until we can be together again."

With that, she walked out the door, unlocked her Escort, and got in. I stood on the porch and watched her wave as she drove away, just like she did so long ago. Only this time, she took my future with her, tucked carefully inside her wallet. I didn't move a muscle, despite the cold wind blowing, as my money, that wall of protection I'd worked so hard to build, faded out of sight.

Minutes later, Granny Po stepped out onto the porch, a terry cloth robe pulled tight across her chest, her wet hair wrapped in a towel. "Your mom didn't leave already, did she? Isn't she staying for breakfast? She didn't want to visit with me?"

"No. She . . . uh, had a lot to do."

"Yeah, I'm sure," Granny Po murmured, the chilly air turning her breath to cloudy puffs. She turned to me. "You okay? You look pale."

I watched as a garbage truck thundered down the highway. "Yeah, I'm fine. Just tired, I guess."

Granny Po nodded. She jammed her hands into her robe pockets, shivering in the cold. "Abbey, is something going on? Your mom's visit was kind of sudden."

There shouldn't be any reason not to tell her. It was my money, after all, but I just couldn't bring myself to tell Granny Po. She would only call me crazy, and deep down I worried she might be right.

The full impact of what I'd done didn't hit until later. All of my money, my security, and my future were gone. My "Millionaire by Thirty-Five" plan, gone. And after Mom buys the house . . . I'll have to say good-bye to Granny Po, to the Widows, and to Gena. To my friends, although I don't think Kym would miss me that much now that she's spending more time with Candice. And to Mitch.

I showed up for work at the salon at ten twenty, feeling as though a steamroller had crushed my skull. A customer yelped when I forgot to check the water temperature before rinsing her hair, and it was way too hot. Another client got annoyed when I accidentally sprayed her face, causing her eye makeup to run. She complained to Gena, who assured her my work was normally very careful, but she still had to pull me aside.

"Abbey, what's going on?" she asked, feeling my forehead with the back of her hand while Granny Po watched from her workstation. "Are you sick or something?"

"No, everything's fine. I'm just tired."

She studied my face. "Abbey, is it because your mother had to leave?"

I turned away, opening a cabinet door and mindlessly straightening the rows of shampoos. I waited a few seconds before trying to speak. "No, like I said, I'm fine."

She put a hand on my shoulder. "Abbey, take the morning off. I know it's hard, being away from your mom. Lord knows I miss my mother every single day. Is that it?"

Granny Po set down her scissors, as though waiting for my answer. I took off my apron and handed it to Gena. "Yeah, that's all."

During the rest of the weekend, I kept thinking, *It's not too late to change my mind.* There was still time, since the check was postdated, the twenty-third of January. I could call the bank Monday, put a stop payment on the check, and forget the whole idea. Things would go back to the way they were. My money would be safe. I wouldn't have to leave my job, or Granny Po.

But Mom sounded so hopeful when she called on Monday evening, thanking me over and over again, saying how she was going to schedule an appointment with the loan officer soon, and asking if I closed my mutual-fund account.

Tell her you changed your mind. Tell her you need the money back.

"Yeah, Mom, that's all taken care of. My investment counselor will take care of closing it and the money will be transferred to my checking account this week. You'll be able to cash it next Tuesday."

For a week I replayed my writing that check, over and over again, like a bad dream I couldn't wake up from. On Tuesday, I ducked into the auditorium during my lunch period, ignoring the group of drama students rehearsing onstage. Just as they finished a scene, I dialed my bank's automated-teller number on my cell phone, punching in my social security number and personal ID. From the menu, I chose the option that provides recently cashed checks. A robotic voice firmly told me that check number forty-eight, in the amount of seventy-five hundred dollars, was posted. Mom had cashed it. The money was gone. And there was nothing I could do about it.

Chapter Twenty~two

All those years of hard work, for what. "Millionaire by Thirty-Five," a waste. I couldn't even stand to look at my notebook, knowing that all my numbers were now at zero.

But I knew I had no choice but to give Mom the money, and part of me was proud. Who knows what she would have done to herself had it not been for me. I knew if something *did* happen, I'd never forgive myself.

She was so excited when she called days later that for twenty minutes she talked about finding a wicker love seat and matching chair dirt cheap at a clearance sale and about the paint samples she'd picked up, and wouldn't sea-foam green look great?

I wasn't exactly a fan of sea-foam green, but said yes, anyway. "How's it going with the real estate lady? What did she say about the loan?"

"Maxine?" Mom said, with the sound of shuffling papers in the background. "I tried to make an appointment with her, but she's been impossible to tie down. January is the busiest month for real estate, so it's been hard. These things take time, sweetheart."

"Oh, of course, Mom. I didn't mean anything by that." It seemed odd, though, that she hadn't met with the Realtor yet. Especially after she'd left in such a hurry when I gave her the check, two weeks ago. Perhaps I did sound impatient. "Sorry, Mom, just let me know what happens when you do, okay?"

She promised, but the next evening, I was still trying to put our conversation out of my mind while watching *Wheel of Fortune* with Granny Po. Outside, roads were blanketed by the falling snow, enough for Gena to send her staff home early, and probably enough to stay closed tomorrow.

Granny Po solved the first puzzle before me, shouting out, "Six of one, half dozen of another!"

She looked at me with a triumphant gleam in her eyes and did a little dance in her chair. "Ha! In your face, Abbey girl!"

I shot her a fierce look, saying she only got lucky, then tried to concentrate on the next puzzle. But my mind couldn't focus. I kept glancing at the framed photograph of my grandmother above the mantel. Her face looked so radiant, hardly the picture of a woman who would one day kill herself.

"Lonely days, lonely nights!" Granny Po hollered, solving the second puzzle. She looked at me with concern. "You feeling all right?"

"Yeah, everything's cool," I lied.

Okay, concentrate, Abbey. But for the rest of the show, I dwelled on how moments like these with Granny Po would soon end. The way we love watching *Wheel of Fortune*, all those crazy hypothetical questions she pretends to hate. I'll be living with Mom, and her wicker furniture. Granny Po solved the bonus-round puzzle a second before the contestant. She leaned back in her recliner and stared at me.

"You sure you're okay?"

"Yep, I'm okay."

"Mmm-hmm." Granny Po tilted her head and tapped the remote on the recliner's arm. "Hey, by the way, Super Bowl Sunday is this weekend. I was thinking of having the Widows over. You wanna watch the game with us?"

"Sure," I said offhandedly.

Granny Po pitched forward and turned the TV off. "Aha, I knew it. You're agreeing to watch football? You couldn't solve even one *Wheel of Fortune* puzzle? And the other day, before you left for the farm, you didn't disrespect me with that *I peed and pooed* nonsense. *And* when Verna McDaniel gave you a ten-dollar tip at the spa, not once did you make that face."

I shifted away from her. "What face? I don't know what you're talking about."

"Oh, yes, you know exactly what I'm talking about," Granny Po huffed. "That *cha-ching* face you make, especially when you get a large paycheck. There is something wrong, and girl, don't make me hog-tie your butt to find out what it is."

I rubbed my temples, knowing I couldn't tell her the truth. Granny Po would be furious if she knew I gave Mom that much money. And how is she going to feel when she finds out I'm leaving? I didn't have to think too hard on that one. Granny Po would be devastated, so I can't tell her. Not yet.

"Abbey, does this have something to do with your mother?" she asked.

Her question caught me off guard. "No, of course not. This has nothing to do with Mom." *Only everything.*

"Well, something is up your butt today, and we're not moving until you tell me." Granny Po's stare was turning lethal. I had to give her something.

"It's just . . . it's just school," I said. "Friends, really. Kym . . . she's hanging out with a new crowd now. Well, not all the time. Sometimes she does eat lunch with us, but only when this snotty girl, Candice, isn't at school. And Sarah's depressed because her boyfriend, John, is now going to another school, and even though they haven't broken up, she thinks it's just a matter of time."

None of these were lies. I was worried about Sarah, and hurt by Kym's turning her back on me after the wart incident, and, thankfully, it was enough to convince Granny Po. She rubbed my knee in sympathy, telling me not to take Kym's actions personally, it had nothing to do with me, and to just be patient: She's probably just going through a stage, and one day, she'll find out who her friends really are.

Granny Po said that Sarah could be right. She and John could break up tomorrow, or five days from now, or five months from now. There's always that chance, but worrying about it won't do her any good. She should enjoy today.

"So what can I do?" I asked.

"Nothing you can do," Granny Po said. "Sarah needs to figure this out for herself. You just be there for her, whenever she needs a friend."

Two more weeks passed and there was nothing from Mom.

I knew enough from listening to Rosemary that buying a house doesn't happen overnight. She would often talk about problems she had buying a new rental property, like with the loan, settlement delays, or title clearance. But I just wanted a phone call from Mom, *anything*, because it drove me crazy being kept in the dark, not knowing what was going on. I left her a message, asking if there were any problems getting the loan that she didn't want to tell me about. And if there were, please call me back.

The next day, at work, Rosemary walked into the spa just as Gena asked me to set the timer for a client getting a perm. "Abbey, dear, I'm going to the bank. You have anything you want to deposit?"

"Yeah, hold on." I ran through the spa to my room and got my paycheck. The pathetically small balance written on my checkbook register made me swallow hard. I tried to not dwell on it and flipped to the back, ripping out a deposit slip.

Rosemary was waiting by the front door when I returned, wearing her favorite wool coat and clutching the leather organizer Gena had given her when the spa opened. I handed her my deposit slip and signed paycheck, but before she turned to go, I touched her arm. There was something that Mom said that had been bothering me.

"Miss Rosemary, I have a question . . . for school," I said, forcing my voice to sound casual. "With all your experience, um, what month would you say is the slowest for real estate?"

Rosemary put my deposit in her purse. "What class is this for, sugar?"

Class? *Which class?* "Economics?"

Rosemary nodded. "Well, that really depends on the market, Abbey. But, on average, I would say January is the slowest."

My temples ached from this information. "Oh . . . January?"

Rosemary buttoned her coat and wrapped her scarf around her head. "Yes, everybody's either too broke from Christmas or too concerned about the cold to want to look at houses. That, and some parents would rather not take their kids out of school during the middle of the school year. Does that answer your question?"

It did.

Gena hustled over in leopard-print heels and put an arm around my shoulder. There was a smile on her face but an urgency in her voice. "Abbey, sweetheart, did you set the timer for Mrs. Dunkin's perm?"

I winced, slapping a hand to my forehead. "Oh my gosh, Gena, I'm so sorry."

Later, Gena pulled me into her office and asked me what was wrong. Maybe I should tell her. She might be more understanding than Granny Po, and could maybe even give me advice. But to tell Gena would be disloyal to my mom.

And I just couldn't do that.

"Well, Gena, I am having problems with my friends . . ."

Rosemary's input nagged at me for days. *Did Mom tell me January was the busiest month as an excuse? Or did she just not know better?*

A few days later, I finally had the chance to ask when she called, late.

"Well, at the beach, real estate is never slow, honey," Mom said, her voice edged with hurt. "But, good news, I met with a loan officer today! Her name is Kelly Harmon, and she says there should be no problem with me qualifying for assistance. Just think, I'll be a home owner before long! Isn't that wonderful?"

"Yeah, it's wonderful news," I said, curling up an edge of Granny Po's red Valentine place mats. Cupid stared up at me, his little finger pointing like I was wrong to accuse her. I covered him with my soda can, regretting my decision to question her. It wasn't as though there was a big rush for me to move, and maybe I should be a little more patient. "I'm sorry, Mom. Just . . . let me know when something happens, okay?"

Almost everyone wore red to school the next day, for Valentine's Day. I wore black.

For a senior class fund-raiser, anyone could prepurchase a carnation for a dollar and have it delivered to a friend or significant other. All morning long, classes were interrupted by seniors, dressed up as Cupid, delivering carnations to the lucky recipients: pink ones for friendship; red for love. Whenever Cupid knocked, girls sat up at their desks, praying a carnation would be for them because the more flowers you had, the more popular you looked. And the girl with no carnation? She would be hating Valentine's Day by the end.

Cupid delivered my pink flower from Sarah during second period. Last year I had two, since Kym bought me one also, as part of our three-way agreement not to look like total losers. But this year, I guess she bought one for Candice instead.

I carried my flower on top of my books into study hall and found an empty table for Sarah and me. She walked in later, carrying the five flowers I had delivered for her.

"Abbey," she said, "that was so sweet; you didn't have to do that!"

Sarah was smiling, but the rims of her eyes were red from crying. She had no flowers from John, which was pretty crappy, considering their one-year anniversary was this weekend. I had hoped John would remember how big of a deal Carnation Day was at Winchester High. He could have easily gotten a friend to buy Sarah a flower for him, but he obviously forgot all about it. "I know. I just thought you might be bummed today, and wanted you to feel extra loved."

Besides, who knows if I'll be here next Valentine's Day.

We both opened our Spanish books in silence as Kym walked through the library entrance, proudly wearing her cheerleading uniform since there would be a JV basketball game tonight. She scanned the room, and waved when she found us. "There you guys are! I was looking for you two earlier."

"Don't you have English this period?" Sarah asked her.

"Yep." Kym put her purse on the table and pulled out a bathroom pass. "I'll tell Mr. Talbot I got my period and had to wait for someone to bring me a tampon. Poor man will be too tripped up to say anything! Besides, I wanted to thank you guys for the flowers. And I'm real sorry for not sending you any. Guess I forgot about our agreement."

She forgot about more than that, but I let it go, trying to do as Granny Po said and just be patient.

"Ooo!" Kym did a little jump, her pleated skirt flaring out. "And guess who else sent me a flower? Jake Spencer, you know, that wrestler I danced with at Camden's party? It's pink, though. Would have been cooler if it was red, but I'll take pink."

Her reminder of Camden's party was painful, but I just nodded and tried to look interested as Kym went down the entire carnation report, telling us who got a flower from whom. Candice got flowers from her entire cheerleading squad and from some guy named Troy. Mindy got one from a senior, blah, blah, blah. Only when she mentioned Paulina's name did I pay attention. "Paulina? Oh, how many did you say she got?"

Kym paused. "Three. And they were all pink."

I kept my face blank, not wanting to let on how much it bothered me that Mitch could have bought her one . . . or maybe *all* of those pink flowers.

Forget it. It doesn't matter, anyway.

Kym soon flounced out of the library, returning to English class, and Sarah went back to studying. Stupid tradition. Who started it, anyway?

Mrs. Cabot shuffled past our table, carrying a stack of books in her thin arms. I remember how the principal had announced that this was Mrs. Cabot's thirtieth anniversary as a school librarian, so *she* would know when it started. Maybe she even knew my mom when she was a student . . . and my father.

A thought crossed my mind. I pushed my chair back and walked to the front desk, where Mrs. Cabot was piling books into neat stacks. With her reddish hair and pale skin, she looked like an older Raggedy Ann. She gave me a warm smile. "Anything I can help you with, dear?"

"Um, yeah, do you keep older yearbooks? From other graduating classes?"

"We sure do!" Mrs. Cabot stepped from behind the desk,

her orthopedic shoes shuffling slightly on the gray carpet as she walked toward a row of shelves behind the periodicals. "What year do you need?"

I hesitated, quickly calculating. Mom dropped out of school the same year I was born, and that was 1990. "Oh, 1987 to 1990?"

Mrs. Cabot stopped, pointing to a shelf labeled ALUMNI. "There they are. You need anything else?"

"That's it. Thanks, Mrs. Cabot."

I waited until she was gone, then took the yearbooks to a secluded table. I peeked around the corner to see if Sarah was still studying, before opening the CLASS OF 1987 book. The freshman pages were near the back, their status at the bottom of the totem pole clear. I flipped to the Ss, scanning for Somers, my mother's maiden name. Mom's face jumped from the page, almost unrecognizable from how she looks today. A clear brightness shone in her eyes, without the anger and despair. She looked just like my grandmother Evelyn Somers. And I looked just like her.

In Mom's sophomore yearbook, there were more pictures of her. One of her posing with the cheerleading squad, their hairstyles almost laughable. She looked happy, just like Kym when she's with her squad. In one picture, Mom stood on the top of a pyramid, pom-poms jutting to the sky; then another of her, in a school play. I left the book open to a picture of Mom leaning against a locker, wearing parachute pants and a striped shirt.

My jaw dropped as I flipped through the next yearbook, CLASS OF 1989. There they were, the golden couple: Grace Somers and Dale Garner. My father, the big senior quarterback; her, the popular junior.

I checked my watch. Not much time before next period. I reached for the last yearbook, CLASS OF 1990. The beginning pages for every yearbook always look the same, no matter what the year. Happy students posing for the camera, mingling in hallways, goofing around on the steps. But the photograph on page thirty-five told a different story. Mom's senior picture.

Her shoulders were bare in the black velvet robe, a string of pearls around her pale neck. Small pearl earrings hung from her earlobes. She looked pretty, but I saw something more. The swelling of her cheeks, the pain etched in her heavily lined eyes. Mom was five months pregnant when this was taken, and I could see that she'd lost hope, like she was dead inside.

There were no other pictures of her. No cheerleading, no school plays, not even a write-up beside her senior picture, because she didn't graduate. But that one picture was enough to remind me just why I had to give her the money. And it was still on my mind when Sarah called later that evening, excited over the dozen roses waiting for her at home, one for every month she and John had been together.

Two weeks later, on the last day of February, Granny Po's answering machine was blinking when I got home from school. Mom's message was brief. "Hi, Abbey, it's Mom. Everything is great, and I'll call you later."

That was all she said. As the days of March passed, my anger grew, and the empathy I felt while looking at those yearbooks faded like the paper they were printed on. Who gave a crap about the wicker furniture, or that she'd decided to paint the interior sea-foam green? What about the house we were putting it in? Is the paperwork finalized yet? If it is, then she's pretty piss-poor at keeping me informed. Shouldn't she pick up a phone and let me know what's going on? I wanted to scream at her, and tell her I'm not some kid she can keep in the dark. I'm her *partner*. I invested money in *our* future, and I demand to know what's going on.

I yelled these frustrations into Mom's machine, not caring if her feelings were hurt. So what if she thinks I'm doubting her? Maybe I am.

But three days later, my anger passed and guilt returned. I left another message apologizing for sounding so harsh, and please, couldn't she just give me a ring? It didn't matter if there were problems buying the house, or if someone else had already bought it and she was just afraid to tell me. It wouldn't matter where we live, any house would do, and we'd paint it sea-foam green, or pink, or whatever color she wanted. *Just let me know what's going on, okay?*

Just call, please.

Granny Po walked into the kitchen, where I was pretending to read at the table. "Hey, we're leaving for bingo in a little bit, okay?"

"Okay," I said, trying to look interested in my book. "You all have fun, then."

Granny Po stood there for a second. "What's with that pissy look on your face? You look all perturbed."

Man, that woman didn't miss a beat. I set my book down, losing my page, but I didn't care. I looked out the back window to where Edith's fence bordered Granny Po's yard.

"I'm angry because . . . because . . . this morning, Mr. Penney brought in a horse that was half-starved. Poor thing could hardly stand in the trailer. We had to half drag him into the barn."

This was true. I'd stayed with the weak horse all morning, watching him eat the mash like he didn't know what food was, and trying not to cry when Mr. Penney said there was a chance he might not make it through the weekend. It infuriated me. If people don't want to take care of their animals, then they should just give them to someone who will.

Guess you could say the same about mothers.

The phone rang, causing me to jump. Granny Po got to it first.

"Hello?" She listened, then cupped her hand over one end. It had to be for me. It had to be Mom. "Abbey . . . it's your father."

I leaned my head back against the chair and stared at the ceiling. Of course it was him, and not my mom. But I couldn't talk to my father. Not today. Not when he was responsible for putting Mom and me in this position to begin with.

"Abbey," Granny Po said. I brought my head back up, staring straight into her eyes with a pleading look. *Please, Granny Po. Not today.* She hesitated, then put the phone back to her ear. "Dale, I'm sorry, but Abbey's in the shower."

Thank you.

She hung up seconds later, then reached out her hand. "Now look, I won't enjoy myself tonight knowing you're home alone, feeling all poopy. So get up, you're coming with us."

"Huh?" No way, the last time I went with the Gray Widows on a Saturday night, a bunch of ladies cursed me out for calling bingo by mistake.

"Don't look at me like that. I promise to not let those loudmouths scream at you this time." Granny Po held up the phone and gave it a shake, reminding me of the lie she'd just told my father. "Besides, you owe me one."

There are some pretty weird bingo superstitions. Like how you should always stick with your lucky bingo seat, *always* circle your chair three times before sitting, make sure your lucky charm is displayed, and never leave your money on the table.

Caddie is a firm believer in all of them. She stood with me while Granny Po was paying our fees, holding one of her fanciest Longaberger baskets, which held all her bingo supplies. Tables were lined up in rows in the church basement. The metal chairs scraped the floor as women of all ages rushed to get ready for the first game.

While Rosemary and Edith ran their desserts to the food table, Caddie pulled out a couple of thick markers from her basket and handed them to me. "Here's your bingo dabbers. Lord, don't let anyone pinch them; it's bad luck, you know. Now, you see those stacks of bingo-paper notepads? You go pick your cards, honey."

I opened the top of my dabber and wondered why they are called dabbers. "Can you just grab me two, Miss Caddie?"

Caddie gave me a blank stare.

"Oh," I said. "Guess that's a bingo superstition, huh?"

Granny Po led us to their customary spot, first row, three tables down from the caller. She darn near snarled at Loretta Scott, who was wearing a pickle-colored blazer and matching trousers, with low heels that looked more orthopedic than stylish. Caddie circled her chair three times, sat, and then began lining up her cards. All six of them. Then she pulled out her lucky charms, six fuzzy-headed troll dolls, and lined them up with pinpoint precision in front of each card.

Maybe I should get some lucky charms. I could shake them over my phone, and then my mother would call. I took out my cell and checked to see if there was service in the basement. There was.

No, stop it.

I didn't want to think about Mom, or my money, or moving, so I put my cell phone back in my purse. Tonight I wanted to just have fun.

After the tenth number of the fourth game was called, I covered my mouth to keep from laughing out loud at how the women seemed possessed by some kind of bingo demon, with veins bulging in their necks, and backs erect and tense, waiting for that one magic number to be called. Maybe I'll have to come more often with Granny Po, who sat hunched over her cards, nervously tapping her dabber on the table, waiting for her last needed number to be called.

"I-17."

"Bingo!" Loretta Scott's loud squawk rang against the cement walls, sounding like a parrot stuck in a door.

"Jiminy Cricket!" Granny Po ripped the top bingo sheet from her pad, wadding it into a tiny ball and throwing it down on the table. "You know she screams like that only to get under my skin, don't you? And that god-awful red velvet cake she brought that everyone is raving about. Looks like someone cut into a huge hunk of raw meat. Caddie, give me a shake. I'm gonna need all the luck I can get."

Caddie took a troll, holding it upside down and waving it wandlike over Granny Po's cards.

I cracked up, getting a few nasty stares from some women at another table, while Edith rolled her eyes and reached out to pinch the top of Caddie's dabber.

The caller announced that the next game will be "eight states," where you have to fill the numbers surrounding the free space. Granny Po rolled her sleeves up and grabbed one of Caddie's trolls for an extra shake. As the numbers were called, the tension grew thicker, each woman clenching her dabber. Just as I marked another square, my phone rang.

Mom.

She could be the only person calling, since Dad doesn't have my cell number and Sarah already called me earlier. I pushed my chair back, leaned down to where my purse was on the floor, and hit the table with my chin. My soda cup shook, but when I went to grab for it, I accidentally knocked it over instead.

"Oh *no!*"

The announcer threw up his hands. "We've got bingo, hold your cards, hold your cards!"

No! Not again. Women began to grumble at their tables, looking around to see who'd won. I stood, struggling to answer my phone by the sixth ring, clean up the soda, *and* tell everyone that I did *not* have bingo. "Just keep playing . . . I'm so sorry . . . I don't have eight states!"

Caddie jumped up to help, and Granny Po waved to the announcer, telling him to keep calling the numbers.

"Well, ladies," he said, "looks like that was only a false call."

"What? Is this someone's idea of a joke?" a lady yelled from the other side of the room.

"Who did that?"

"That girl over there did it! Look at her, on the phone like some typical teenager."

"Isn't that Polly Randall's girl?"

The rest I couldn't hear. I left the mess to Caddie and ran out to the empty hallway, pressing the phone to my ear. "Hello? Hello? Is anyone there?"

"Abbey, what's going on?" Mom. Finally.

"Mom, thank God you called."

She apologized for not getting back to me. I leaned against the wall, then slid down to sit on the cold floor and listen. Her excitement was evident, explaining how she'd let the lease run out on her apartment, and how she had temporarily moved in with a friend until the house was finalized. I was so happy to hear this, and yet, a burning ache closed over my heart.

What did I want? I'd spent weeks worrying that Mom wasn't doing anything to buy the house. Now she'd given me an update, and I felt anxious instead of relieved.

"Abbey . . . you still there?" There was a muffled sniff and her clearing her throat on the line. "Honey, don't you want me to get this house?"

"W-what?" My breath quickened. "What makes you say that, Mom?"

There was the sound of ice clinking in a glass. "I don't know, I just got a feeling, I guess. Like you're having second thoughts or something and you don't want to move here to be with me. Would you rather stay in Winchester with Granny Po? Gena, maybe?"

Her voice dropped when she said "Gena," making me feel horrible. And so does Mom, if she thinks her own daughter doesn't want to be with her.

"No, Mom! Of course I want to live with you. I'm just tired tonight. And I guess it seems like it's taking so long. But I want us to be together, really, Mom. I wouldn't have given you the money if I didn't."

"Are you sure, Abbey?"

I closed my eyes, picturing my mother's face right now, frightened and uneasy, her forehead wrinkled with worry. She needs me more than Granny Po or the other Widows do.

"Yes, I'm sure."

Chapter Twenty-three

The first day of spring came and went, but it wasn't until April that warm weather finally arrived. Granny Po broke out her bunny-appliquéd sweatshirts, and we spent one evening decorating for Easter, stringing pink lights around the railings and hanging colorful plastic eggs from branches of her redbud tree. A yellow blow-up rabbit was tied up like a hostage to the trunk, its ears bouncing in the wind.

The number of pedicures booked at the spa had increased, even though it wasn't quite warm enough to break out the sandals. Gena's manicurist was on her fourth pedicure by the time Granny Po walked into the spa, wearing the same floral smock she used to wear when it was Polly's Parlor. She handed me a still-warm loaf of zucchini bread wrapped in aluminum foil and pointed out the window. "I think that's Mitch pulling in to mow the lawn, so you take this on out and ask him to deliver it to Harry, you hear?"

I hesitated after taking the bread, and looked out the window. Sure enough, there was Mitch stepping out of his car.

Granny Po shooed me out the door, where a wreath of flowers hung on a nail. Mitch was unlocking the storage shed as I walked up. He looked up and smiled in that same, natural way, but there was still an awkwardness between us that just wouldn't go away. Or maybe it was only me.

I handed Mitch the bread. We made pleasant small talk about the horse that came to the farm last month half-starved and how it looked like he would survive after all. Then we talked about the quarter horse Lena and how an older woman was so excited to adopt her. Then Mitch started up the mower, drowning out any more words I might have said.

The next weekend, Gena was busy at her station, doing a series of different hairstyles for an extremely fussy bride-to-be who simply could not decide which look went better with her veil. Granny Po was perming a friend from bingo, and every now and then would run to her kitchen to check on the red velvet cake baking in the oven. And I was rinsing a client's hair, trying to look normal, trying not to think about how it had been weeks since I'd heard from my mother.

Weeks. Without one single word.

Granny Po dashed back from the kitchen just as her timer rang. From the manicure table, Rosemary watched as she unrolled a wave rod and checked the curl. "So, Polly. Red velvet cake, huh?"

Granny Po furrowed her brow and refastened the rod. "Yeah, red velvet, what of it?"

Rosemary blew on a nail. "Oh, nothing."

Caddie caught her eye and smirked. Granny Po put her hands on her hips. "And just what are you two all giddy about?"

"Well," Rosemary purred, "gossiping is not how one should behave in polite society; *however,* I've got it on good authority that a certain Harry Penney loves red velvet cake. And you, my dear, hate it."

"I do not," Granny Po huffed.

"Oh, you lying sack of dung," countered Edith. "You said at bingo not long ago that you hate red velvet cake. How exactly did she put it, Abbey girl?"

Oh no. Getting involved in their tiffs was never wise. But . . . getting Granny Po riled up would be a great way to get my mind off things. "Like someone cut into a huge hunk of raw meat?"

Granny Po opened a drawer, pulled out disposable gloves, and put them on with a snap. "I was referring to Loretta Scott's horrendous piece-of-crap, my dear. Mine, however, is divine."

"Mmm-mmm," Rosemary cooed. "So, for what occasion did you make that divine cake if it wasn't for our Mr. Penney?"

"Wait," Gena laughed. "She'd be Polly Penney! That's a riot!"

"Good gravy, are you out of your mind girly-girl?" Granny Po pointed at Gena. "I don't want to be no Polly Penney!"

Gena pointed back with the curling iron she was using to twirl the bride-to-be's tendrils for hairstyle number six. "That's what you get for all the teasing about Eric. Don't dish it if you can't take it."

"Well, *you're* dating the guy. But I am *not* interested in no stinking husband," Granny Po exclaimed. "Took me thirty years to recover from the first one, God rest his soul."

"God rest his soul," repeated nearly everyone in the entire room, except the bride-to-be.

"Besides," she continued, "if I was, don't y'all think I'd be smart enough to hide it from you vultures?"

She had a point. Granny Po went back to her perm, barking for me to go get the mail. I ran out quickly, past the slightly deflated bunny hostage, hoping not to miss any of their bickering. I grabbed our mail, and Gena's, as well, but almost dropped it all when I saw the letter on the bottom of the pile. From Mom.

I walked slowly back to the porch, sat on the steps, and opened it.

April 12

Dear Abbey,

Oh my gosh, I can't believe how screwed up things are! I moved out of my friend's apartment at the beginning of April, and the witch never bothered to forward your messages. I only found out when her boyfriend came into the bar I'm working at and told me. Right now, I'm staying with a coworker, but you can reach me on my new cell phone, 443-555-5972.

Things got a little shaky with the deal, but as soon as I know something, I'll let you know. I love you, sweetheart.

Mom

That was it. No details, just a small letter, six sentences long. I read it twice, three times, trying to make sense of it. Shaky? Is that all she can say? Things are a little shaky? After all this time, I wanted to shake her myself and rattle her head until she knew the true meaning of shaky.

My chest ached with a familiar tightness as I went back into the spa, trying to think of what all could have gone wrong with Mom's loan, and why she didn't think enough of me to keep me informed. Gena came over to get her mail while Bridezilla went to the bathroom. She showed me a brochure she'd gotten from a new salon in Trecos Valley called Movies, Makeovers, and More. The salon was tripped out like a Hollywood movie studio, with sixteen-foot screens and individualized rooms with their own plasma televisions.

Gena gave me a wink. "You know, as a business woman, it's my duty and responsibility to stay abreast of all the new trends, right? So I really should take a day off and check this out. Care to join me?"

"Sure," I said, feeling my mother's letter in my pocket and sinking down on the love seat. "Sounds fun."

Paul walked over, giving me half a chocolate-chip cookie. He stayed thin by pawning half his food off on someone else. He sighed and brushed away my overgrown bangs. "Girl, look at you, after that amazing cut I gave you! It's been months, and I can't even see your eyes now. How about a trim after closing, hmm?"

"Uh, sure, that'd be great. Thanks, Paul."

Edith plopped down beside me, taking the rest of the cookie. "Abbey girl, can I interest you in a trail ride? I guarantee ya it will shake off whatever's been getting you down today."

I cringed. "Thanks, Miss Edith, but no."

"Oh come on," she pushed. "Nothing will happen. That Ragman is too fat to run away or anything. Won't you do it for me, for your old pal Edith, just for the shits and giggles of it?"

Shits and giggles. That got a smile out of me. But before Edith could confuse it as a yes, I shook my head no. Hard.

"Well, you can't blame an old girl for trying, can you?" Edith sighed, then grabbed the new tabloid that came in the mail and flipped through the pages. "Okay, then, we'll try this. Here we go, Abbey. Hypothetical question of the week: If you were forced to eat only *one* food for an entire year, what kind of food would that be?"

Caddie gave an exasperated sigh. "Oh Lord, here we go with those silly questions. I'm supposed to choose only one food? Why, there's just no way!"

Gena poked a large pin though the French twist she rolled the bride-to-be's hair in, the seventh attempt to make her happy. "Hmm, something healthy. How about tomatoes?"

"Steak," Granny Po said, holding a roller in her lips. "Can't live on no darn vegetable."

"Tomato is a fruit," Gena countered, holding a mirror up so the bride could see her hair from behind. The bride pouted with a scowl, saying she wanted something with a little more pouf. Gena agreed graciously and pulled the pins out to try again with hairstyle number eight.

"These mini-cheesecakes of Caddie's," said Rosemary, peeling the wrapper from another and popping it into her mouth. "My darling Thomas loved cheesecakes, God rest his soul."

"God rest his soul."

"Fair fries!" Caddie clapped her hands in front of her. "You know, the kind they serve at the 4-H fair every summer? Oh, Lord, *Lord.* Sheer heaven. Salty, crisp on the outside, moist on the inside. And you can get cheese fries, gravy fries,

fries with vinegar, and oh, fries with Old Bay seasoning. So many yummy choices!"

Edith nudged my arm, staring at me hard. "Abbey girl, what about you?"

It was hard not to cry. Here I was in a room full of people who cared about me. Gena, asking me to go to that new salon. Paul, sharing his cookie. Edith, pushing me to ride, even though the notion terrifies me. But it shows she cares just the same.

And what do I get from my mother? Shakiness.

The room seemed to grow silent as all eyes focused on me, waiting for an answer. Granny Po's alarm went off, but she ignored it. I forced a smile, showing that I was fine, just fine, and answered. "Okay, how about spaghetti with meat sauce. Carbohydrates from the pasta, protein from the meat sauce, and antioxidants from the tomatoes."

"Perfect," Gena shouted. "I want what she's having!"

Rosemary giggled. "I bet our friend Mr. Penney would pick red velvet cake!"

The last of the Easter eggs Granny Po and I had carefully dyed were now beginning to rot and were thrown out. The bunny hostage was tucked away for another year, the redbud tree was now in full bloom, and the concern I'd had for my mother faded to doubt, after weeks without her returning my calls.

The one woman who *did* call me was Gena, on a Thursday night. "Hey, Polly told me you don't have school tomorrow, so would you care to take a little road trip with me?"

"Where to?" I asked.

"Movies, Makeovers and More. Remember the brochure?

I thought we'd go check it out, for *business* research only, of course."

"Of course," I replied. "And what kind of research are we doing?"

"A facial and a mani-pedi. You in?"

I was so in.

Gena picked me up at ten, since we both had eleven o'clock appointments. She put the top down on the Jeep, and the warm air felt so good on my face.

"I thought we'd take the scenic route and drive through the valley," she said, her hair tied down with a chic scarf and her voice raised above the wind.

After thirty minutes, we turned into the "valley," a long road sandwiched between gorgeous horse farms with beautiful barns, elegant and pristine. We saw Thoroughbred broodmares grazing, their foals prancing in circles around them. Gena explained that this is where the Maryland Hunt Cup Race is held and how she used to go to it with her ex-husband.

As we drove around a sharp corner, she pointed up the hill. "See that mansion? That's Cal Ripken's house. Or *was* his house, depending on which rumor you believe. I hear it has a basketball court and a bowling alley in there."

The house was amazing, but my mind was still on Gena's ex-husband. When she talked about going to the Hunt Cup with him, there was no eye-rolling nor dark scowls when she said his name, like when Mom mentions my father. Even though Gena's ex treated her horribly, there was no bitterness, no anger. Maybe it had something to do with her new relationship with Eric, but I doubted that was the reason. Gena was just that way.

Still, I was curious. "Uh, Gena, how's it going with Eric?"

Gena gave me a quick smile, then turned back to the road. "It's good. He's such a nice guy, and I'm taking it slow, but it's going good."

I nodded, looking out at another horse farm, which had a pond with a fountain in the middle of it. Gena started to sing along to a Shania Twain song we both liked, and I leaned back in my seat, enjoying the morning and the sound of her voice.

The salon was a combination of a Hollywood movie experience and upscale spa, where the stylists had their own rooms, each with a huge window overlooking the sixteen-foot movie screen in the large waiting room. While Gena's salon was full of down-home charm and camaraderie, this one was sleek, stylized, and high-tech. And both, in my opinion, were fabulous.

Gena and I looked over the price list while waiting for our appointments, with *Titanic* playing on the movie screen. "Not bad prices, really. I expected them to be higher."

A hostess brought us both water with lemon. I thanked her and pointed to the list. "Uh, Gena? Am I reading that correctly, or does that say 'male Brazilian wax'?"

Gena cringed. "Yeah, Loretta Scott would love that."

Our facials and nail treatments were fantastic, and I thanked Gena several times for treating me as we hobbled back to the Jeep, wearing flip-flops to keep our toenails from getting scratched.

"My pleasure," she said, putting on her seat belt and then adjusting her rearview mirror. "So, what did you think?"

"Awesome," I said, looking at my newly polished nails. "Definitely a cool experience, sort of multitasking—getting

your nails done while getting caught up on your movies—
but . . .”

"But what?" Gena asked, pulling out of the parking lot
and heading back toward the valley.

"But I like yours much better. I mean, come on, they
didn't have a single mini-cheesecake!"

Gena laughed. "Well, thank God for Caddie's cheesecakes! I'll stay in business after all."

Her comment was lighthearted, but it still made me pause
at the thought of what would happen if Serenity Spa did leave.
It was ironic. In October, I hadn't wanted to give Granny Po
Gena's card because I'd thought she would take the beauty
shop away from us. But it's still my home.

For now. At least, I think so.

Gena braked for a red light, and watched as a young
mother led her two reluctant children across the street. She
then reached behind my seat for a CD case and set it on my
lap. "Go ahead, you pick the tunes."

Gena had a little of everything: Coldplay, folk music by
Jonatha Brooke, Alison Krauss bluegrass, an Elvis gospel
collection, and Aerosmith's *Greatest Hits*. On the back of the
Aerosmith CD, "Sweet Emotion" was listed, my mother's favorite song that we used to listen to so long ago. Seeing it
made me feel emotions that were anything but sweet.

Gena mistook my hesitation. "What, you can't find anything you like? Man, I didn't think my music was that out of
touch."

"No. It's all great. Really."

I tapped the CD with my fingers, and then put it back.
Gena gave me a playful swat on the arm. "Hey, what's wrong?
You didn't inhale too many fumes in there, did you?"

I pulled out a Frou Frou CD. The Jeep vibrated as she drove over railroad tracks and shifted into third gear. Maybe I would never be able to talk to Gena about the problems with my mother, but there was something I could ask her. "No, I'm fine. It's just, um, have you . . . ever made a mistake?"

She snorted. "Oh please, you do recall my life story, right?"

"No, I don't mean that. I mean something big, something you . . . regret. And I know what you said before, about all your mistakes always working out for the best. But . . . what if they don't?"

Gena turned down the radio and braked slightly around a turn. Her face seemed to cloud over for a second. "Regrets. Well, I could regret being married to Rick, or opening that salon in Baltimore, but I don't. They were big mistakes, but I see it as God's way of putting me on the right track."

"So, there's nothing you would do differently?" I asked.

"Well, sure. I should have worn more sunblock," Gena said, "and taken my education more seriously. I could have spent more time with my mom before she died, and made more of an effort to keep in touch with old friends. But it doesn't get me anywhere beating myself up for past mistakes. That's just life."

My heart skipped a beat when she mentioned her mother. Gena then gripped her steering wheel harder, biting down on her lip with a serious expression on her face. "I do, however, have one giant regret. Something I so desperately wish I did differently."

"What was that?" *Please, give me something.*

Gena looked at me briefly and took a deep breath. "Not

making you do bikini waxes like I threatened to do for tattling on me about Eric."

She was only being funny, but instead of laughing, I felt tears gathering in the corners of my eyes. I wanted to tell her about my mother, to tell *someone* what's been going on, because I just couldn't take it anymore.

Gena noticed my tears. "Abbey, you don't have to tell me what you're going through, sweetheart, not if you don't want to. But this will pass, I swear. It will pass, and maybe one day you'll be able to look back and realize why it happened. Just be patient."

I have been patient, for nearly four months. How much more patience do I have to give?

I tried to wait. I tried to be patient. I tried not to lose faith in my mom and to understand that she was doing the best she could, knowing that if I lost my hope, I'd have nothing.

But as the month of May came to an end, no amount of hope or patience could control the paralyzing doubt that raged in my head. The anxiety I'd been holding on to since January swelled to a point where I couldn't breathe. I dialed her cell number. After five long months of waiting, I heard an automated voice tell me the truth I'd been trying so hard to avoid.

Her cell was no longer in service.

Chapter Twenty-four

Eight o'clock Sunday morning and Granny Po still wasn't up, probably sore from planting all the flowers in front of the house last night. I cracked open her door and saw her sprawled on the bed with her mouth gaping open.

"Granny Po? You okay? Do you need some coffee or anything?"

She cracked open one eye, moaning as she turned onto her side. "Good Lord in heaven, I'm hurting, girl. Plum tuckered out. Remind me next year to hire Mitch to do all the gardening."

I leaned against the door frame, watching Granny Po rub her weathered hands together. A yellow and blue quilt lay rumpled on the floor beside a basket of unfinished knitting projects that she'd abandoned a long time ago.

"Hands hurt?"

Granny Po nodded, her hair a mangled knot. "Darn straight they do. Like I shucked an acre's worth of corn."

My eyes wandered from Granny Po's nightstand to her

dresser, every inch of surface cluttered with framed photographs, bottles of lotion, porcelain knickknacks, and jewelry boxes. The pictures were mostly of me, taken over the years, with the Widows in the background.

"Okay, Abbey. Just what is up your rear end?"

Granny Po's abruptness snapped my attention back to her. "Huh? Nothing's wrong."

"Don't tell me nothing's wrong, child, because I know better. There has to be some reason why you're mooning around my door. You've been off kilter for some time now."

I wanted to tell her. That's what I came in here for. To spread the pain to somebody else because I just couldn't carry it by myself anymore. But the words wouldn't come out.

"No, I'm fine. Just tired."

Granny Po fluffed her pillows. "Just tired, huh?"

I forced a smile and stood up straight. "Yeah, that's all. You want some coffee, or what?"

"If you're serving. My butt only plans on getting up when I gotta pee."

"How about I bring you a bucket for that?"

Granny Po gave me a double thumbs-up. "Perfect."

In the kitchen I measured the coffee, then leaned against the counter while it slowly brewed. Maybe I didn't tell Granny Po about the money because I didn't want to get Mom in trouble.

I walked to the front window. Flowers now lined the front walk, and cascading petunias in a riot of blooms hung from plastic baskets. Gena's Jeep was parked in the driveway, the morning sunlight reflecting on the hood. The spa wouldn't open for another hour, but she always came in early.

Instead of telling Granny Po, I thought I should just forget about the money. Maybe Gena would let me work full-time once summer vacation starts. There's only one more week of school left, except for seniors, who graduated last night. And maybe I could work part-time for Rosemary. Since decorating the spa, she'd had five interior-design jobs. She might need some help. By the end of the summer, I could have half my money back.

I could just start all over.

Granny Po's old coffeemaker finished brewing with a gurgle and a hiss, but instead of filling her mug, I crossed over to the spa. Gena's funky Celtic music softly played, the rooms feeling bare without any people. I walked slowly to her office, mentally preparing my plea to work full-time. But when I saw Gena at her desk, the words choked in my throat.

She looked up at my soft knock.

"Hey there, toots! I didn't expect to see you until ten." She stood to pull a chair close to her desk, waving me in. I walked in, then sat, twisting the bottom of my T-shirt in a knot.

"So, you ready for summer vacation?" Gena asked. "When's your last day of school?"

"Um, next Friday."

Gena reached up to tighten her ponytail. "I'm thinking of running a special promotion for the beginning of summer. Think you could design some flyers later today?"

"Yeah, sure." I looked at the papers stacked on her desk, and the small bouquet of fresh daisies. "What did you have in mind?"

Gena leaned back in her swivel chair and clasped her hands behind her head. "Something that involves highlights and facials. Gotta get that summer glow ready!"

I nodded, my throat swelling. Tears slowly gathered in the corners of my eyes.

"Maybe ten dollars off highlights, or a free pedicure. Or a combination of the two with a manicure."

Tension built in my neck, leading to a dull ringing in my ears. Gena rocked back and forth in her chair.

"I have appointments only until twelve, so I'll work out all the details later this afternoon. And then we'll—oh my gosh, Abbey! Are you crying?"

I buried my face in my hands, trying hard to swallow.

"Oh honey, what's wrong?" Gena pushed away from her desk and placed a chair next to mine. The pressure of the last six months poured out once my head hit her shoulder. The years I wasted praying Mom would come back for me. The guilt I had clung to for not taking better care of her, even though she left me alone in the dark like a toy she didn't want anymore.

"Try to breathe, Abbey," Gena whispered, rubbing my arm with calm fingers. Muffled footsteps came from outside the office. I looked up to see Granny Po standing in the doorway, dressed in her nightgown and faded slippers.

"You didn't bring my coffee. I got worried." Granny Po stepped forward and sat on the corner of Gena's desk. "And it's time you started talking."

My forehead pounded inside my skull. I was too embarrassed to talk, too ashamed to let her know I'm nothing like the smart, driven person I once so arrogantly claimed to be. Granny Po reached forward and lifted my chin. "Please, Abbey."

I took a deep breath and shut my eyes. It was time.

"It's gone. All of it, gone."

Gena took my hand. "What's gone, honey? Did you lose something?"

"My money. Mom. My life savings . . . everything."

Gena looked at Granny Po and me in confusion. "What do you mean, your money is gone? Did you lose it, Abbey? Honey, sometimes accidents happen, but you can't beat yourself up like this."

Granny Po stood up and paced the room, a hand pressed to her forehead. She walked back and kneeled in front of me. "Abbey, please, *please* tell me you didn't give money to your mother. Please, tell me you didn't."

Her face darkened when I nodded.

"Good Lord, I knew something like this must have happened." Granny Po hit her fist on Gena's desk, scattering papers to the floor. "Son of a . . . How much did you give her, Abbey? Just tell me the truth. *How much did you give her?*"

"Seventy-five hundred."

The truth was out. Gena drew in a sharp intake of air, while Granny Po's face went absolutely rigid.

"You gave her . . . What were you thinking? Why didn't you talk to me about this . . . after she came back in January. It was then. I should have known it. Dammit! I should have known! And the way Grace went zooming out the next morning. No wonder she couldn't wait to get out of here."

Gena handed me a tissue, putting an arm protectively over my shoulder. "Yelling isn't going to help, Polly. I'm sure Abbey feels terrible as it is."

Granny Po wheeled around. "Don't try to calm me now, missy; I'm way too pissed. The nerve of that Grace, taking your money like that. She has *no* pride! No pride whatsoever, stealing from her own child. Uh-uh. She can't do this. No sir, not while I'm still alive."

Granny Po paced the room again, muttering under her breath and twisting her nightgown. It was almost a relief, tossing someone else the reins and letting them take control.

"Okay, Abbey, give me her phone number. I'll take it from here."

I shook my head, my chest too tight to talk.

"Why on earth not? Don't tell me. The phone's disconnected, isn't it?"

"Yes."

"Son of a *bitch*!"

Gena stood up, facing Granny Po with furrowed brow. "What are we going to do?"

"We? I'll tell you what *we* are going to do. There's been enough hurt in this family. I will *not* let anybody do this to my Abbey, no matter who they are." Granny Po stabbed a finger at Gena's chest. "You. Got gas in your Jeep?"

"Yeah. Why?" Gena said, hands on her hips.

"I'll tell you why. Because we're taking a little trip." Granny Po looked down at me. "Stop crying, Abbey. Don't be the victim. Is Grace still living on the eastern shore? Like she said at Christmas?"

I held the tissue to my mouth. "I guess . . . She never said otherwise."

From my pocket, I brought out the last letter from my mother and handed it to Gena. She flipped it over, reading the envelope. "No return address, postmarked from Ocean City. Didn't she tell Edith how she was working in Ocean City and living in Dewey Beach?"

"All right then. We'll start in Ocean City." Granny Po nodded, her face set and determined. She looked at her watch. "Go change your clothes. Something decent but comfortable. It's going to be a long drive."

"What are you going to do?" I asked, in a small voice.

"We're going to find your mom," Granny Po said.

"But how?"

Granny Po looked away. "I'm not sure. But I do know I can't stay here. And on the way, you're going to tell me everything."

Gena went to her desk and picked up the phone.

"Wait, Gena, you have appointments this morning," I said. "You can't just cancel them!"

She hit a speed-dial number. "I'm calling Paul. He'll open the spa for me and take care of the appointments, so go, do what Polly says."

Paul must have answered. "Hey, it's me, Gena. I have a favor to ask."

I walked in slow motion out of the spa, waves of dread throbbing in my head. *We're going to find Mom.* My bedroom door was open, the blankets and sheets still twisted and bunched from last night. I crawled into bed and buried myself under the covers, wondering what is going to happen now. *Maybe I should have taken care of this myself and not involved Granny Po. Maybe I should have given Mom more time. What if she planned on surprising me after school ends next week?* But it was too late. The ball was rolling and there was no going back. I sat up, placing my feet on the floor and curling my toes in the carpet.

"Abbey, come on! It doesn't take twenty minutes to throw on some clothes!" Granny Po yelled down the hall. "And don't forget a jacket, in case it gets chilly."

I walked to the closet, slowly dressing in a T-shirt, jeans, and flip-flops. On the closet floor, wedged to the side of my shoe rack, was a gray sweatshirt. I hesitated, then pulled it out. A terrapin growled on the front with UNIVERSITY OF MARYLAND in red. My father's sweatshirt, the one I took from the town house so long ago.

I pressed it to my face, breathing in deeply. It smelled like he did, like crisp fall evenings, motor oil, and cigarette smoke. Why hadn't I gotten rid of this years ago, when it was nothing but a painful memory of the past?

"Abbey!" Granny Po walked into my room. "Aren't you ready?"

The doorbell rang. Granny Po rolled her eyes and moaned. "Oh heck. I told 'em not to come!"

"Granny Po! You didn't!"

She looked at me with a weak frown, fingering her messy hair. "Abbey, you know what would happen if they didn't know where I was today! Good grief, you'd have better luck shaking a booger off your finger than not having those three get involved."

Before we even made it down the hallway, the front door slammed open as Edith, Caddie, and Rosemary barged in, almost running in to Gena. From the look of horror on their faces, I knew Granny Po had told them everything.

Caddie ran forward. "Oh, baby girl." She sniffed and wiped her eyes. "This is awful. Just simply awful!"

Rosemary threw her purse on the sofa and embraced me.

She must have been working, since she was dressed in stained capris. "Are you okay, sweetheart?"

Edith slammed the door shut, her hair sticking up in the back. She stared at me hard for a few seconds before hugging me, also. "I can't believe the bitch took your money."

"Edith!" Gena said, quickly shaking her head. "Not helping!"

Edith ignored her. She looked at Granny Po. "We ready to go?"

I clutched the sweatshirt as Granny Po pointed a finger at Edith. "Oh, no, I don't think so. This is not a road trip, Mrs. Jones. We don't need any more distractions."

Edith planted her hands on her hips, shaking her head from side to side. "Don't you be pointing at me, Mrs. Randall, 'cause I *do* think so. Somebody hurts my Abbey and I'm gonna be involved whether you like it or not."

Rosemary linked arms with Edith. "Double for me."

Caddie blew her nose loudly. "And we can take the Cadillac. There's even snacks that I keep in the trunk, you know, for emergencies. If I'm stuck in a snowdrift or something."

They stood firm, like three ticks latched to a dog. Granny Po sighed and looked at Gena.

"Fine," said Gena. "But *I'm* driving the Cadillac."

Rosemary, Edith, and Caddie sat crammed in the back, passing a box of doughnuts.

"Tell me, Caddie," Edith said. "It's June. Why do you have an emergency food stash for snowdrifts in your trunk?"

I watched Caddie from the rearview mirror fumble for an answer. "Well, then, it's for when I run out of gas. What are you complaining about? You seem to be enjoying them."

"So have you, my dear," Rosemary said, shifting uncomfortably. "If you would have laid off the chocolate éclairs, we'd fit better in this seat."

Granny Po paid no attention to the backseat bickering. Instead she stared ahead at the road that would lead us to the eastern shore. "How long is it going to take?" she asked Gena.

"Three and a half hours if I watch the speed limit. Three if I don't."

"Then, don't." Granny Po leaned against the passenger door so she could look at me. "Okay, Abbey, I want to hear everything. Starting at the very beginning."

All the talking stopped, each ear now tuned in to me, waiting anxiously for my story to begin. Oh well. I took a deep breath and told them everything.

Looking at road signs, with my father's sweatshirt rolled under my neck as a pillow, the anxiety in my stomach grew with each passing minute. Edith snored in the back, making me wish I could just fall asleep and then wake up and find this whole mess was nothing but a nightmare. A long, crazy nightmare.

Thirty-seven more miles to Ocean City.

Oh my gosh, what have I gotten myself into? Driving half-cocked without a clue about where we're going. Without my mother's address or phone number. Or even where she works, except that it's a bar. And if we do find her, what am I going to say?

Gena must have noticed my tension. Her hands tightened on the wheel. "Abbey, we're in Salisbury, so do you need me to stop? For another bathroom break? Something to drink?"

No. I want to turn around. I want to go back home.

"Okay," I said. Anything to delay this trip.

Gena put the blinker on, looking over her shoulder before changing lanes. "There's a McDonald's ahead. Is that okay?"

The thought of eating turned my stomach, but I nodded. Gena pulled into the parking lot, Caddie's boat of a car taking up two spaces. "Pit stop, ladies. Wake Edith up."

Rosemary nudged Edith's arm. "Hey, buzz saw. Gotta pee?"

"Huh? Oh. Yeah. Had to since we left the house."

Gena stretched her arms to the afternoon sun. "Hmm. You can almost smell the sea air."

Granny Po held the door open for me, her face pale and drawn without makeup. "No, smells more like greasy fries and exhaust fumes. Abbey, you want something to eat?"

"No," I said, putting on my sunglasses. "I'm not hungry."

"I am," Caddie said, tugging at a sandal, her feet swollen against the leather straps. "Just hearing you say fries reminds me of the boardwalk fries Gary and I ate once at the beach. Not as yummy as fair fries, but a darn close second."

Edith rolled her eyes. "And you wonder why he had a heart attack, God rest his soul."

"God rest his soul," everyone repeated, except me. I shoved my hands into my pockets, leading the way across the parking lot. From behind us came the squeal of tires and a blaring horn. We turned around to see a dusty Bronco jerk to a stop, with at least six guys hanging their heads out the windows.

"Hey, grannies! We got something for ya!" One guy pulled

away from the rear window so another could stick out his bare butt, reaching back and spanking his white cheeks. "How's 'bout some of this!"

"Oh my dear Lord up above in heaven!" Caddie covered her eyes while Granny Po pushed me behind her. Edith stepped forward to help block my view as Rosemary let out a loud gasp, pointing to the Bronco.

"Oh no. No, no, no! This is terrible, just *terrible*!" Rosemary put a hand to her mouth as she watched the Bronco speed away.

"Yes, it is terrible." Caddie clutched her cross necklace. "Young men behaving like that."

"No! Not that! Didn't anyone read what was written on their back window?"

Granny Po snapped, "No, I was a bit too distracted by butt flesh to do any light reading, Rosemary Lewis."

"You don't understand!" Rosemary cried. "Good Lord, it's *Senior Week*!"

GO CLASS OF '06!

OCEAN CITY BOUND.

SENIORS RULE.

I knew about Senior Week, but never in my life did I ever think I would be experiencing it with four senior citizens and a thirty-two-year-old.

Teenagers clogged the highway, blaring their horns and laughing, in cars packed with sleeping bags, boogie boards, duffels, and coolers. Their vehicles' windows were covered with graffiti, with things like SENIORS ROCK etched in block letters. Granny Po rolled up her window to keep out the loud music blaring from an overloaded SUV, but I could still feel its exhilarated pulse.

I wished I could trade places with them.

Traffic inched onto the drawbridge, where we could finally see Ocean City's skyline bordering Chesapeake Bay. I remember how, when I was eight, the panoramic view took my breath away as Dad drove Mom and me over this bridge on our first and last vacation as a family. It felt like we were entering a magical kingdom, with roller coasters, people parasailing, and brightly colored kites dancing in the sky.

But now the town didn't cast the same spell. Instead of enchanting, it seemed noisy and cheap, almost tacky, like I was no longer childlike enough to see its beauty.

Granny Po gasped as a girl wearing a bikini top stuck her whole upper body out the car window, then sat on its the ledge.

"Good heavens, look at that nonsense!" Granny Po elbowed my side. "Didn't anybody realize it was Senior Week?"

I should have figured it out, since graduation was last night.

We crossed the bridge and turned onto Route 528, one of the two main roads in Ocean City that run parallel to the Atlantic Ocean. Beach shops, liquor stores, gas stations, and nightclubs lined the crowded streets. I looked at the shabby apartment buildings, wet beach towels drying on the porch rails, and seniors drinking from plastic cups. A clump of girls dressed in bikinis paraded down the sidewalk, almost causing a carload of guys to wreck. Gena slammed on the brakes, throwing us against our shoulder straps. Granny Po responded by shaking her fist at them, screaming about their indecent behavior.

I slunk down in my seat, covering my face with one hand.

"Look at that boy!" Granny Po grumbled. "I swear, he's stone drunk! And that girl, she's half-naked. Abbey, don't you dare ever, *ever* let me catch you acting this way. You hear me?"

I was doing nothing but sitting in the car, and yet I was the one being lectured. "Granny Po, please."

"And don't even think about coming here after you graduate, young lady. The answer is *no*."

"Oh, Polly," Gena said, braking again to avoid a herd. "They're just letting off some steam, and I say let them. After the summer ends, it's back to the real world. They should have fun while they can."

"Amen to that, sister," Edith called from the backseat.

"If they live that long!" Granny Po huffed, adjusting her seat belt. "Let's find Grace and go home. I'm not spending one night in this town."

At the sound of my mother's name, my stomach hollowed. She could be anywhere, and if we found her, I'd have to confront her face-to-face.

"What?" Gena leaned forward to stretch her back. "With all this traffic, I've been driving for over four and a half hours. There's no way we're going back tonight."

Edith felt the same way. "Yeah, Polly, my hemorrhoids couldn't take it."

"Miss Edith, too much information," I said, flinching at the thought.

"All right, fine." Granny Po huffed. "Let's get a hotel room, and *then* we'll find Grace."

Easier said than done. We scanned all the signs along the road. NO VACANCY. NO VACANCY. NO VACANCY.

"Hold on!" I said, pointing out the window. "That one on the right has openings!" The vacancy sign flickered on and off above a faded green building with dried-up geraniums hanging from paint-chipped rails. Gena swung the Cadillac into the parking lot.

"This does not look good." Caddie's lip curled as she pointed to the overflowing trash cans. "Oh my. That can't be hygienic."

Granny Po turned in her seat. "Who's going in?"

Not a hand went up. I shrugged when she looked at me. "Can't, Granny Po. I'm a minor."

"I know that! Good grief." Granny Po moaned. "*I'll* go. But I'm gonna look at the rooms first before paying."

Edith patted her shoulder. "If you're not back in fifteen, we'll come getcha."

"Big of you."

She was back in ten, nearly running to the yellow Cadillac. "I can see why they have vacancies. The pillowcases are wrinkled, so they surely weren't washed; there were ashes on the floor; the showers looked like someone slammed a diseased artichoke on the tiles; and I swear I saw a bug bigger than my toe!"

"Crap," I said, pressing my head back against the seat. On the other side of the road, a group of girls came out of a surf shop, laughing and clutching their purchases. A bar next door pumped out rock music, to which a young couple danced on the sidewalk. There's nothing but happy, sun-soaked people in this town. Except us.

"Doesn't anybody here know *anybody* who owns a beach house?" Caddie whined from the back. "Rosemary, don't you have connections?"

Rosemary pointed a finger to her cheek. "Gee, I know. Loretta Scott does. Why don't we call her?"

"I'd rather rot first," Granny Po muttered.

I sighed and rolled my head toward Gena. "Any ideas, Gena?"

Gena leaned her head back, inches from mine. "Well, if you want the lowdown on any town, you ask the locals. They know everything from where the cheapest gas is to where to get the best pancake breakfast. Let's go find a place where the locals hang out."

Gena pulled back onto the highway, nearly cutting off a car full of seniors. Five red lights later, she pointed to a diner painted lime green with lavender trim. A blinking neon sign flashed BREAKFAST, 24 HOURS.

"Perfect," Gena said, putting on her blinker and parking.

While everyone walked in, I stood on the sidewalk, looking at the diner's bold paint job. Lime green and lavender. Mom was right. You can get away with any colors at the beach. A surge of bitterness pulsed through my veins. You can probably get away with a lot in this town.

No wonder she likes it here.

And if we don't find her . . . No. We'll find her. She can't get away with everything.

I angrily threw open the door. A blast of air-conditioning, country music, and fried food hit me in the face. Granny Po and the others were being seated at a large round table by an older waitress in a Baltimore Orioles baseball jersey. Dyed red hair poked out from under her baseball cap, trying to hide the wrinkles around her eyes. "You ladies want some coffee?"

"Hon, you have no idea how much." Granny Po fell into her chair, setting her purse on the graffiti-ridden table.

"Just a Coke, please," I said, thinking hard about everything my mother had said about her life here, searching my brain for any clue that would help us figure out where she's working.

Bartending. Mom loves bartending, so it has to be a nightclub or a bar.

"You got it, tootsie." In a few minutes, she returned, maneuvering her loaded tray with the grace of a seasoned pro. "What brings you ladies out to this crazy scene? Don't you know what week this is?"

"Lord, don't we," Granny Po said. "But we had no choice."

The waitress smiled. "Neither do I, honey. But at least I ain't cocktailing anymore. Old farts like me are too tired for that."

Older people. That's right! In Mom's last letter, she'd said how her ex-roommate's boyfriend came into the bar she was working at. Could Mom have been talking about the same place she was working at Christmas? I replayed what my mother said that night, struggling for every detail. Yes, now I remember.

"Wait!" I touched the waitress's arm before she could wheel off to her other customers. "I need your help. About nightclubs. Which ones in town would, ah . . . older people go to?"

Edith smacked the table, almost knocking over her coffee. "Dang it, you're right, Abbey girl! Grace did say something about serving older people. Good thinking."

"Ah, so you're here to find somebody. A bunch of bounty hunters, eh?" The waitress rested a hand on my chair, ignoring the customers waving her over. "Let's see. Older crowd. Not too many of them in town. Oh yeah! There's The Echo, over on Forty-ninth. Good karaoke on Monday nights. Beach Elite is a fancy nightclub on the top floor of this one pricey hotel, but heck, I can't remember which one. And there's another, called Barnacle Bar, somewhere near Ninety-first, bay side. I'll ask around the kitchen for any others."

Gena thanked her, then asked where a tourist could find a decent, *clean* hotel.

"Clean? Oh honey, if you want clean, you're going to have to shell out the bucks. Try some of those swankier high-rise hotels farther uptown. You're going to pay through the nose, but there should be some rooms available. The young folk can't afford them."

All eyes turned to Rosemary.

"Hmph. Bet you're glad I came now, aren't you, Polly?" Rosemary patted her purse.

One swipe of a credit card and we had two rooms. Rosemary swallowed hard at the $462.50, but she only rubbed my back when I apologized. "You're worth every penny, kiddo."

Granny Po pushed us toward the elevator. "Come on, now, we've got things to do! Let's get Abbey settled in the room and head out."

I planted my heels deep into the plush carpet, like a stubborn horse refusing a jump. "No! I'm going with you!"

"Young lady, I will not have a fifteen-year-old girl traipsing around in some bar. End of story. I will be the one dealing with my granddaughter." She stabbed the elevator button with her finger.

"But it's my mother we're looking for. My money she took. I *am* going."

"And I said you're *not*!"

Tears threatened my eyes. I lowered my voice, looking deep into her eyes. "Granny Po, please. I have to go."

The elevator door opened but nobody moved a muscle. Granny Po took a deep breath and watched the doors close a few seconds later. "Okay, Abbey. You win."

Edith let out a whoop, taking my arm and pulling me to the exit door. "Come on, gals. My money's on the Barnacle."

"I'll take that bet," answered Rosemary.

Caddie brought up the rear, grabbing a handful of mints from the hospitality table. "I really don't think this is an appropriate time to gamble, is it?"

But that's all this trip is. Nothing but a gamble.

Chapter Twenty~five

Edith won.

In a swamp of sour beer and blue-haze smoke, the bartender at the Barnacle wouldn't admit whether he knew Grace Garner or not. He didn't have to. I could read it in his sleazy face.

"Grace? Grace Garner?" He ran a hand over his goatee. Other than Gena and me, he was the youngest person there, early thirties maybe. Old men wearing plaid shorts on white legs sat on bar stools, looking like, well, barnacles stuck to a boat's bottom. Explains how they came to name the bar. "Nope. Can't say that I recall any Grace Garner."

"Are you sure?" I asked. "She said she worked at a place like this that serves older customers. Probably as a bartender." I inched away from a customer tapping his shoes off-beat to an oldies tune, his eyes stuck on Gena like a buzzard to a carcass. Another customer leered at me with a creepy, toothless grin, but Granny Po moved in between us, flashing him a look that could bring down a plane. She had given me strict orders before we walked in not to talk, breathe, or touch anything, a rule I quickly ignored.

"Nope. Never heard of her."

Rosemary fumbled in her purse and brought out a twenty. "Will this refresh your memory?"

I tried to hide my smile. Rosemary looked pleased with herself, like she'd always wanted to do that.

The bartender took a long drag from his cigarette, blowing smoke out of his nostrils like a cartoon bull does before charging. His eyes scanned us each in turn, then he swiped the money from Rosemary's hand. "It helps. I'm starting to get a vision."

Rosemary rolled her eyes, mumbling to herself and opening her wallet again.

He held his hand up. Each finger bore a ring. "No, not money. I want a dance. With her."

"I don't think so." Gena huffed.

The bartender laughed. "Don't flatter yourself, sweetheart. I didn't mean you." He pointed at Caddie. "Her."

I couldn't tell who was more shocked. Gena or Caddie. Caddie's mouth dropped open, her ears crimson at the tips. "Why, I never . . . Oh heavens. Young man, you should be ashamed of yourself. I am old enough to be your mother!"

"That's how I like 'em. Why do you think I work here, huh?" He crossed his arms across his chest. "You dance with me, and I'll tell you what you want to know."

Granny Po pulled Caddie back, and all of us huddled around her.

"Polly, you don't expect me to dance with that boy, do you?"

"Good grief, it's just a dance, Caddie."

"But my husband . . . I'm a respectable widow!"

"What's your husband gonna do, divorce you?" Edith shook Caddie by the shoulders like a trainer prepping a boxer. "Come on, get out there and take one for the team! And I swear on my mother's grave I'll never tell a soul."

Caddie brushed Edith's hands off. "You hated your mother. What good will that do?"

"Miss Caddie." I reached for her elbow. "Please. I'll wash your Cadillac all summer."

She looked at me with nervous eyes, then glanced at the leering bartender. "Fine. I'll do it. Just for Abbey, though. Not you bunch of old pimps!"

The bartender reached overhead to put a CD in the stereo, a slow, soulful groove. With the flip of a switch, a shiny disco ball above the dance floor began to spin, fragments of light flashing. "Madam, care to join me?"

Caddie walked toward his open hand, like a lamb to slaughter. She looked over her shoulder at me. "Abbey girl, you owe me big-time."

"Yes, ma'am, I do."

He spun Caddie around, almost knocking her rear end into a chair. "By the way . . . name's Arnold." Hair escaped from Caddie's clip as he whisked her into his arms, starting a weak two-step. They staggered across the dance floor, Caddie glancing at us every other step.

"Don't you let that hand go any lower, young man! Oh, heavens to Betsy!" Lights began to pulse blue, green, and yellow, Caddie teetering like an antique top about to fall over. Her eyes pleaded for mercy with each spin.

Granny Po gave her a thumbs-up. "Doing great, Caddie-O!"

"Atta girl, Caddie!"

"Oh my heavens, don't you dip me . . . my back! Watch out for my back. Abbey, I want my car waxed, too!"

"Yes, ma'am."

Arnold spun her in a slow circle, as the music began to fade. He stretched her down in a low dip, his goatee almost touching her nose. "You dance divine."

Was that a blush?

He stood her up when the music ended, pulling her hand to his lips. "Many"—*kiss, kiss*—"many thanks."

Caddie straightened her cardigan, nearly running from the dance floor. Arnold took his time walking to the bar, bowing at the applause from the seated barnacles.

Gena was not amused. "Okay, gigolo. You got your dance." She tapped a finger on the sticky bar. "Now. Tell us what you know about Grace Garner. Does she work here? Where does she live?"

He winked at Caddie. "Grace quit bartending here a month ago, after she moved. She gave me the address, but I threw it away."

"Do you remember anything about the address? Street name?" I asked.

Arnold paused, as if he noticed me for the first time. "You look like Grace."

I held my breath in the smoky haze, wondering if Mom had ever told him about me. But he dismissed me by pouring himself a draft. No, she probably hadn't. "The address," I repeated.

"Yeah, I remember something. The street name starts with an *H*, I think. Bay side." He picked up a rag, throwing it over one shoulder. "That's all I know. Now, how about your phone number, in case I see her again?"

He looked straight at Caddie when he said that.

Granny Po pushed her toward the door. "I don't think so, big guy."

We were almost outside when I remembered something and ran back to Arnold. "Wait, her car. What is she driving?"

I held my breath while he poured a drink for a customer. "Some piece of junk. But I remember she was looking at one of our waitresses' car that was for sale."

"What kind was it?" I asked, even though I already knew the answer.

"A Ford Mustang."

I sat in the backseat, by the window. Arnold said she moved a month ago. But I remember Mom saying something about moving into an apartment in March. Or did Arnold mean she just quit a month ago? I leaned against the door, angry for not asking more questions. And what about the car? The same kind she always nagged Dad about.

"Can't you drop me off at the hotel?" Caddie said, using a towelette on her hands and face. "Lord, I feel so dirty! That boy smelled like a wet dog!"

Granny Po snapped her seat belt. "There's no time. It's almost seven o'clock. You're just going to have to wallow in your sin, Sugar Momma."

"Polly!"

"Caddie has a boyfriend . . . Caddie has a boyfriend," Edith sang under her breath.

"You promised! No teasing, y'all! It's not funny."

Gena held a hand up. "Ladies, not now, okay?" She nodded in my direction.

The teasing stopped as Gena headed toward Dewey Beach. I pressed my forehead against the cool window, with Caddie's leg pinned against mine, watching Ocean City flash by. Hotels. Beach shops and restaurants. People having fun, enjoying the evening sunshine. A family sat on a porch eating ice cream, reminding me of the photograph I saved of Mom, Dad, and me.

The buildings began to dwindle until there was nothing but stretches of sand dunes on both sides of the highway. A couple walked along the ocean, pants rolled up and darkened with saltwater. On the other side of the highway, Jet Skis skipped on Chesapeake Bay like an advertisement for the perfect summer day.

"You okay, baby girl?" Caddie patted my knee.

No. I'm not okay.

"Why don't we just go home, forget about all this?" My voice faltered, the pent-up anger I'd felt before quickly fading. Maybe I'd rather go home and live with her lies than go forward and learn the truth.

Gena slowed the Cadillac, switching to the outside lane. "It's your choice, Abbey. Say the word and we'll turn around."

I was scared to go home. Scared to go forward. What if I upset her again, like the last time? What if we can't even find her? Granny Po turned in her seat. "Abbey, hon, it makes no never mind to me. Maybe I shouldn't have forced this trip on you."

But she was right to come. Deep down, I knew it was time to face my mother.

I took a deep, staggering breath. "No. Keep on going."

Dewey Beach is a speck of a town compared to Ocean City, but still large enough to get lost in. Gena maneuvered the car bay side, through developments, up and down back streets, through alleys, mumbling to herself when we came to a dead end. We all looked for any street starting with *H*.

I was also looking for a Mustang.

Caddie pointed to the right. "What does that street sign say? I don't have my glasses."

It said Hickory Lane. With an *H*. There was a pizza parlor on the corner, called Big B's Pizza. My chest tightened and a sickening ache grew in my stomach. *Pizza parlor.* At Christmas, Mom had told me about there being a pizza parlor down the street from the house she wanted to buy. *This* pizza parlor.

No . . . she couldn't have.

My heartbeat quickened as Gena turned by a group of taunting boys on skateboards. The blacktop turned to gravel, tires crunching as we passed the beach homes, each more run-down than the last. At the end, on the right corner of the cul-de-sac, was a faded rancher. With a porch and blue shutters. And a burgundy Ford Escort parked to the side.

Mom.

She didn't blow my money on a new car. Instead, she got the house. She got her dream. And it didn't include me.

A wave of nausea snaked its way through my body. I was the one who listened to her problems, who tried to make her happy. It was me who saved her that night, holding a towel to her slashed wrists while screaming at the 9-1-1 operator. I hated my father for her. Defended her. Waited for her. I lost Mitch because of her.

And yet . . . I was the one she left. Again.

Gena stopped the car. Granny Po stared at the mailbox, seeing the name GARNER spelled in gold stick-on letters. "Son of a—, I *cannot* believe what I'm seeing."

She yanked her seat belt off, grabbed the door handle, and threw the door open. "Abbey, you wait right there, you hear? It's time for your mother and me to have a little chat."

I scrambled after her. "No, Granny Po, wait! Don't do this; I need to see her first."

She wheeled around, fire coming out of her eyes. I shut the door and stood with weak knees, leaning against the car for support. "Please. This is between us."

Granny Po scowled and then stepped aside. "Fine. Go ahead. But in fifteen minutes, I'm coming in."

Chapter Twenty-six

Maybe I was wrong.

Maybe Mom was only renting this house, and the blue shutters were a coincidence. Maybe there are ten Big B's in town, and by some fluke chance, one happened to be at the end of the road.

Small pebbles crunched under my feet as I walked up the driveway. Shadows spread across the withered yard, ending in jagged forms over concrete sidewalk. I noticed sandy flip-flops on the porch steps, and a Budweiser beach towel hanging on the rail, as if she had just returned from the beach. Two shabby bikes were leaning against the hedges, rusted from the salty sea air.

My legs felt like dead weight as I forced myself up the steps. A wooden plaque hung on her front door. I stood paralyzed, reading it.

HOME SWEET HOME.

She did it. This is her home. With no landlords, no rent. *She did it.*

All these years, I swore to protect myself from men. And yet, with all my walls and armor, someone did break in and hurt me. But it wasn't a guy, or some stupid curse I swore had plagued all the women in my family. It was my own mother.

Blood pounded at my temples when a radio was flipped on inside and I heard rock music coming through the cedar plank walls. It sounded like the Guns N' Roses album Mom used to listen to constantly. And then I heard singing. Happy singing.

I lunged forward to the door and ripped her sign off the peg, clenching it with my fingers so tightly, the wood bit into my flesh. Every ounce of hesitation I felt earlier disappeared. All those months of waiting, afraid she'd try to take her life again, and she had no concern for mine.

Damn her.

Mom wasn't coming back for me. She had done nothing but string me along for the past six months, making me wait like a shivering dog longing to come in out of the cold. I threw the sign, watching it crash against the porch rail. The bones in my knuckles felt shattered when I pounded on the door.

"Hold on!" Footsteps approached from inside. "What, did you forget your key?"

She opened the door. I stared her hard in the eye. "No. I never got a key."

Mom reeled back in shock, almost dropping her wine cooler. "Oh my God. Abbey."

Neither of us spoke. Her tanned skin glowed beneath a white tank top and jean shorts, and cheap highlights, probably from a drugstore kit, now streaked her hair. She looked like a relaxed local, someone who doesn't have a care in the world, certainly not about her own daughter. From where I stood, I could see a man's jacket hanging by the door, and motorcycle boots lined up underneath it. A new rush of fury almost knocked me down when I remembered there were two bikes outside. *Two bikes.*

"So, those boots are yours, right?" I asked through clenched teeth.

She bit the inside corner of her lip, flicking her eyes at the boots, her mind probably spinning some kind of story to explain their presence, like how a friend left them after a visit and must have driven home barefoot.

"Just tell me whose they are, Mom!"

She exhaled. "They're Hank's. But Abbey, honey, it's not what it seems. Please, come in and we'll talk, okay?"

Mom stepped back to let me in. I barged past her and slammed the door shut, hard enough to knock a cheaply framed picture of the ocean off a green wall. Sea-foam green, just like she promised we would paint the house. Everything was just like she said it would be. The seashells. Wicker furniture. Everything but me.

Mom set her drink on the small kitchen counter and nervously cleared the coffee table of empty cups. "Hank . . . can leave such a mess." She then grabbed a pack of cigarettes that were beside an overflowing ashtray, and fished the last one out. The flame of her lighter shook as she lit it.

I stabbed the off button on her stereo and glared at her.

"So. Do you own this house?"

Mom broke my gaze and trained her eyes on the front door like a trapped deer about to bolt.

"Mom, do you own this house?" I shouted.

"Yes." Her voice was small, helpless. "Please don't yell, honey. It's not how it looks."

"Let's see. I gave you money for a down payment. For our

home. Together. You bought the house, never told me, and got some asshole to take my place. How is it supposed to look, Mom? *What am I supposed to think?*"

Mom puffed hard, then blew out a straight line of smoke. "Abbey, please. Just let me explain. There's a good reason for this."

"Let's hear it." I crossed my arms over my chest, my breath hard with anger. "Let's hear the excuses. I just can't wait to hear what you come up with this time."

She sank down on a wicker chair, burying her face in trembling hands. "Abbey . . ."

I reached forward and yanked on one of her arms, causing ashes to fall to the floor. I wanted to see her face, watch as the lies spilled from her lips. "Well, come on! Let's hear it."

Mom leaned over to pinch the ashes off the carpet, anything to avoid looking at me. "Yes, I bought the house, but I wanted to wait and get settled before you came, so everything wouldn't be a mess. And then Hank . . . he wanted . . . he moved in and it just got too hard . . ."

Her voice trailed off.

"So, it's because of Hank." The sarcasm dripped like tar from my tongue.

"Yes! Oh honey, I didn't want this to happen, I swear. I thought if Hank and I had our relationship more established before you came out, then we could all live here together. You remember how it was before? On those rare times when your father wasn't such a jerk and we lived like a family? That's all I wanted for us again. But then Hank and I started having problems and he became so demanding . . . and made it impossible for me to tell him about you, even though I really wanted to, I swear."

I reached for a framed photograph on top of the television. Her and Hank. Surrounded by people at a bar, maybe the Barnacle. "Right. It's not your fault, is it, Mother? It's all Hank. Mean, big Hank. Just like my father made your life miserable. Like my grandfather did. And every other man you've ever come in contact with, right?"

I flung the picture at the wall. Glass shattered, leaving a dent in her perfectly painted wall.

"Abbey . . ."

"Stop it, Mom! Stop it! I am so sick and tired of you and your lies. How it's not your fault. *Never* your fault because you're just the helpless victim. Isn't that right?"

Mom stood, pacing the room as though wanting to escape. I stepped in front of her, blocking her path.

"So what is it, Mom? You have nothing in your miserable life, so you figure I have to have nothing? Is that it? What kind of person thinks that? What kind of *mother* does that to her child?"

Her face, once so angelic in my memory, now aged before me. Harsh lines, shallow skin, hollow eyes. "Don't you dare talk to me like that. I did not raise you to speak so meanly."

"That's just the thing, Mom, you *didn't* raise me. Granny Po did." And Caddie. Rosemary. Edith. And now, Gena. "You were too busy raising yourself. I was just along for the ride, for the sympathy, for the *excuses.*"

Mom sucked in her breath and dropped down on the wicker love seat, probably the one she was so excited about finding way back in January. She stubbed out her cigarette and reached for another but found the pack empty. It felt as though I was seeing her for the first time, with a sharp and painful clarity. I couldn't hold back the sobs anymore.

"I'm sorry, Abbey," Mom said softly.

"No, you're not," I whispered. "I don't believe you. Not anymore."

The muscles in my legs ached as I knelt, picking up the broken picture frame. She looked away as I pointed to the photograph. "Looks like you made your choice, didn't you, Mom? Well, you know what? You can keep the money. You can stay in this house with your lousy boyfriend. But you'll never have me."

I walked to the door, then stopped. There was more I needed to know.

"What about my dad?"

A seagull's cry sounded through the open window as Mom clenched her hands into tight fists. "I don't want to talk about your father," she said, her voice low.

I stood rooted in the spot, unwavering. "I do. I want to know if my dad ever wanted me. If he paid child support. I want to know the *truth*."

The pulsing tick from a hanging clock echoed. Mom looked up with a piercing gaze. "Don't you understand, Abbey? I was protecting you."

"Protecting me? Protecting me from what? Mom, for once, will you help me understand?"

"You'll never understand!" Mom stood, her face flushed. "You'll never understand how the real world works, Abbey! I had to protect you, all your life, even when I was pregnant with you. My own mother wanted me to get an abortion, and when I refused, she wanted nothing to do with me. And years later, when I left your father, I did it because I didn't want you to grow up around a drunk who resented having a family. God knows *I* know how horrible that is, having a parent who resents you. I felt that every day of my life with my mother."

She stopped, looking around the room with her lips quivering. "Your father could have come after us, Abbey, but he never did. He should have realized we were really gone and done anything to get us back, but he didn't. Yeah, he sent a few child-support payments, but there was no point in letting you know that. Because then, lo and behold, he sends divorce papers, like he wanted to completely wipe me out of his life to marry some other woman. Not only that, but after two years, he wanted joint custody of you. Two years! He didn't deserve you; he didn't deserve anything! I had to protect you and, dammit, if he didn't want me, he sure as hell wasn't going to get you!"

A gasp escaped my throat. "He wanted joint custody?"

The words fell on me like a rock. No, that couldn't be. I was there, in Granny Po's house, a few days after Mom had left me on her doorstep. I heard her talking to my father. *Dale, are you sure you don't want custody of Abbey? Have you thought this through?* There's no way I could be mistaken about that.

Mom stood up, taking a few hesitant steps toward me. "You may not believe it, but I really did do you a favor, Abbey."

I backed away. My skin felt pierced by a thousand needles as her words sank in. No wonder she never changed back to her maiden name; she was waiting for him to come to her. And when he didn't . . .

"Abbey . . ."

All these years, she had me believe my father didn't want me. Did he?

"Abbey, honey, please say something."

Mom stood with her hands crossed over her chest. I came forward and reached for a hand, turning it over to look at the scar on her wrist. It was a faint line, from a wound that was only superficial, just deep enough to scar. I looked up at her face, seeing a pathetic mix of desperation and sadness. My voice was a bare whisper. "Mom, you didn't do me a favor, and you know it. You didn't want me happy, because you weren't. *That's* the truth."

She could try to deny it, but I saw a flash of guilt cross her face. She knew it was true.

"Sweetie—"

"Don't 'sweetie' me. All those years of *lies*. All those years you made me believe I had no father. Made me hate him as much as you do. How could you do that, Mom? To me? How dare you say you wanted to save me from my father's resentment when you ended up resenting me more than anybody!"

"No, that's not true!" Mom spun on her heels, stepping with an unbalanced stride to the window that overlooked the bay.

"Yes, it is." I crossed the room, standing right behind her. "You saw me living with Granny Po and that I was happy. You were able to see how much Gena meant to me, and that killed you, didn't it? And what about my savings, Mom?"

She faced me. "I don't know what you're talking about."

"Did you see it, Mom? When you left me your number on the notepad that you got from my desk drawer, did you see my ledger and know how much money I had? Is that why you came back so willingly in January when I was upset about Camden?"

"Stop it!" Mom cradled her head with her arms, falling to her knees. "Stop, Abbey, please! I can't take this, I swear!

You're making me out to be the enemy. Just like your father did. Just like everybody does."

She started to cry, rocking back and forth on the carpet. Part of me wanted to fall at her knees, apologize, and throw my arms around her in a childlike attempt to make everything better. But just like I was no longer childish enough to be spellbound by Ocean City's skyline, with all its flying kites and parasails, I could no longer sympathize with her. Not anymore.

I took a last glance at the bay rocking peacefully outside her window and the small boat tied to a neighbor's dock— just like she said we'd have one day. But I could never belong here, or with her.

"Never mind, Mom. I don't want to know. It would only make me hate you more."

I could feel her eyes on my back as I headed for the door.

"No, wait, don't go!" Mom got up and tried to follow. "Please . . . Abbey, don't leave me! *I can't live without you!*"

I turned around. Mascara streamed down her cheeks. "No, Mom, you can. You've lived without me for years. This time, *I'm* the one leaving. I want you to watch *me* walk away, and know exactly how it feels."

Granny Po was on the porch when I opened the door, her hand raised to knock. She looked at me, then turned to Mom's tearstained face. "Oh Grace, how could you?"

I stepped out onto the porch, into Granny Po's warm embrace. "Please, Granny Po, let's just go home. There's nothing more that needs to be said."

Chapter Twenty-seven

The answering machine was blinking when we arrived home after midnight, but neither of us bothered to listen to it then. I didn't have to, since I already knew what it would say—how sorry Mom was, and how she desperately needs me. Anything to wind that veil of guilt around my head, making me doubt who was right and who was wrong. But it wouldn't work. She can't play that card on me. Ever again.

Granny Po mumbled something about talking in the morning as I crawled exhausted into bed, still wearing my father's sweatshirt. But in the last seconds before I fell asleep, I could hear Granny Po, playing the message, over and over. Mom's voice was muffled and incoherent, but certain words came through with perfect clarity.

Sorry. Desperate. Need.

In the morning, Granny Po knocked softly on my door, then entered with two cups of coffee. She looked older today, the dark smudges under her eyes proof she couldn't sleep, either. "Here, I brought this for you."

"Thanks," I said, as she set the cups down. "What time is it?"

"Ten thirty." Granny Po turned on my lamp and helped me sit up, fluffing the pillows behind me. She gave me the coffee, and the steaming mug warmed my cold hands.

"Do you think Rosemary is mad about the hotel rooms she paid for?"

"No, of course not." Granny Po reached out to pick lint off my sweatshirt. "Honey, Sarah called a few minutes ago. She wanted to know if you'd like to go with her to a double header today, but, I, ah, told her you weren't feeling well. Unless, of course, you want to go."

Yesterday's events flashed again in my head. The mailbox with Mom's name on it. Hank. The lies, my father, and that pathetic excuse of protecting me, when *she's* the one who dumped me on Granny Po's porch like trash. I couldn't go to a baseball game today and see Sarah and John together. I didn't want to go horseback riding, like Edith suggested last night. I didn't even want to go to the farm, in case Paulina was visiting Mitch again, although it was funny the way she tiptoed around the barnyard in her strappy sandals. I just wanted to lie in bed all day.

"No," I said, trying to keep the tension out of my voice. "No . . . I've got a headache."

"Okay, I'll check in on you later, then." Granny Po squeezed my hand and left.

The pain at my temples swelled to a throbbing ache. I turned my lamp off and grabbed the photograph of my parents and me off my nightstand. In the near dark, Mom's sweet smile made me want to vomit.

Liar.

The frame crashed to the floor as I ripped it open, then tore the picture with frantic motions, shredding it smaller and smaller until the pieces scattered on the floor like crumbs.

Mom's scarf still hung from my bedpost, the one she'd left behind because she couldn't get away fast enough. The familiar stench of cigarettes almost gagged me as I ripped it down, eyeing a loose stitch. With each jerk and pull, the loose thread grew longer, the fabric unraveling in my hand until a knot stopped my destruction. I pulled, wrapping the yarn around my fingers till they turned red, and then I threw the scarf into the trash.

My worn-out MBTF notebook was sitting on a shelf. I pulled it out and flipped through all my grand plans and dreams. But just before tearing all the sheets out, I stopped. Screw it. I wouldn't let her destroy my life any further. I'd start over. I'd work as many hours this summer as Gena would let me. Maybe I'd even write a bestseller, titled *Just Say NO: To Loans, Gifts, and Other Stupid-ass Mistakes.* And on the inside cover, a picture of her face with a huge *X* crossed over it.

I can't live without you.

Bullshit. Even if she was crazy enough to try to kill herself again, I couldn't care less. Mom could go ahead and saw her wrists in two. She might as well. She was dead to me already.

Friday afternoon. Final bell in ten minutes. Mrs. Langdon was flipping through a magazine, occasionally glancing at her watch as students raced around the room for last-minute yearbook signings. The fact that she seemed even more eager than us to end the school year pissed me off. It's not like we forced her to take the job.

A heavyset girl wearing a Frederick Keys baseball shirt bumped into my desk, knocking my yearbook to the floor. She picked it up, and for a second I thought she might ask me to sign hers. But she only handed it back and apologized before working her way back up the aisle. Whatever. It's not like we even really knew each other, and she probably still believed those stupid rumors. Earlier, at lunch, Kym stopped by our table, scribbling out a quick message about good times, keep in touch, XOXO, even though she's more concerned about her new group of friends. Sarah filled an entire page, ending her message with *Abbey, I'm so happy we got to know each other better this year. We'll have a blast this summer! Sarah + John forever.*

I opened my yearbook and flipped through the pages. My stomach churned, looking at photos of happy students, joyful teachers, and pep rallies. All the group pictures of various clubs I never bothered to join, the jocks and their sports trophies, the clusters of friends hanging out on the steps.

Why don't they show what high school is *really* about? Like pictures of students in detention. Or the girl crying by a dented locker, her heart broken for the first time. What about an outcast, sitting alone on the outskirts, tormented for being different, or the scared freshman antagonized by the worldly sophomore?

Or the stupid girl, who believed all her mother's lies?

My photograph appeared only once, categorized alphabetically with the rest of the sophomore class, like I'm part of the herd. What's going to happen twenty years from now? Will I have a daughter who'll look through these pages, trying to figure out if her mother was ever once happy? Will she stare at my picture, just as I did at my own mother's picture?

The final bell rang. End of another year. I grabbed my backpack and drifted with the wave of students to the front lobby, where Sarah was waiting to hug me good-bye, promising to call me later. As my bus pulled out into traffic, I thought for a second, and then turned to the index to find out what pages Mitch was on. There he was, wearing a wide, goofy grin and posing with friends, as though they didn't have a care in the world.

I tossed the yearbook down beside me, leaned back, and watched the miles pass by. The bus driver slowed, flashing yellow caution lights before jerking to a stop. The door *whoosh*ed open, letting in a cool June breeze.

A junior ambled down the bus aisle, deliberately slow, yelling promises to a friend to meet at the mall. I wanted to kick her down the steps. Anything to just get home. But once she'd stepped off the bus, I could see the sign her lingering body had been hiding.

GRANITE HILL METHODIST CHURCH.

An arrow pointed down the side road. Two miles.

The bus driver shut the door.

Granite Hill Church, where Granny Po refused to set foot because of Loretta Scott. It's been so long since my mother had taken me there, at least six years. I remember how Mom had stood for what seemed like hours, staring at my grandmother's headstone as though hidden somewhere on the concrete were the answers to all her questions. Did she ever find them?

I had to find out for myself.

The bus started forward.

"Wait!" I grabbed my backpack. "I'm getting off, too."

The driver braked, then turned in his seat, scratching his balding head. "You got permission?"

"Yes," I lied.

Maybe it was against the rules, but he didn't seem to care. "Fine. Just get going. We're holding up traffic."

Without thinking twice, I bolted from my seat and off the bus. I stood at the side of the road as the bus lurched away. *This is not a good idea.*

In three miles, the bus will stop in front of the spa, and Granny Po will be watching out the window. But my seat will hold only the abandoned yearbook I left behind.

Sweat trickled down my back by the time the red-brick church came into view. Behind it, the cemetery was nearly deserted. A man stood before a headstone adorned with flowers, his eyes cast down in prayer. He obviously had a good reason to be here.

What was mine?

Answers. I wanted answers. There had to be a connection binding the four generations of women in my family together. More than teenage pregnancies and failed marriages. There had to be more buried beneath the surface than just bad luck, or bad men, or some curse.

And maybe it was buried here.

At the upper end of the graveyard, a group of trees stood clustered like an oasis. I picked my way through the dense grass toward them, remembering how there were trees near my grandmother's grave when I visited with my mother, and she had yelled at me for peeling the bark from one. Beneath the shade of an old oak tree I found her headstone, mildewed and silent.

Evelyn Grace Somers
Born 1957   Died 1993
May God have mercy on her soul

The cement felt cold and rough to my skin as I traced the words with my finger. *May God have mercy on her soul.* Nothing else. No "devoted wife" or "beloved mother." It was sad, to have no inscriptions that defined her life . . . or what she meant to the people she left behind.

I took a few steps back, then sat on the hard ground, with my spine pressed against a tree's rough bark. With my eyes fixed on her grave, I searched for the missing clues, for the answers to my questions. But there was nothing. Only a swarm of gnats that persistently circled my head and patches of weeds swaying in the soft breeze. It wasn't until an hour had passed that I realized why. Someone else needed to be here with me.

Granny Po.

Caddie answered the phone at Serenity Spa. "Oh, thank the sweet Lord! I thought you were dead. Abbey, dear, pardon my language, but where in the *hell* are you? Do you have any idea how worried Polly is? She's been frantic."

"I'm sorry, Miss Caddie."

"Sorry doesn't cut it, toots," Caddie barked in a voice I'd never heard before. "And, pray tell, why isn't your cell phone working? Didn't Polly give you it for a reason?"

I explained how students weren't allowed to have phones

on at school and that I didn't think to turn it on. Caddie told me to wait, she needed to get Granny Po on the phone, but I quickly stopped her. "Can you just tell her where I'm at and ask her to come get me?"

"Fine. Where are you, Abbey?"

My voice shook. "Um, Granite Hill Church . . . at the cemetery."

Caddie paused. "Oh Lord, no wonder you want me to tell her, baby girl. Guess I better ask Gena to drive."

Minutes later, Gena's black Jeep pulled into the parking lot, and Granny Po sprung out with an agility I'd never seen before. "Girl, I have half a mind to kick your scrawny butt all the way back home."

Gena got out and shut her door. "Polly, this was not the approach we agreed on."

"Tough. Abigail Lynn Garner, do you have any clue how scared I was when you didn't get off the bus? And why am I spending money on that cell phone every month if you don't know how to use it? And of all the places to run off to, why here, huh? *Why here?*"

Granny Po's hair stood up in messy clumps, and there was a coffee stain on the front of her rose-appliquéd sweatshirt. She hurried to where I was, almost knocking down a wreath planted by an older grave. "Young lady, you have no idea how worried I was. I thought you ran away. Or that you . . ."

She stopped midsentence when her eyes locked on her daughter's headstone.

". . . that you . . . done something . . ."

Oh, no. She was afraid that I'd done something drastic.

Just like my grandmother. Tears sprang from her eyes as she pulled me close.

"Granny Po, I am *so* sorry. I am so sorry to make you worry."

She clung to me and kissed the top of my head. "You can't do that to me, Abbey. Ever."

Gena walked up beside us, her thumbs hooked in the waistband of her jeans skirt. "You okay, sweetheart?"

With my head still on Granny Po's shoulder, I nodded. "I'm really sorry, Gena."

She smiled and brushed hair from my forehead. She looked down at my grandmother's headstone. "Evelyn Somers? Who was that?"

The air was muted by Gena's casual comment. Granny Po released me, and knelt by the headstone, saying nothing as she pulled out a few stray weeds. Then she raised her face. "Gena, Evelyn was my daughter. She killed herself when she was thirty-six."

Gena brought a hand to her mouth. "Oh, Polly, I'm so sorry. I had no idea."

Granny Po fished out a wrinkled tissue from her pocket and dabbed her eyes. "That's because I never talk about it. I thought it would help me forget the pain. But it doesn't work, does it, Abbey?"

"No, it doesn't," I said softly.

My arms were chilled from the breeze, despite the June sun. Gena motioned to her Jeep. "You know, I have a sweater buried somewhere in there, Abbey. Why don't I get it for you?"

Not waiting for an answer, Gena went off to search for the sweater, but I knew she wouldn't find one. It was only a ploy to give Granny Po and me privacy, and I loved her for that.

Once Gena climbed back into her Jeep, I sat cross-legged by Granny Po in the damp grass. Neither of us spoke, not sure where to start. From the road, we heard a car with a busted muffler roar past the church. She mumbled how the fool driver should get a ticket, while I concentrated on the words carved into the headstone.

Granny Po picked up a weed and aimlessly twirled it around her finger. "Abbey, I'm, uh, real sorry you lost your money, honey. I know how hard you worked for it."

But somehow it didn't seem as important to me now, not when we were sitting by the grave site of her dead daughter. "Thanks, Granny Po, but it's not the money. It's the fact that my mother . . ."

A sob cut my words short.

Granny Po tossed the weed and gathered me in her warm embrace. "She lied to you, baby. And I'm so sorry."

I leaned against her strength, letting go of all the angry tears I'd been holding in all week, while Granny Po rocked me gently. With her, I felt loved. Safe. Like the comforting feeling when someone covers you with a blanket at night, kissing your forehead when they think you are asleep. But there was nothing she could have done to stop my mother from hurting me. Or my father.

My father.

I pulled away. "Granny Po, that day you talked to my father. About custody. What did he say?"

She looked confused. "What day, honey?"

"*That* day. The day after my mother left me here." I got up on my knees, turning to face her. "Last week in Ocean City, Mom told me that Dad wanted partial custody in the divorce papers. But after Mom left me, you called him and I heard what you said. You said, *'Are you sure you don't want custody?'* I heard you!"

Granny Po nervously fingered a button on her shirt. "Abbey, I, that was so long ago. I can't remember."

"Yes, you remember." I pleaded. "Then you came to me later and said it was best if I lived with you for a while until things straightened out. So why? Why did he ask for custody in the divorce papers if he never wanted me in the first place? Was it just to hurt my mother?"

Granny Po closed her eyes and pressed her fingers against her eyelids. "Oh Lord."

Just tell me, please!

She lifted her chin, tucking a stray hair behind her ear. "Abbey, I did call your father. When he heard about Grace's suicide attempt, he thought taking custody of you would . . . upset her more. It was an unstable time for everyone, so it *was* best if you stayed here."

For a second, I was stunned, but so what if he didn't want to hurt Mom. Neither did I, but that didn't do me any good. "Yeah, best for who? For him? And unstable, why, because he was marrying that other woman and didn't want any extra baggage?"

"Lord, child, I'm sorry but yes," Granny Po said. "That was part of the reason as well. After your mother left him, his drinking problem got worse. When Sharon came along, yes, it was his replacement family."

"I knew it," I said through clenched teeth.

"No, honey, wait . . . Listen to the rest." She took a shaky breath before continuing. "Maybe I could have convinced him to come for you, but at the time, he was such a confused young man . . . I couldn't bear your living with a drunk, not after all you'd been through."

My knees ached from the way I was sitting, but I couldn't move.

"But then," she said, "he called me, after he quit drinking. It was part of his recovery. He confessed that the only reason he married Sharon was to get a family back, so it didn't surprise me when they divorced. He missed you so much, honey, and Grace, too."

"But . . . why didn't he ask for custody after he became sober?"

Granny Po rested her hand on the side of my face. "Because he wanted to make sure he was completely recovered first. And he knew how upsetting it would be if you were uprooted again. Instead, he wanted to build a relationship with you, slowly."

I tried hard to take everything in. All the times Granny Po had encouraged me to talk to my father. How she didn't allow me to change my name to Somers, my mother's maiden name. And how she said she'd attend his Alcoholics Anonymous meetings with me, if I wanted to go. It all made sense, except one thing.

"But . . . what about you? I still don't understand why you never told me, after everything we've been through."

Granny Po frowned at the headstone of her lost daughter, the color drained from her face. "I should have told you, Abbey, and I wanted to a thousand times, but Dale asked me not to."

"Since when do you listen to other people?"

She turned, tears streaming down her weathered cheeks.

"I agreed with Dale because . . . because you were my second chance. To do things right, not like with Evelyn. I was thirty-four when my husband died, and Evelyn was eighteen. She was married with a baby by that time, and still resented me for not supporting her relationship with Elton. I could have tried harder to make things right between us, but I was too busy trying to save my own rear, opening the parlor, and paying off Ralph's debt. So I wasn't there for her, not when she was a scared new mother, not eighteen years later when she was so depressed after kicking her own daughter out of the house. Maybe if I was . . . she wouldn't have killed herself."

Granny Po now gripped my face with both hands, a desperate urgency in her eyes. "Don't you see, honey, how resentment over the past affects the future? I know what your mom did was terrible. But don't hate her, like Grace hated her mother. And just like my own daughter hated me."

How many times before has Granny Po told me that? To not hate my mother? Now I understood why. My mother hated my grandmother. My grandmother hated Granny Po.

I hated my mother.

That was the connection. All these years, I swore never to let my guard down, never to fall for some guy and be like the women of my family. But I was protecting myself from the wrong things. *Hate* was what truly bound all three generations of women. Hate and resentment. And I was at risk of becoming the fourth.

Granny Po's lower lip began to tremble. "Abbey, I'm so sorry. When Grace left you here, I swore to do right by you, somehow, to make up for all the mistakes I'd made with my own daughter. But it looks like I didn't do a very good job, did I?"

I thought of how Granny Po never let me out of her sight without my cell phone, how she supported my desire to work, and how she always made those egg-custard pies for me. I wrapped my arms around her shoulders, pressing my cheek into her neck.

"No, you did the best job. And I'm so sorry to make you worry today."

Granny Po pulled back, wiped her eyes, and laughed. "Worry? Girl, please. I was looking forward to watching *Wheel of Fortune* without you and all your cheating."

"Sore loser," I said.

Granny Po nudged me with her elbow. "Well, come on, then, let's go home and have ourselves a face-off tonight."

"Okay, but first, here's the hypothetical question of the week." I paused for a second, thinking of Dad and all those months he'd tried over and over to come back into my life. Maybe I could try as well. "If a certain someone admitted that she threw away her father's phone number, would you give it to her . . . and promise not to push her into calling until she's ready?"

Granny Po hoisted herself up off the ground and held out her hand for me. "Well, I'd say yes to the certain someone on both counts. Hypothetically speaking, of course."

We stood together for a while, staring at my grandmother's headstone, both of us lost in our thoughts. Granny Po wrapped her arm around my waist and, in a regretful voice, said, "I wish there was more written on her headstone, about how wonderful she once was."

Her deep remorse saddened me. "It's not too late, Granny Po. We could get another. And visit her more often."

She wavered for a second, then grinned. "You always

were the smart one, Abbey girl. It *is* time for me to be with my daughter again. And would you . . . would you come with me here next Sunday? To church?"

"What about Loretta Scott?" I asked.

Granny Po snorted. "Shoot. After all these years, I can handle Loretta Scott. Besides, just wait until I find my old recipe for the next fellowship luncheon. French pound cake with Grand Marnier butter cream. Loretta won't know what hit her!"

"You can't bring a cake with alcohol in it!"

She leaned over with a wicked grin. "Says who? Might be just the thing she needs. You ready to go home?"

Yes. Now I was ready to go home.

Chapter Twenty-eight

I couldn't dial his number.

Each time I tried, my stomach would churn, just thinking about what to say. Yes, my father had had a drinking problem, and he'd worked hard to become sober. But it took so long for me to finally learn the truth that I just couldn't flip the switch and instantly forgive him.

The phone rang, causing me to jolt upright in bed. For a second I thought it could be my dad. I waited until the fifth ring to pick it up. "Hello?"

"Hey, Abbey. What's up, girl?" Sarah sounded excited, like she was busting to tell me something. "You enjoying our first days of summer freedom?"

"Wow, not as much as you are. What's got you in such a great mood?"

"Hold on a sec." I could hear the sound of her door closing and then the squeak of bedsprings as though she flopped onto her bed. "Okay, well, John and I *both* got jobs at the community pool for the summer, can you believe it? I'll be getting paid and be able to see him at the same time! Maybe I can sneak you in sometime and we can swim together."

"Yeah, that would be great," I said, even though I planned on working more hours at Gena's this summer.

"And . . . don't be mad," her singsong voice lowered to a quiet hush, "but John's friend Will—you know, they used to hang out when John was still going to school with us? Will's working at the pool, too, and John and I thought it'd be really cool if we all got together, you know, like on a double date. Nothing serious, or anything."

Will Grover? Will was cute, in a quiet way. He was the one who tried to bail me out when Mrs. Langdon caught me daydreaming in class.

"Did you say anything to him about me?" I asked.

"No," Sarah said, "I wanted to speak with you first. I'm not trying to push you or anything, Abbey, but I thought it would be fun, all of us hanging out."

It could be fun. Will seemed nice. It wouldn't hurt to let go for once. To just go on a simple double date and stop worrying all the time. Gena would. But I couldn't say yes. I'd never be like Gena, no matter how hard I tried. "Sarah . . . I, uh, don't think so."

She seemed to understand, and we spent the rest of our conversation talking about her music lessons and about the movies we both wanted to see. But in the back of my mind, a profound realization overtook me. I'll never be normal. My mother's words, and all her warnings, will haunt me forever.

Before hanging up, Sarah lowered her voice. "By the way, you'll never believe this," she said, "but I heard that Kym is dating Camden Mackintosh. Can you believe it?"

Yes, I could, because she'll never learn. Kym was so focused on being popular that she refused to see him for what he really is, just as I had refused to see my mother for what she is.

Gena handed me my paycheck at four, the end of my work shift. I quickly filled out a deposit slip to give to Rosemary later tonight and looked at the balance of my savings account. It was $942.85, a far cry from my January balance. A cold knot formed in the pit of my stomach. No. I had to stop thinking about my mother . . . and my money.

Granny Po called me to the kitchen, handing me a basket full of homemade corn muffins to take to Mr. Penney. She threatened to cut off all my hair while I slept at night and choke me with it if I dared spill one word about it to the other Widows.

"Fine," I agreed, "but tell me. Why, exactly, do you send him so much food?"

Granny Po gave me a reassuring pat on the hand. "Abbey, dear, please. You know I simply appreciate it when a man likes my cooking. No, child, having you in my life is all I need right now, thank you very much."

"Same here," I said, knowing she really didn't have a thing for him, but still wondering about the "right now" part. "And it's a good thing. I'd hate to have to change my name to Abbey Penney."

Granny Po snorted. "Better than Polly Penney. Now, if you've got your cell phone, and if you've peed and pooed, then go before they get stale."

Bodie jumped off Edith's porch, knocking over an art easel that someone set up, probably one of the 4-H volunteers. He raced to greet me with his tail wagging. As I approached the barn, Ragman poked his head up, with blades of grass hanging from his mouth. He ambled to the fence, whinnying softly. I caressed his soft, whiskered muzzle with one hand.

"Sorry, baby, I don't have any treats."

Ragman shook his head and blew out hard from his nose, spraying me with snot. Good thing I protected Granny Po's basket.

"Guess I deserve that, huh, for not wanting to ride you." Ragman stomped his back foot as though he agreed with me. I was about to give him a small piece of corn muffin when the barn door opened and Mr. Penney walked out.

"Abbey! Darned pleased to see ya. Is that food in your hand?" Mr. Penney's face lit up when I handed him the basket. He took a huge bite of the largest muffin and proclaimed its excellence. "You working today, Abbey?"

"I can. Do you need me to do anything?"

He wiped a crumb off his whiskers. "Nope, not now. I gotta run and get some worm medicine, so maybe later you can help with that."

Great. Worm medicine.

I waved as he drove away, then went back to Ragman. How many times had Edith tried to push me into riding him? Too many to count. He gazed at me with a soft eye, looking nothing like that maniac pony my father put me on. Ragman's the safest horse here, but I always say no. No to riding, no to the date with Will, no, no, no.

And I was suddenly sick of it.

I was sick and tired of all my stupid fears and sick of not being normal. It was time to get over my mother once and for all.

Before I could chicken out, I climbed the fence, took off my belt, and looped it around Ragman's throat. He lumbered beside me to the small stable and stood patiently while I put on his halter and snapped on the cross ties. Edith's saddle was heavier than I'd imagined, but Ragman gave me a forgiving look when I heaved it to his back and the stirrup hit his other side with a *thunk*.

"Sorry, boy."

I had learned a lot about tacking horses since first coming to the barn, but cinching up the girth and putting on his bridle were difficult. Difficult, but not impossible. I led him to the mounting block, my nerves strung tighter than Granny Po's clothesline as I put my left foot in the stirrup, then swung into the saddle.

Don't think . . . be tough.

Ragman moved forward when I touched his sides with my heels, his long rolling stride heading for the worn-out path that followed the fence line. I took a deep breath and dropped my hand to his roached mane, letting him decide where to go.

There. This wasn't so bad. It was . . . nice.

Ragman circled the pasture, occasionally shaking off a cluster of flies pestering his ears, which reminded me I forgot to put on fly spray. At the far corner of the pasture was a pond, where tall clumps of weeds dotted the gnawed grass. I let Ragman take me there, and loosened the reins so he could dip his head down for a drink. Just as I swatted a fly from his neck, Ragman snorted, then tensed.

"What's the matter, boy?"

A black snake darted out from the weeds. Ragman bolted sideways, with ears pinned back, then spun on his haunches.

The saddle slipped. I flew to the ground—hard—landing on my back. I gasped for air, the wind knocked out of me, as Ragman pranced in a circle, his head arched high in panic.

Clouds whirled above me and I heard the snake dive into the water. Ragman stepped closer, lowering his muzzle to my forehead. He breathed in deeply, but I was too stunned to move. *Lie still,* was what my father said after the pony threw me all those years ago. *Lie still, so I can see if anything is broken.*

Minutes later, I flexed my feet and moved my hands. No, nothing was broken. I could stand up if I wanted to. But instead, I stayed on the hard ground and cried. For so long, I'd been afraid to ride, always fearing the worst would happen. Well, the worst did happen. I was thrown. Thrown *hard,* but nothing was broken.

And for years I was so afraid of being like my mother that I hoarded every dime possible, thinking a large bank account would protect me. But what I had feared the most did happen. In some ways, I am like my mother—guarded and resentful over things that have happened in the past. Now she's gone, and so is my money.

And yet, I'm not broken. I can stand up and move on . . . if I want to.

A screech of brakes came from the driveway, followed by the sound of a door slamming. Footsteps pounded on the gravel like thunder. "Abbey? Oh my God, *Abbey!*"

I turned my head to see Edith, climbing the fence and jumping to the ground. She ran toward me, her hands clenching with each pump of her arms. Ragman stepped back as she knelt beside me. "Don't move, baby, don't move."

She ran her hands down my arms and down my legs, just like my father had. I lifted my head, pulling up to my elbows. "I'm okay, Miss Edith. I'm not hurt. Just shaken up."

Edith pulled me close, her body shaking. "Oh Lord, I thought you were dead. If anything happened to you, Abbey . . . It's all my fault! I shouldn't have pushed you to ride. I . . . I . . ."

Edith began to cry.

I wrapped my arms around her, the woman who rarely cries. Maybe my real mother was gone, but I had five women who took her place: Granny Po, Caddie, Rosemary, Edith, and Gena.

"It's okay, Miss Edith, nothing was your fault. Ragman only shied because of a snake, and the saddle slipped."

Edith sniffed and looked to where Ragman was standing off to Ragman's side, the saddle now hanging upside down below his belly. "Oh, would you look at that goober horse. Child, I bet you forgot to check his girth again before getting on, since he always blows up."

Blows up? I laughed at Ragman, standing with his back feet parked out, the saddle hanging like a child with a full diaper. "I think I forgot that step, Miss Edith."

She hugged me tightly, then leaned back. "You ready to get up? We gotta rescue that fat boy over there."

Edith pulled me up, my back sore but otherwise okay. We undid Ragman's girth, letting the saddle drop, and then she lifted it onto his back. As she tightened the girth, she said, "I won't push you, toots, but after a hard fall, you gotta cowboy up and get on again. Before the fear can sink deep into your soul. What do you say?"

She put the reins over Ragman's head. He turned his soft eyes toward me, as the truth of her words made my skin tingle.

"Come on, Abbey," she said. "You can't let one snake scare you."

No, I can't. Not anymore. Not Camden, not my mother and all the bitter stories she wove about my father. Whether or not they were true didn't matter. It was time for me to stand up and move on. I put my foot in the stirrup and pulled myself back into the saddle. Edith patted my leg, and as we headed back toward the barn, she started to hum a tune that sounded so familiar.

She hummed louder. Yes, I knew that song. It was "Happy Trails," from those Roy Rogers shows.

Roy Rogers. Westerns.

My heart started to pound louder than Ragman's hoof beats. There's something else I've lost besides my savings and my mother. I've lost the tumbling tumbleweeds and get along little dogie. And right then and there, I knew I had to get it back.

But what if I'm too late?

"Miss Edith," I said with sudden urgency, "can you drive me somewhere? Now?"

Ragman would have gotten us there sooner. Her Dodge pickup rattled like an old tractor down the highway. I clenched my hands, willing her old truck to go faster, at least the speed limit.

"Abbey, relax! You're making me nervous."

I sat back in my seat, trying to glance at the dashboard without being obvious. Only fifty in a fifty-five-mile zone. "Okay, but can you drive just a little bit faster, please?"

Edith didn't know exactly where Mitch lived, just his street, from when she'd dropped him off one night when his car had a flat. I closed my eyes and asked God to help us find it, feeling the same breathless panic in my chest as when the wind was knocked out of me.

I had to see him. I can't let fear hold me back anymore.

Edith put on her blinker, turning into the quiet development where Mitch lived. I searched each driveway, looking for his car. Sweat beaded at my temples as my anxiety grew, pushing her truck forward, past the two-story colonial, past the kids playing basketball, past all those barriers that have held me back for too long.

"Wait, this looks familiar," Edith said, turning onto a small side street. "Yes! There's his car."

His Chevy was there. I didn't wait for Edith to put the truck in park. The door swung open as she braked, the hinges pushed to their max. My feet pounded on the driveway, up the sidewalk with neat bushes planted on each side, up the porch steps. Without thinking, I pushed the doorbell.

Mitch answered moments later, wearing a tank top and faded jeans. He looked at me through the screen door. "Abbey? What are you doing here? Is there something wrong at the farm?"

I almost wanted to spin on my heels and get out of there. Almost.

"Abbey?"

I wrapped my fingers around the railing like talons grasping for support. "I need to explain why."

"Why what?" Mitch opened the door, the confusion on his face clear. Of course he was confused. It'd been a long time since I canceled our date, and he's moved on. But I had to make him understand.

"About Camden. And why I accepted a date from him . . . instead of you."

Mitch stepped out onto the porch, letting the screen door slam shut behind him. "Abbey, you don't need to explain anything. Really, it's okay."

"No, it's not." My voice sounded like it came from miles away, but it was too late to turn back now. "Mitch, I knew Camden was a jerk. But I opened myself up to him only to prove a point, that my mother's theories were right and no guy can be trusted. With Camden, it was safe. There was no chance of my heart being broken, because it was never on the line to begin with. Not like with you, because if I gave you my heart . . . and things didn't work out, I'd be crushed. Devastated."

He looked deeply into my face, sending an ache that hurt worse than being thrown from Ragman. Worse than having Camden tell people I had warts, and worse than my mother only doing what I thought she'd do all along.

I buried my face in my hands. "I screwed up."

Mitch said nothing.

"Tell me, Mitch. I screwed up, didn't I? It's too late."

Mitch still said nothing. I looked up as he shoved his hands into his pockets, his brow furrowed. The look on his face said it all. I was too late. And Paulina wasn't.

"I'm sorry, Mitch." And with that, I turned to go. He didn't speak until my feet hit the porch steps.

"So," he said, "you don't blame me for moving on."

Tears fell down my cheeks. Of course not. What did I expect—him to ask me out again after I've turned him down so many times? Once you've been bitten many times, you stop trying to pet the dog. I turned back to face him. "No, I don't blame you for seeing Paulina and giving her those three carnations."

He nodded. "Right . . . and you know I care about you, Abbey. You've always been a great friend."

Friend.

Mitch reached for my hand. Squeezed it hard. "But sometimes, friends turn into something more."

Huh?

He stepped closer.

"Abbey, I bought Paulina only one pink carnation. The rest she bought herself."

Oh.

"Besides, where've you been? We broke up a month ago."

And with that, Mitch tilted my chin up and pressed his lips to mine. I drenched myself in this moment, committing every move, every action to memory. How it felt when he placed his other hand behind my neck, fingers threaded in my hair. The sweet smell of his cologne and the aroma of lilies planted in the flower bed. The look of promise in his eyes when he pulled away, and the drop of my heart when he reached down to pick me three flowers.

And the sound of applause. Coming from the front seat of a rickety old truck.

Chapter Twenty-nine

It seemed fitting to walk into Gena's office after the spa closed that day, just as I did weeks ago on the morning we drove to Ocean City. Because now . . . I needed to go back.

Gena hung up the phone as I sat down. She spun her chair around to face me with an overly enthusiastic grin. "Hey there, Abbey! You got any plans for tonight?"

A blush rose to my face. I could tell by the twinkle in her eye that she knew about Mitch. So did Caddie, who kept pinching my cheeks, sniffing at how her little girl was growing up. Rosemary was ready to spirit me off in her car to go clothes shopping, and Granny Po, at this very moment, had *two* egg-custard pies baking in the oven for me.

"Edith told you, huh?"

"Oh, yes she did, sweet thing," Gena said with a sly grin. She did a little dance in her chair and sang, "Abbey's got a boyfriend . . . Abbey's got a boyfriend."

Even though I knew I'd be the target of their teasing for at least the next two weeks, it felt so good to hear that. So *normal.* It was now clear why I didn't want to double-date with Will. The only one for me was Mitch.

"Well," I said, "you know what Edith's punishment for tattling is, don't you?"

"Bikini waxes," we both answered at the same time.

Gena smiled and leaned back in her chair. "Well, I can't guarantee you won't get anything from the Gray Widows, but I promise not to tease you anymore, okay?"

"Thanks," I said, pulling up a chair and wincing from my bruised back. "And I have a favor to ask you."

Gena tapped her pen against the wood, her face going from a teasing grin to a frown in two seconds. "Well, I hope that you aren't asking to work more hours, sweetie, because I'm afraid I cannot allow it."

I thought of my plan to be a millionaire by thirty-five. I can still work hard to reach my goal, but this time for the right reasons. For my future, not just as a way to shelter myself from the past. "No, I wasn't thinking clearly when I asked for all those hours. I wasn't thinking clearly about a lot of things. That's not the favor."

"Okay," Gena said. "Then, fire away."

I took a deep breath. "Can you drive me back to Ocean City? I need to see my mom."

The sight of Ocean City's skyline took my breath away.

As Gena and I drove onto the drawbridge, I felt like a kid entering the magical kingdom with its colorful buildings and fishermen lined up along the bridge, patiently waiting for a bite. Boats sailed by on the water beneath us, and planes dragging advertisements flew overhead.

Maybe I'll come to Ocean City one day for a real vacation, with Granny Po and the others. Or Mitch. Or . . . with my dad.

But not yet. There's still a lot of talking to do.

Last night, when I finally got up the nerve to call my father, I couldn't speak at the sound of his voice. We had too much damage, too many layers between us. But before I could hang up, he said my name.

"Abbey? Is that you?"

My heart skipped a beat; he knew it was me. "Yes . . . how did you know?"

"Caller ID."

"Oh."

He must have sensed my disappointment. "But I had a hunch it was you, even before I looked. Is everything okay? Are you okay?"

I clamped my hand over the mouthpiece, squeezing my eyes shut.

"Honey? Are you crying?" The sound of him turning off the television brought tears to my eyes. "It's okay, sweetheart, I'm here. Your dad's here."

A cluster of seagulls swooped down as I walked up her driveway. Mom, wearing a pink waitress uniform, answered the door before I knocked. She gripped the doorknob, waiting for me to say something.

"Hey, Mom."

"Oh, Abbey. I . . ." She choked. Mom straightened her uniform and invited me in. Gena had parked a little up the road, hidden from my mother's sight, but I could still see the Jeep's front fender. Once she told me I was strong. But today I didn't need strength. This time I was not here to fight.

Mom's house was different. The stereo and kitchen table were gone, as well as the Budweiser signs on the wall and the heavy boots by the front door. "No Hank?" I asked.

"No Hank."

Looks like Hank didn't leave with his hands empty, but the wicker sofa and chair she so proudly bought in January were still there.

"Did Granny Po come with you?" Mom asked.

I almost smiled at the memory of Granny Po, who was primped and ready by seven this morning, wearing a brand-new dress and slingback heels I convinced her to buy. "No, she and Miss Caddie had church. They went to Granite Hill, where your mother is."

"Oh. That's . . . nice." Yes, it was. And next Sunday I'll go, too.

Mom picked up a cigarette pack from the kitchen counter, tapping one out and then putting it back. "I'm trying to quit." She nervously clenched her hands and motioned me outside. We stood on opposite ends of the shaded back deck made of weathered gray planks that had raised nails and splintered edges.

Wind from the bay blew across our faces, as she turned to me, tears welling in her eyes. "Abbey, I asked Hank to leave. And I've been thinking of you so much."

"No, Mom. Please stop. Let me talk." I collected my thoughts, remembering everything that had happened since last October when I answered the door and found Gena on the other side. A lifetime ago. "You hurt me. You stole from me. You lied to me . . . about so much. You made me hate my father and blamed everybody else for everything that has gone wrong for you."

Mom looked down at her worn and scuffed sandals. "You don't understand what I've been through."

"I do understand. More than you think. How hard it must have been when your own mother threw you out. All the problems you had with my dad and his drinking. You were hurt before, but it doesn't justify what you did to me, your own daughter, when I've done nothing but love you."

Mom turned away, her eyes scanning the bay. "I know, honey. I'm so ashamed of what I did, and if there was any way for me to take it all back, I would. I'd do anything." There was a sincerity in her voice that I'd never heard before, as though all her barriers had vanished as well and, for the first time, the real Grace Garner was talking. "The thing that hurt me the most was watching you walk away and knowing it was all my fault. I . . . love you, Abbey. More than you'll ever know."

"I do know, Mom."

She does love me. And it was true what she said about always trying to protect me. Mom protected me the minute she dropped me off on Granny Po's porch, knowing that would be the only way I'd get the kind of life I deserved. And maybe, in a sad way, my grandmother tried to protect Mom as well, by thinking she'd have a better life if she aborted me.

There was hope in Mom's eyes when she said, "Do you ever think you could forgive me enough to live with me again? This house was supposed to be our home. Is it too late for that?"

"I do forgive you. But, no, I can't live with you now."

My words were harsh, but Mom had to hear it. I reached out and covered her hand. "What you did to me was horrible, but I forgive you, Mom. For taking the money, for lying about Dad, I have to forgive you. If not, the rest of my life would be ruined by anger, resenting you for anything else that goes wrong. I want more than that."

I looked out at the bay, a warmth swelling in my heart. "And there's a guy I know. We used to be friends, good friends, but now we're much more. And like Granny Po said, maybe we could break up tomorrow, or five days from now, or five months from now. Maybe we won't. But if I get my heart broken, then I'll pick myself up and be strong on my own until the right one comes along. I just can't be like you, Mom. Not anymore."

Gena was right. Sometimes it's the dead ends in life that put you on the right path. And this path has led me straight to Mitch.

"Then it *is* too late." Her voice was shaky, weak. "I've lost you forever."

I squeezed her hand. "No, Mom. I know you love me, but I need more than that. I need you to prove it."

"How?" she whispered.

"You can prove you love me by loving yourself. By not moving to a different town every time something goes wrong. By not blaming other people and learning how to stand on your own two feet. And maybe by learning what it means to be a friend. To me."

As hard as it was to leave her, there was no choice. Mom had to learn the hard way, by losing everything, just like I did. And her everything was me. I pushed away from the railing and began walking away.

"I love you, Mom. Always will. But I won't let you hold me down any longer. So until you're willing to try, I'm going to walk away from here. And not look back."

Chapter Thirty

Welcome to the 109th annual Carroll County 4-H and FFA Fair,'" Rosemary read from the large white sign posted at the fairground's entrance. She pulled a compact from her purse, checking her lipstick while Caddie cruised for a parking spot.

The grassy field was already packed with cars, trucks, and vans, the ground between the rows worn to dusty strips. Caddie found a spot she liked, taking up two spaces so nobody could ding her Cadillac.

"Look at all these cars! How on earth are we going to find Edith in this mess?" Caddie said, stepping out into the blistering heat.

"She's going to meet us at five o'clock by the French-fry stand," Rosemary answered. "Abbey, darling, when's Sarah coming? She's such a nice girl."

"Around six, six thirty, after she gets off work." Sarah and I made plans to meet at the fair, earlier this morning when she called to say that Kym had just found out for herself what Camden Mackintosh was really like. He held out as number one on her list for six or seven weeks, until she caught him making out with another girl in the backseat of his car. I called Kym after talking with Sarah, to tell her that we would be watching the mule pull tonight and to stop by if she wanted. Why not. There's always room in our crowd.

Granny Po straightened her hat and stretched her muscles, taking a deep breath. "Smell the country perfume of manure. Good grief, I love this. Fair week. Best time of the year. Brings back so many memories."

"Rosemary, did you say Edith's meeting us at the French-fry stand?" Caddie's brow furrowed. "Lord Almighty, I live for fair fries. And now I can't have even one with this diet Gena has me on."

Gena reached into the trunk for a folding chair, looking at Caddie's worried face. "Ah, the famous fair fries you've been talking about. Are they wedge cut or shoestring?"

"Right in between. Not too greasy, perfectly crisp, and moist on the inside."

Gena shrugged. "Diet, schmiet. I'm buying."

Caddie breathed a sigh of relief, straightening her pink bowling shirt with the words GUTTER GALS embroidered on the back. Gena convinced her to start exercising more, so she's now bowling Saturday afternoons in a women's duckpin league.

Smiling, I watched the four women weave in and out of the parked cars, each one so different and yet the same. No, Mom wasn't abandoning me on that rainy night long ago. She was giving me a chance.

The fairground midway was bursting with activity; the smell of funnel cakes, pizza, sawdust, and livestock filled my lungs.

We made our way past children with balloons tied to their wrists, 4-H'ers rushing to show their next exhibit, and parents with strollers. An old farmer by the dairy barn took off his hat and brushed the sweat from his forehead, probably thinking of days long ago, while a group of kids crowded around a small calf in the petting zoo.

Gena stopped to smile at a toddler trying to handle his ice-cream cone as the loudspeakers announced the start of another pig race. Then we saw Edith standing by the French-fry stand, wearing a floral skirt and cute leather flip-flops instead of her usual jeans and boots. My jaw dropped and Granny Po stepped back, as though she wasn't sure it was really Edith. Rosemary opened her mouth, but Edith stopped her with a pointing finger.

"Just shut up about it, all right? Gena took me shopping, that's all."

"Well, I think you look lovely," Caddie said, stepping in line for fries.

Edith pulled Caddie away. "No time for food. I need to show y'all something before the mule pull starts."

We set up our chairs on the grassy knoll, then weaved through the crowd to the large red building housing 4-H entries. Crafts, photography, woodworking, sewing, art—if you could make it, it was in that building. Edith led us over to where the senior citizens' crafts were displayed.

"Why is she dragging us here?" Granny Po asked.

Edith stopped and turned to a wall of acrylic paintings. There, among the paintings of flowers, landscapes, and children, was a painting of a house along a highway, flanked by large oak trees. Pots of geraniums hung on the front porch, lace curtains billowed from an open window. And there was the white, rusted sign in front, BEAUTY SHOP FOR RENT . . . FULLY EQUIPPED, INQUIRE WITHIN."

Home.

It was so beautiful, I couldn't speak. Now it all made sense—the book of art Gena had given her, the easel set up on her porch. "Miss Edith, you painted this!"

She nodded, with a slight blush.

"Edith . . . oh my . . . it's wonderful." Granny Po's chest heaved. "My old shop."

Edith's face softened when she looked at her work. "This shop, it's the world to me. Where we came together, the most unlikely batch of women, and formed a family."

She reached for Gena's hand. "Then you came and made it better. You gave Polly here a job, since she never was ready to retire. Got Caddie to take better care of herself. And Rosemary, going back to decorating. Became such a dear friend to our girl Abbey, and convinced an old horsewoman like me to have the guts to try something like this."

Edith sighed and looked at the painting. "Yeah, the old place sure looks different now. But the heart of it never changed. No remodeling can take that away."

Gena smiled. "And I know the perfect place to hang it. Right in the reception area, above the desk, if that's okay with you."

Edith nodded.

I pointed to the bottom right corner. "But the BM? What does that stand for?"

Edith took off her straw hat, running a hand through her hair. "I didn't know if I'd have the nerve to show y'all this. So I used the initials of my middle and maiden names. Barbara Miller."

Granny Po squinted close. "It could also stand for *bowel movement.*"

Edith swatted her. "Now, why ya gotta go there? A perfectly touching moment and you had to ruin it."

Hundreds of people gathered on the two large hills flanking the show ring, with some grass-stained children rolling down them despite the announcer's warning it could spook the mules. Some brave couples danced to the bluegrass music, while many older folk sat along the hilltop. Remembering a display we'd all seen earlier, Caddie's face still glowed as we made our way to our chairs. "Did you see me? My picture was there, right there. Oh my goodness, they actually had my picture up!"

Rosemary saw it first, just after we left Edith's painting. A display set up with white balloons and draped chiffon showed pictures of all the farm queens for the past sixty years. Caddie glowed when she saw herself posed on a stage with a tiara on her head. Gena took Caddie's picture beside it, posing just like she did years ago with her one foot cocked daintily in front of the other.

I leaned over and hugged her. "Yes, and you were gorgeous. Still are. A real beauty queen, no matter what Granny Po says."

She gave me a wink, making me wonder if she was the one who had told Gena about Edith's love of art. The same way she told her about Rosemary being a decorator. Come to think of it, Caddie was the one who helped me convince Granny Po to let Gena rent the spa in the first place.

Maybe our innocent little Caddie isn't all that naive after all.

The mule pull was about to start, so Edith put her straw hat upside down on the ground, pulling five dollars out of her dress pocket. "Okay, ladies, it's time. Place your wagers. I'm putting five on Charlie Hawkins, the one with the two brown mules on the end of the ring."

Caddie squinted, looking down at the show ring. "Oh my, that Charlie certainly is a muscular fellow. Reminds me of Cecil Kelley, the man who owns the bowling alley. Did I ever tell you about him? He was so nice to show me how to clean my bowling balls the other day."

Edith raised an eyebrow. "Did you offer to clean his?"

Gena waved a finger at Edith. "This is a family event, remember."

Edith stuck her tongue out at Gena. "Anyway, Charlie Hawkins was the one who owned that champion team Jan and Jacob—those cute mules who creamed all the bigger ones."

"Oh yeah," I said. "They were awesome. What ever happened to them?"

Edith took a sip of her soda. "Jan's retired from the mule biz, living a life of relaxation on Charlie's farm. And Jacob, well, he moved on to higher pastures, God rest his soul."

"God rest his soul."

Granny Po threw her money into Edith's hat, betting on a pair of heavyset sorrel mules. Caddie neatly laid hers in. "I'm for those darling buckskins in the middle."

Gena bet on a pair of bay mules. "So, is this like a fair tradition, gambling on mules?"

"Oh, yeah." I laughed, sticking with the smallest mules, who looked too determined not to be powerful. "And at the pig races. They're mighty big around here."

My heart swelled as I looked at the women surrounding

me. Granny Po offering Rosemary the rest of her cone, and then Rosemary, usually the prissy one, taking a huge bite. Gena chatting away with Caddie, both on their second round of fries, and Edith, who was walking down the hill to talk with Charlie Hawkins.

And my mother . . . in a way, Mom's here, too.

I slipped my hand into my purse to touch the folded paper, just to make sure it was still there—a check from my mom that arrived this morning. For only a hundred dollars, but accompanied by a handwritten chart, detailing how over the next several years, she'll pay me back. No words, no promises, just a plan. A *long-term* plan.

It's a start.

"Um, Abbey?" Gena discreetly pointed to her watch. "You better go."

I stood and slipped away, walking through the crowd, past the dairy barn and livestock building, to the lower parking lot to meet Mitch. He was about fifteen minutes late by the time he pulled in, driving slowly behind a mule-driven wagon full of shouting kids.

"You're late," I teased, as he opened his car door.

He kissed my cheek, his touch still making me weak. "I'm sorry, but an emergency came up. Have I missed anything?"

"No," I said. "Just paintings, farm queens, mules, and clean balls."

"Okay." Mitch laughed. "Is that supposed to make sense?"

I gave him a coy smile. "Yeah, after a while it makes perfect sense."

Mitch took my hand and pulled me toward the backseat

of his car. "I've got plenty of time. But come on, I need to show you the emergency that held me up."

I didn't know what to think as he reached into the backseat, pulling something wiggly from a cardboard box. He placed a fuzzy puppy in my arms. It was an Australian blue heeler just like Bodie, with a black head and blue-tinged body, who instantly nestled against me. "Oh my gosh, Mitch! Where did you get him . . . or her?"

The puppy licked my nose, its tail wagging in my arms. "I was the last one to leave the farm, and there she was," Mitch said. "Someone dumped her by the farm's sign, and I didn't have the heart to take her to the shelter. Not tonight, at least."

I held her in front of me, gazing into her eyes. *Abandoned, huh?* The tiny puppy reminded me so much of Bodie when he was first abandoned. Back then, I was furious over someone dumping an animal like that, without knowing if anyone would care for it. But not this time. I was grateful, because if this puppy needed a good home, she certainly was at the right place.

"Mitch, she's not going to the shelter, not ever."

Mitch scratched the puppy behind her ears. "Oh yeah. Granny Po will have a heart attack if you bring a dog into the house."

"Don't worry," I said. "She'll say yes. Eventually."

The puppy jumped in my arms when the announcer blared the start of the mule pull. I glanced at my watch. "Oh, we have to go. He's going to be here soon."

"Who's he?" Mitch asked, locking his car door.

"My . . . dad. My dad is going to be here soon."

The words felt alien on my tongue, but in time I'd get

used to it. I had invited him to the fair, where it's crowded, where it's too noisy to have any deep conversation that we aren't yet ready for. But where we could just be together, like a family.

It's a start.

Maybe that's why I never got rid of his old sweatshirt. Because I wished this day would come. Dad did make mistakes in the past. The drinking. Putting me on that god-awful pony. But after all our falls, he was the one who was there, trying to fix what was broken.

Mitch and I walked through the crowded midway, past the pizza and pit-beef lines, to where the Gray Widows and Gena were sitting on the grassy knoll. Caddie turned around and gave a little squeal when she saw my bundle, but quickly dropped her smile when I put a finger to my lips.

Granny Po was sitting forward in her chair, yelling at those buckskin mules to *pull, baby! Pull!* I gave Mitch a wink, then leaned over to whisper in her ear. "Granny Po, remember that day when we all talked about our favorite smells?"

Granny Po wheeled around, her eyes bulging at the squirming puppy in my arms. "Oh, hell no, Abbey!"

"Hypothetical question of the week: Is there anything, *anything* more precious in the world than the smell of puppy breath?"

⊱ Acknowledgments ⊰

Many, *many* thanks to Pam Smallcomb, for inviting me to lunch all those years ago and being my friend/mentor/therapist ever since. To the brilliant James Proimos, for all those necessary kicks in the rear and for hooking me up with one killer agent. I am beyond grateful for Rosemary Stimola, my killer agent, and to Lara Zeises, for her selfless advice and support. Thanks, also, to my critique group: Andrea Rice, Carole Shifman, Marianne Floyd, Lyn Seippel; to reader Bethany Brown; and to Dawn DeMario and Michael Hollingshead for their spa expertise.

A very special thanks to my wonderful editor, Karen Grove, for believing in my story, and to the folks at Harcourt for bringing it to life.

Thanks also to my father, Alfred Barnes, for his encouragement; my brother, Al Barnes, and his wife, Jenny, for their faith; my stepfather, Al Roberson, for feeding us when I was on deadline; and my mother, Betty Barnes, for her countless readings and endless support.

Bob, Broc, Cooper—you guys have been there for me every step of the way, and I love you for that.